ANOMALOUS READINGS

ANOMALOUS READINGS

THIRTEEN CURIOUS AND CONFOUNDING TALES

ROBERT J. MCCARTER

LITTLE HUMMINGBIRD PUBLISHING

Dedicated to Roni for always being there ready to read.

INTRODUCTION

These stories are anomalies, divergences from where the bulk of my writing has taken me. If you've read any of my "A Ghost's Memoir" books starting with *Shuffled Off* or my first short story collection *Life After: Stories of Life, Death and the Places in Between*, you know what I'm talking about.

By and large those are stories of life, death, and transitions, full of ghosts and grief.

There are some ghosts in these stories, but not *those* ghosts, not the kind I've written about before. There is grief too (which is rather hard to avoid in the human experience), but different shades of grief. There is lots of science fiction here, but with themes untraditional for me (and perhaps more traditional for sci-fi at large).

In "Gossamer Threads" you will find a very unusual, and karmic, apocalypse. "For a Horse Named Corwin" is a gritty sci-fi/western with a genetically enhanced, talking horse. Exploring an AI controlled post-apocalyptic world is "The Judgment of Edward Tillingham", and "Designation Null" is the dark cousin of my much lighter android story, "Probability: Resolve."

You have probably already picked up on this, but these stories are, by and large, darker than my usual fare, going into territory that I wouldn't have strayed into earlier in my writing. There's some humor and horror (together, of course) and a hard-boiled detective trying to stay ahead of his inner demons.

I hope you enjoy these anomalies. As with *Life After*, each tale is followed by a short backstory for those of you that like to know the story behind the story.

Enjoy!

Robert J. McCarter, May 2018

PART ONE

JACK WHO WORKS THE BEANSTALK

JACK WHO WORKS THE BEANSTALK

JACK LOOKED SMALL FOR HIS AGE, WHICH WAS FINE BY HIM. Looking like he was ten when he was twelve was a competitive advantage. He had more experience, he knew more. When you're competing for scraps from tourists, or the proceeds of an occasional lift, you took what you could get. And today he needed it all. Mary was counting on him.

Jack ran his fingers through his stringy brown hair, his sharp blue eyes watching everyone and everything. His face was dirty, his clothes ragged, and he walked with a slight limp. All of it on purpose.

His mouth still had the metallic tang from the cheap antibiotics he had taken and he wasn't quite healthy, but he was well enough. Jack stood in his usual spot, under the scant shade of a mesquite tree in front of the Martian beanstalk terminal high on the slope of Pavonis Mons. The beanstalk rose before him out of sight; at first appearing large, about eight meters in diameter, but then thinning to an apparent thread as it reached to the red-tinged heavens. Several times a day cars slid down it bringing visitors or cargo from orbit.

From here you had "the best view in the universe," as he was fond of telling travelers. Pavonis wasn't nearly as tall as Olympus Mons, but sitting on the equator it was ideal for the beanstalk and there was water below the surface from ancient glaciers for the city. You could see New Chicago arrayed on the southern slope of the volcano below, and beyond it green patches of agri-land and the still mostly red expanse of Mars. And beyond that you could just make out the bulk of the CO_2 mines as they continued to work, thickening the still thin atmosphere.

Jack longed to ride up that beanstalk, to escape to the moon, to the asteroid belt, or even Earth. But a sonofawhore like him never got to leave. He was destined to have a hard life of subsistence on a Mars that the rest of the solar system was no longer so enthralled with.

"Hey, mister," Jack said to the man who had just exited the towering glass-faced terminal, its Gothic-inspired architecture harking back to when Mars's future was much more promising. The man was dressed well but simply, and carried a metal brief-case. "Mister, do you need a guide? I'm the best, none better in all of New Chicago City."

The man, who had a bland, forgettable face, looked down at the boy and their eyes locked. Jack always made eye contact with his clients. He knew it made him appear trustworthy, and he got to learn about them that way.

"What's your name, boy?" the man asked.

"Jack, my name is Jack. What's yours, mister?"

"Jack?" the man asked, shaking his head and smiling, pointing over Jack's shoulder at the beanstalk. "You're Jack, there's the beanstalk. That's good. I like that. Aldan. Call me Aldan."

Jack's brow furrowed; he didn't understand what was so amusing about his name. "OK, Mister Aldan, where can I take you?"

"You don't know about *Jack and the Beanstalk*?" Aldan asked.

Jack shrugged, sticking to business. "I'll give you a good deal, only 50 creds for the day."

Their eyes had remained locked for the entire exchange. That never happened; nobody looked you in the eye for that long. And Jack noticed something odd. The man had exited the terminal out into the bright Martian sunshine, but the irises of his gray eyes hadn't constricted, not one bit. He would either have to be so high on kethylin that he couldn't walk, or he was an artificial.

"50 creds, huh? Looks like you could use more," Aldan said with a smile. "How about 75 a day for the next two days."

"Sure, Mister Aldan, sure," Jack said with a smile that masked his concern. No one ever offered more, ever. And while he had heard rumors of artificials, he had never seen one.

Most days after an exchange like this, Jack would have come up with a convenient illness and begged off. But not today, even though he was barely well. He needed the money and Mary needed him.

ON EARTH, IN CHICAGO, THEY WOULDN'T HAVE REALLY called it a car. It was a three-wheeled, open-air cart with a large solar panel on the top. It was adept at navigating the narrow sloped streets and sharp turns.

"Come on, Mister Aldan," Jack said, tugging on the man's sleeve as he moved quickly, his limp becoming more pronounced. "Come meet Junior, best driver in all of New C."

Junior had brown skin, with bright green eyes, and was leaning against his car working his teeth with a bit of wood as the two approached.

"Junior," Jack began, "this is Mister Aldan, and he has important business here, real important business. He needs a driver and I told him you were the best."

"Happy to help," Junior said with a tip of his wide-brimmed hat indicating for the others to get in his car before following. "Where can I take you, Mister Aldan?"

"To the Maze, please," Aldan said casually, pointing down to the chaotic jumble that clung to the western edge of the orderly New Chicago streets.

Junior threw Jack a piercing glare. "Uhh, Mister Aldan," Jack said, "that is not a safe place. Are you sure you want to go there?"

"Sure," Aldan said, "I got the best guide and best driver in all of New Chicago; it shouldn't be a problem, should it?"

Jack swallowed, forced a smile on his face, and said, "Nope." He studied the man further. He was tall and thin and he sat with his hands on his lap, and both feet on the floor looking forward. His metal briefcase sat between his feet. Jack stole a few glances at the case; it was made of a burnished metal with two small black rectangles along the top edge. Jack figured they were fingerprint readers. He began regretting the 75 creds a day; he should be getting more for this kind of work.

"So what's your business in the Maze, mister?" Jack asked once Junior had started driving. Jack knew Junior didn't want to go, his tensed shoulders as he gripped the steering wheel told the story.

"I promised my aunt I would look up a relative of ours."

"Yeah, what's his name? The Maze is pretty big and if I can tell Junior which way to approach it, that would really help."

"I think they call him Carl," Aldan said.

Jack saw Junior's shoulders rise up another notch. "Carl, huh? He doesn't go by Carl the Caterer, does he?"

"Yes. That's it."

Junior gasped and Jack saw his knuckles go from brown to white as he gripped the steering wheel. Jack "accidentally" kicked the back of Junior's chair.

"OK, mister," Jack said with his heart beating fast and a smile on his lips. "Junior, go around the south end. You can park there and I'll walk Mister Aldan in."

"Your funeral," Junior mumbled.

Jack led the tall man through the Maze, Jack's right hand holding Aldan's sleeve. They walked on compacted red dirt, down the narrow winding streets and alleys. The ramshackle buildings rose above them, each one unique in materials and construction. Shipping containers were the basis of many, but the materials varied, from sheets of steel, to tarps, to cardboard, to irregular red bricks. The place was hot and stunk of perspiration and urine.

As they entered a larger street from an alley, a wave of Condenados swept by raising their bottles and singing, "Martian scum and villains all. You sent us away, but we stand tall. Proud we are and victorious. Someday Earth will bow to us."

Jack spun around and quickly went back into the alley. Aldan spun smoothly and followed. The Condenados were gangs of young people, predominately made up of criminals exiled to Mars. New Chicago once had a large penal colony, but when the economy had collapsed, all the prisoners had been freed to fend for themselves.

"You know, mister," Jack began, once again looking his client up and down, "you're not normal. I didn't tell you why I had you by the sleeve; you just did what I needed you to. Just like that, not a word said."

"And?" Aldan asked.

"And what? You're not normal, mister. No other client has ever acted like you. They need to be babied and coddled and explained every little thing. Think they know best when they ain't never set foot on this planet before."

"So, I guess I am glad that I am not normal."

Jack stared at his eyes, at those unchanging pupils. "Look, you seem like a good sort, so I'll just tell you. Carl the Caterer, despite his pleasant name, is just about the nastiest guy in these parts. He runs a bunch of gangs and controls much of the Maze."

Aldan nodded his head and said, "Yes. I know."

"And I would wager the full 150 creds you're gonna pay me that he is not a relative."

Aldan just smiled, showing his perfect white teeth.

Jack looked at him hard again, but Aldan didn't say anything else, so Jack grabbed his sleeve and pulled him deeper into the Maze.

The rest of the journey was quiet and without incident. Jack led them in an even more circuitous route than was strictly necessary. They had picked up a tail when they entered the Maze, and it took a while to lose them. His client was compliant, he was perfect, and this did not sit well with Jack. He worried about the moment when he wasn't compliant and perfect. He didn't want to be around for that.

They arrived in front of an unusually well-built red brick building; on it hung a sign that said, "Carl's Butcher Shop and Catering."

"OK, mister," Jack said. "Here we are. This is as far as I go."

"I may need you, Jack. I will double your rate if you come in."

Jack paused a moment thinking of Mary, his harried frown turning to a smile. "Sure, mister, but I get my first day's pay once we get out of this place."

"Of course," Aldan said. He handed the briefcase to Jack and added, "I think I might need both hands free." He then squared his shoulders, pushed back the blanket that served as a door, and strode in.

––––––––

JACK WAS SCARED, THERE WAS NO DENYING IT. HE DID HIS best to hide it, but he knew anyone with even a bit of skill reading people could sense his fear; he stunk of it. He hung back for a minute after Aldan had entered, clutching the cool metal case to his chest. He thought about running, he though hard about it, and twice he almost did run. His right foot leading away from this place, only to have his left foot bring him right back.

Sounds escaped the building. Harsh words, grunts, and crashes. These made Jack want to run away and go in, too. Who was this Aldan? Was he in over his head? By running he might survive, but not get paid. By going in he would get paid if he survived. Jack could not turn away, not today. So, he took a deep breath, and with a more exaggerated limp than usual, he strode in.

The scene inside was chaos: three large men on the floor unconscious; an overturned table with playing cards and chips strewn throughout the room; and in the middle of it, facing another man, stood Aldan. But to Jack's eyes he was a different man. His relaxed hands looked deadly instead of docile, his long thin body looked dangerous instead of weak, his cool, even tone sounded powerful instead of passive. Jack silently cursed himself for missing the commotion while locked in his own indecision. *Don't get yourself killed, Jack*, he thought.

"You agreed to these terms," Aldan said to the man in front of him, who Jack recognized as Carl the Caterer.

Carl was a large man, with a red-stained white apron pulled taut around his massive belly. He had brown eyes and sagging jowls, with sweat running down his cheeks. He stood in front of a small glass case with cuts of meat arrayed under bright lights. Meat was scarce and expensive on Mars and butcher shops even scarcer. Jack's nose filled with the blood of the dead animals and it made him want to run.

"You're making a mistake, mister," Carl said, using the word "mister" as a curse. "You won't leave the Maze alive."

Aldan's head jutted back, indicating the bodies on the floor, "Either comply with the terms you agreed to or I will just take what I came for."

With a sharp nod, Carl moved behind a counter that held an archaic cash register.

"I'll need that briefcase now," Aldan said, extending his hand behind him while keeping his eyes on Carl.

"Sure thing," Jack said, quickly delivering the case and moving back several steps.

Aldan placed the case on the counter, putting his thumbs to the two black rectangles. It popped open. Carl took the case behind the counter, put something in it, and returned the case to Aldan.

"Your payment will be made as soon as the delivery is complete," Aldan said as he backed out of the room, never letting his gaze leave Carl.

Once outside, he turned to Jack and said, "Get us out of here by the most direct route, please."

"Right away," Jack said, grabbing Aldan's sleeve and moving forward quickly, his limp forgotten.

DURING THE TRIP TO THE CAPITAL, ALDAN'S NEXT destination, everyone was silent until after they arrived and Aldan had taken the case up the ornate red stairs to the capital building.

Jack sat there staring at the tall columns and dome of the structure. He had only been in the city center once before. It wasn't the kind of place that wanted people like Jack. He wondered at his client, a man who gladly stood against Carl the Caterer. Even the Condenados stayed out of Carl's way.

"Who the hell is he?" Junior hissed. "Him just being waved through all the checkpoints like he's the bloody king of England or somethin'."

"I think he's an arty," Jack whispered.

"No... Impossible," Junior whispered back. "They don't make anything nearly that human looking."

"He is, I swear. You should have seen what he did to Carl's thugs. And watch his pupils, they never dilate or constrict. It ain't natural."

"How do you know he's not an andy?"

Jack snorted, "Why would they wanna make an android that lifelike? Nah, I've been watching him, talking to him, whatever kind of brain he's got, it used to be a human brain."

After a pause, Junior looked around and said, "What are you going to do?"

Jack shrugged and rubbed at his long brown hair. "I need the creds, Junior. I gotta stick with him."

Jack sat in a chair next to the hotel room's window watching the street far below and listening to the sound of Aldan's humming in the shower. He was mad at himself for getting roped into this—and so easily.

"Don't my 150 creds get me twenty–four-hour service?" Aldan had asked. They stood in the lobby of the towering hotel in New Chicago.

After a pause, Jack shook his head and said, "No, mister. I don't do that kind of work. If you need companionship I can help you acquire it, but I am not available no matter what the creds."

Aldan had paused for a long time, a deep frown on his face— the first Jack had seen. "To keep watch, Jack. That's all, just watch."

Jack had nodded and he had followed Aldan up to the hotel room. They had ordered room service and eaten well before Aldan went into the bathroom.

Jack was still nervous sitting there, wishing he had a way out. He had heard the stories. He couldn't believe all the stupid things he kept doing; he would get himself killed, and if he did, what would happen to Mary?

At least he was warm. The Martian nights got cold, the temperature dramatically dropping at sundown. Surprised by a small rustle, Jack looked up to see Aldan standing in front of him fully clothed—much to his relief. Jack was mad at himself again; he kept getting lost in his head and missing what was going on.

"So, *Jack and the Beanstalk*," Aldan began sitting on the bed. "It's an old story, written about four hundred years ago, about a young man named Jack who trades his cow for magic beans. The beans grow into a giant beanstalk which Jack climbs."

Jack smiled, beginning to understand Aldan's amusement when he found Jack in front of the Martian beanstalk.

"Up there he finds a mean giant, fabulous treasures, and has a grand adventure."

"What's it like?" Jack asked, the words tumbling out of him. "Earth and Jupiter station. The outpost on Ceres. Have you been to those places? Have you met any of the Xinis, the aliens? Do you get to travel everywhere?"

Aldan smiled and laid back on the bed, telling Jack about each of the places he asked about in his slow, steady tone. Wonders that Jack knew he would never see.

———

THEY CAME IN THE EARLY HOURS OF THE MORNING, AN HOUR before dawn.

Jack sat on watch, his head full of exotic places and strange aliens. He studied the man as he slept and was disappointed; Aldan's face was slack, his strange eyes twitching under their lids, his chest rising and falling evenly. It was entirely normal.

Jack had really hoped Aldan was an arty. Now that would be something, a story he could tell. Just a guy with artificial eyes with busted iris, that was interesting but it wasn't—

Jack heard scuffling outside the door and hissed, "Aldan!"

Aldan woke swiftly and was on his feet. "Get in the bathroom," he said calmly as he stuffed some pillows in the bed, making it look occupied, and then he smoothly moved across the room and placed himself flat against the wall by the door.

Jack moved into the bathroom but kept the door cracked; he wasn't going to miss the action again.

Aldan let both of the big men enter the room and fire into the bed before he attacked.

He moved with a catlike grace sliding into position behind them as they fired. His leg swept out, toppling both men as soon as they started to lower their guns. His fist then jabbed down twice, once on each of their heads, and the men were silent.

"Look, mister," Jack said, "I got a deadline. Can you just pay me so I can take care of something?"

They were in a dark room in the Maze, with a dirt floor and an old cot and a threadbare blanket as a door. Jack had an arrangement with the owner and slept there at times. He had slipped the wrinkled crone a few extra creds to keep her quiet about the guest. She had given Jack a knowing, sneering look as they went into the room.

"It is too dangerous, Jack."

"The place I gotta go is in the Maze, not far from here, and someone will die if I don't get this done. You'll be safe here. I gave the crone enough creds to buy her silence for at least a couple of hours."

Aldan was silent for several minutes, his unchanging eyes fixed on the boy. Jack didn't care, he didn't waver, he kept staring into those eyes.

"OK," Aldan finally said, getting up. "But I am going with you."

"That was quick," the crone cackled as they left. Both the man and the boy ignored her.

"Where is she, where's Mary?" Jack asked the short

man. He had dark eyes and a pinched face and was leaning against the door to a little pawn shop deep in the Maze.

The man's dark eyes darted around, fixing themselves on Aldan. "Who's the tourist?"

"He's... He's with—" Jack began.

"I am here," Aldan said, "to advocate on behalf of my client, in the case that negotiations should break down."

The dark-eyed man shook his head and shrugged his shoulders. "Sorry, kid, you didn't come up with the creds fast enough, she's gone. Someone probably ate her by now."

Jack's face scrunched up as he tried in vain to hold back the tears. "You... you bastard. I'll... I'll..."

"What are you going to do, little man?" he said, looking at Jack's balled up fists. "You gonna hit me with those?"

Jack let out a wail and swung first his right fist and then his left, but the dark-eyed man was faster, his foot came up and hit Jack square in the chest. Jack fell back into the dust, tears running openly down his cheeks.

No sooner had Jack hit the ground than Aldan had the man pinned face down in the dirt next to Jack, one knee leaning on his back, and a hand squeezing his throat.

"Now," Aldan said smoothly, his head close to the dark-eyed man's, "begins the phase of the negotiations where you tell Jack exactly what he wants to know."

THEIR JOURNEY HAD LED THEM THROUGH MUCH OF THE Maze. From the crazy one-toothed old man who normally deals in ancient artifacts, to the lovely one-eyed woman who normally deals in the sex trade. They had all had Mary, if only briefly. In between their stops searching for Mary, they dodged Carl the Caterer's men and the various gangs.

"Ah, yes," the man with the pipe said. He had a small junk shop built from a shipping container. "She's in back. Don't know why I bought her, it's not as if I know what to do with her. Besides, I don't need another mouth to feed."

The negotiations were swift; the man with the pipe was willing to sell Mary for what he paid, which was about the same as Jack had been paid by Aldan.

After the funds were exchanged, the man came out with a cage that contained a small simian: Mary. When Mary saw Jack, she screeched and jumped up and down in the cage.

Jack rushed forth, opening the cage, and the monkey climbed up to Jack's shoulders, holding onto his hair with one hand and jumping up and down and screeching loudly.

Aldan smiled.

"You know what your problem is, Jack?" Aldan asked as they walked away down one of the wider streets of the Maze away from the junk shop.

"No, mister, what?"

"You've got a heart."

"Look, mister, I really appreciate your help. I want you to know this is not the way I normally conduct business. It's just that... I had to get Mary back."

"How did you lose her?" Aldan asked.

Jack shrugged, "Got sick, had to put her up as collateral for the meds. I wouldn't have done it, but without me she woulda starved or been eaten."

Just then the monkey screeched and the boy and the man noticed the figure standing several meters in front of them dressed in his bloody apron with his meaty fists on his waist. Jack looked around and saw three thugs behind them with weapons drawn.

"Don't worry," Carl said to Jack, a grin on his face, his lips smacking, "I'll take good care of Mary after we are done conducting our business." Turning to Aldan, he said, "I want my merchandise back."

Aldan shrugged, "It has already been processed. Your payment has been made."

The street had been busy and when the guns came out some people had run away, but others had stayed, pressing themselves against the ramshackled walls of the buildings that lined the street.

"The payment was insufficient." Carl sighed. "I'll guess I'll have to take my payment in flesh. You'll be coming with me now."

Jack looked up at Aldan and saw something in those unchanging eyes: a warning, an admonishment.

Aldan took a graceful step forward and said, "We got off on the wrong foot. Why don't—"

"Stop!" Carl yelled, holding his hand up. "One more move and we'll just take care of things right here."

Jack watched as Aldan stumbled and fell forward as if caught off balance by the Mars's low gravity and the demand to stop. Jack dropped, shielding Mary with his body as the shots rang out.

When Jack looked up, Carl the Caterer was lying on the street dead, his blood soaking into the red dirt. Aldan had vanished. Carl's men cursed and ran away.

JACK GAZED UP AT THE BEANSTALK AND THOUGHT, *SOMEDAY I'll climb it like the boy in the fairy tale. Someday I'll find my riches.* Mary's return had boded well for Jack. He had made enough each of the last three days to keep them fed and sheltered.

He didn't notice the man approaching from behind him, but Mary did. She let out a brief chirp from her perch on Jack's shoulder. Jack turned and saw Aldan.

"Mister Aldan," Jack said with a grin. "I am so glad you're all right."

With a small smile, Aldan said, "I couldn't have done it without you, Jack."

"Well, mister, next time you come back, look me up."

"I will."

"Can I ask you a question?" Aldan nodded, so Jack continued. "I've been thinking, and you didn't come all the way out here to take something from Carl and deliver it to the capital. Anyone coulda done that." Aldan's face remained impassive so Jack continued, "You came here to piss Carl off so that he would do something stupid and get himself publicly killed, and not by you."

Aldan smiled, full and wide, and then took a small slip of paper out of his pocket and handed it to Jack.

"What is this?"

"An access number. Memorize it and destroy it. If you get tired of being Jack who works the beanstalk, dial it up. Tell the person who answers the following three words: Aldan, Mary, Carl."

"What?" Jack asked. "Who do you work for?"

"Can you remember that, Jack?"

"Sure, mister. Sure."

"Good," Aldan said as he strode towards the terminal. "We could always use a man like you."

Puzzled, but pleased, Jack watched him go into the terminal and imagined himself riding up the beanstalk and getting into a spaceship bound for exotic destinations and glorious adventures.

BACKSTORY—JACK WHO WORKS THE BEANSTALK

WE'RE STARING OFF EASY HERE WITH THE ANOMALIES. FOR me, this YA (Young Adult) sci-fi is unusual because of the YA and harder sci-fi nature of it. Contemporary fantasy (i.e. ghosts and such) are easier to write, no pesky research and looking up details. Getting sci-fi facts right (or right enough) is a lot of work.

This story started as an image: a street urchin plying his trade on Mars. The allusion to Jack and the Beanstalk just fell out of that and while the story doesn't parallel the fairy tale, this Jack still longs to rise out of poverty and achieve greater things.

This story received an honorable mention in the Writers of the Future contest.

PART TWO
THE DOUR MR. M

THE DOUR MR. M

"She's going to die," Mr. M. said, his lean, middle-aged face serious as he stared at the old woman who had a grimace ruining her once lovely face. She was on a narrow bed, the sheets tucked in around her neck.

"No shit," I answered. Mr. M. had a habit of stating the radically obvious like he was conveying the mysteries of the ages. Like, "Well, you know, the sun will be rising in the morning." Or, "You've got to pay your taxes, no real choice there." Not that he said either of those things, not his area. His prognosis concerning my mother was his area.

"When?" I asked. She was suffering, the tears slowly leaking out her eyes, her quivering jaw, darting eyes, and clenched expression made that clear. Her damaged brain brought her nothing but fear now. Her breath was sour and caustic, the scent would linger in my nose long after I left. Death would be a relief—for me and I do believe for her—if nothing else.

Mr. M. shrugged his thin, bare shoulders, his washed-out blue eyes briefly connecting with mine. "'But of that day and hour no one knows, not even the angels of heaven,'" he said, his voice dry as he quoted the Bible. Something else I didn't like about him. The Bible seemed unequipped to explain the breadth human suffering, especially what this disease was doing to her.

Lately, I've been referring to my mother by her first name—Olivia—because the Alzheimer's took my mother away long ago. Her grey hair was short and plastered to her head from too long in that bed.

The room was nice enough. A twin bed, a nice blue recliner, pictures on the wall of tropical locations my parents had visited after retirement. It was most of her world at this point, which made the room seem small and mean.

"It won't be soon enough," I said, regarding how long to Olivia's death. This wasn't life. This was suffering.

Mr. M. raised an eyebrow and stared at me. I sat on the bed, holding my mother's hands. Her joints were large and arthritic, but her skin still so smooth. He stood on the other side of the bed, nude. Mr. M. didn't believe in clothing, calling it "a useless shield against the vagaries of living."

"Are you planning something?" he asked, a small spark in those dull blue eyes.

I shook my head and looked back at my mother. "It's okay, Mom. I'm here. I won't let anyone hurt you."

But the truth was I was desperate to end her suffering, and the suffering of those that loved her—especially mine.

I met Mr. M. about three years ago, just after we had moved my mother into the memory care unit. I was lying in the snow, staring up at the startling blue sky and snow-covered pine trees, disoriented and confused.

"You fell," he said, his middle-aged, dour face floating into view surrounded by that blue. Without that expression, he might have been handsome, his face gently wrinkled, crowned with short salt-and-pepper hair.

I nodded. I had fallen. I was up on the roof trying to remove two feet of snow that my old house couldn't handle. At first I thought he was a neighbor.

"You're dying," he said. His face was passive as he delivered his prognosis, kind of like he was telling me it had just snowed, or that spring was still ten weeks away.

A shiver ran through my body, the cold snow that pressed against my back was sucking the warmth out of me. I tried to move and an electric spike of pain stabbed at my gut.

"It's a tree branch," he said, like he was reading the telephone book. "It has run you through. You are bleeding quite a lot."

I sucked in a breath and could smell the clean, cold air, tinged with iron. I couldn't see it, but I imagined a red stain seeping into the perfect white snow.

"Help me," I said, my breath gushing out in a cloud of condensate.

"Everyone dies."

I blinked, noticing for the first time that this man was nude, in the snow, early in the morning, with the temperature well below freezing. He didn't seem cold, and I didn't notice any condensation as he exhaled.

"Who are you?" I asked as I started to fumble for my phone. It was in my jacket pocket, wasn't it? My arms were clumsy and my hands stiff in their gloves.

"You can call me Mr. M."

"You... you're not real, are you?" My teeth chattered as blood flowed out of me and the cold creeped in. My wife and daughter were still asleep. I heard shoveling close by, but my house was set down from the road and no one could see me. I pulled a glove off and got my phone out of my pocket, but it slipped.

Mr. M. shrugged his bare shoulders. "What's 'real' anyway?"

"Help!" I tried to shout, but it came out thin and weak, barely a croak. "Help me!"

"They can't hear you," my naked companion said. "It's just you and me. Don't worry, though, I won't leave you."

I panicked, my bare right hand fishing in the snow for the phone. Where was it? I had to find it. It seemed like hours passed, my hand numb when I finally found the glass and plastic rectangle. I pulled it up in front of me; it was covered in pink and red snow.

"It's best to just relax," Mr. M. said as I fumbled to unlock the phone. I pulled the glove off my left hand with my teeth, drawing my password pattern, once, twice, three times... I couldn't get it. My hands were not working right.

"Tap where it says 'emergency,'" Mr. M. said.

I did and the dialer came up, but I couldn't manage to get 911 dialed properly, my hands shaking, my teeth chattering.

"Here, let me," he said, his pale finger stabbing down on the three digits. "Not sure if it will help."

"Nine-one-one, what is the nature of your emergency," a female voice said from my phone. I could barely hear it; the phone wasn't in speaker mode.

"Fell," I croaked. "Bleeding. Help me."

"Sir," the tinny voice said, "I can't hear you. What is the nature of your emergency?"

"Dying," I tried to shout, but it was a croak. "Help!"

The phone slipped from my hand back into the snow. I could barely hear indistinct mumbling.

I looked back up at the sky and the passive face of Mr. M. I couldn't struggle anymore; I didn't have it in me. The sky was so blue, so beautiful. I love mornings like this after the storm has broken, when the air is crisp and fresh, the snow clinging to the pine trees like puffy cumulonimbus clouds. The world is so beautiful.

My vision began to tunnel in and the last thing I saw before the darkness came were the pale blue eyes of Mr. M.

MR. M.'S EYES ARE WATERED DOWN, AS IF AT ONE POINT THE blue had been vibrant, like the winter sky on a mountain, but he lost something and the intensity bled out, like a slow tire leak you don't notice until it becomes dangerous. Some mornings, my eyes look a little like that too. Not that they were ever very intense— passion is something I long for in my life, but I don't fully understand.

After that visit at my mom's bedside, I kept thinking about the tiny spark in Mr. M.'s eyes when he thought I might do something to end my mother's suffering. As if that, and only that, could breathe life into his tired soul. And I would do it—end her suffering —if I could. That's what I told myself at first, that I would do it, but there wasn't really a way. The truth was there were many ways, just not any that were without significant risk. To my mother and to me. Well... mostly to me. She's barely there, her brain finally approaching the end of its long, slow digression. One of these months she'll forget how to breathe, or better yet, contract pneumonia and pass from that. But any action I could take would risk jail, and that puts my family at risk.

That's what I told myself, but a little niggling voice inside of me told me that if I was a passionate person, I would figure out a way. I could end her suffering humanely and not get caught.

These thoughts flitted through my mind on my next visit. Her hand was so warm, the skin smooth like expensive leather. The tendons stuck out and the skin clung to the bone as she had lost a lot of weight. She was dying, there was no hope for improvement, and yet every day, three times a day, the caregivers shoveled food into her mouth. And she ate, mostly from reflex, I think. I wanted to yell at them, to tell them to stop, that we all just needed to let her go. But I didn't even have the courage for that.

She moaned and her eyes flickered open, their glassy brown depths unfocused and then, for a moment, her eyes snapped onto mine like she recognized me. Her lips moved, pursing and then breath puffing out in a weak "p" sound.

"I'm here, Mom. It's Peter."

She continued the p-puff and I had to pull back, the scent of her breath rotten, cloying, and slightly metallic.

Mr. M. sauntered in, his hands behind his back, his naked form gaunt and pale.

"I'll be your lookout," he said with a thin, toothless smile. I had never seen him smile before.

I shook my head and looked back at my mother.

"Your work is suffering. Your marriage is stretched to the breaking point. Your daughter misses you. These people will do everything they can to preserve her 'life.' They can't help themselves." He actually used air quotes when he said "life."

I shrugged. It was all true, but what could I do? Leave her here to die alone? Take a pillow and smother her?

"It's wrong," I said.

"Ending suffering is never wrong."

I didn't look away from my mother's drawn face until I heard him shuffle away.

Is Mr. M. a hallucination? I've tested him many times, the first was on the slopes in Aspen, Colorado. My recovery from my fall had left me, if not passionate, then more energetic than my stable and steady norm. The ambulance had gotten to me just in time, and it was strange to know I had Mr. M. to thank for that. After I recovered, I took my wife and daughter for a nearly spontaneous skiing trip. I was enjoying a brief moment of solitude looking down a route much steeper than I was comfortable with, when Mr. M. showed up walking through the snow.

"I want to show you something," he said, his voice dull like an old kitchen knife.

I looked around, and since no one was near, I followed him to a nearby fir tree. Under it was the half-frozen remains of a rabbit, it's back end torn, a garish, ragged red. "He didn't run fast enough," he said, his pale eyes finding mine. "You never know when you won't be fast enough."

I sighed and dug my poles into the snow, ready to push off down the slope, the terrifying grade be damned.

"Test me," he said, suddenly right in front of me.

"What?"

"You don't believe I'm real, so test me."

I shrugged and thought for a moment. "Describe the next person I will see."

He nodded and smiled. "Hot pink down jacket with blue ski poles."

I shook my head but waited the two minutes it took and there she was, a teenage girl dressed just as he promised.

He did it three more times and would have done it more, but I couldn't take it. I shoved off and started making my way down the slope, slowly cutting from side to side to regulate my speed. About halfway down, some kid slammed into me and sent me sprawling.

Mr. M.'s pale face appeared above mine as I sucked in cold air, my lower back feeling as if someone had chopped it with an axe. "You never know when you won't be fast enough. But don't worry, my friend, you aren't dying... this time."

———

Mom was asleep in her bed, her brow furrowed even in slumber. I sat there next to her in a hard, wooden chair staring at a piece of paper in my hand. On it was a list of times with a few words scrawled next to it. Like "4:15 p.m. 'Yes, you do live here, Margaret,'" or "4:33 p.m. 'You're not George! Where's George!'"

My hands looked older than they used to. Boney with prominent veins on the back and spots you might prefix the word "age" to. They didn't look like they were mine anymore. They were shaking a little, like fall leaves in a slight breeze. You see, I never did believe that Mr. M. was real. Despite the predictions in Aspen and the many other times, I was convinced that fall I took off the roof, the stick running me through, and facing my own mortality had jarred something loose in my psyche. I was sure that the predictions were a trick of memory. Even though I remember seeing him, remember him making predictions, there was still no objective proof.

But this piece of paper and the picture on my cell phone were that objective proof. I had written the note the last time I had seen him, yesterday morning when I was home sick in bed. He told me that I wasn't dying and I would be fine in the morning. He told me to write down the times and phrases. He had me take a picture of it with my phone so it would have a time/date stamp, and when I began to doubt, I could know it wasn't just a trick of memory.

He made me promise something before he did it, though. He said, "Peter, you promise me you'll end your mother's suffering and I'll prove I'm real beyond any shadow of a doubt." That little spark danced in his watery blue eyes.

So I promised, sure I was promising myself, and that nothing would come of it.

And like clockwork, each of the eight phrases were said at the exact time predicted. The last one was my mother. George was my father's name and he's been gone five years now. The picture of the piece of paper is on my phone.

Mr. M. is real. Real. And I promised to kill my mother.

"WHAT ARE YOU?" I ASKED MR. M. AS THE DISTANT, warbling cry of an ambulance got slowly closer. I could barely hear it over the ringing in my ears. My mouth tasted funny, like talc or something, undoubtedly from the airbag deploying. My front right tire had blown, my car ramming into an ancient oak tree. Blood dripped down my face into my mouth, the taste of iron overwhelming the talc.

This was six months after that Aspen ski vacation.

Mr. M. shrugged from the passenger's seat, nude as always. I don't know why, but "naked" seems wrong to describe his state. Naked implies a vulnerability that was completely lacking.

"You don't know?" I asked, struggling to focus my eyes so the two Mr. M.'s turned into one.

He ignored my question. "You might die, chances aren't very good, a brain aneurism is highly unlikely from the blow to your head, but..." He ended in a hopeful tone with a small shrug.

"What are you?" I said, gritting my teeth.

"It's not a simple question," he said. "What are *you*?"

I wasn't sure I heard him right. It was the simplest of questions. "I'm Peter Maan. I'm a middle-aged white man that teaches high school history and lives on planet earth."

"Are you sure?"

I closed one eye and wiped the blood from my forehead, it was flowing at an alarming rate, but at least there was only one Mr. M. now. "Yes. I'm sure."

He harrumphed, as if my assurance held no weight with him. "Well, I'm not sure that's what you are, and I have no idea what I am."

"Are you real?"

He sighed. "We've been over this. From you're rather unimaginative perspective, yes, I am real."

"What are you?" I asked again. The ambulance was close and I didn't think I had long with him. My stomach was roiling, the smell and taste of blood mixing with what must be a nasty concussion. The world began to spin, darkness creeping along the edges of what I could see through my one eye.

"I am Mr. M.," he said with the saddest of smiles as I passed out.

To the small matter of killing one's mother in a humane and undetectable way, I say, no!

First off, killing is wrong. In all cases. Even to reduce a suffering you know will never abate. The suffering of a brain slowly eating itself on its way to forgetting how to breathe.

Secondly, it's against the law. Even if it wasn't morally wrong, risking my family's future is just stupid.

I was pacing outside the facility that housed the body of the woman that once was my mother, the summer sun beating down, bright and unrelenting in a washed-out blue sky. Sweat trickled down my back, and my mouth was dry.

I had a plan. It would work. The chances of getting caught were slim. I hadn't done one google search, checked out one book, talked to one person—save Mr. M.—about this. There was no evidence of planning, no clear motive, just a few trips to the library and a couple cash purchases while I was out of town.

But, first off, killing is wrong, and second off, there was a chance I could get caught.

I kicked at the cracked blacktop—it too was sweltering in the heat.

"You would put down a pet, in fact you have." This was Mr. M.'s counter to my "first off." And "I will watch" was his response to my second. But I didn't trust him, the way his watery, washed-out blue eyes sparked at the thought of this act meant there was something in this for him. Something dark.

I fingered the pill container in my pocket. It was stainless steel and slightly cool to the touch. I just had to slip the two pills into her mouth, let them melt, and bye-bye, Olivia.

Bye-bye, Olivia.

She doesn't know me. When she is aware, she's afraid. She doesn't have a life anymore. What was left of her was suffering. I wouldn't put a dog through this, but I would put my mother through it?

So, my "first off" was bullshit. Nothing in life is that black and white. And my "second off" was a bit out there too. Slipping two pills in her mouth, not very high odds I'd get caught. Was I hiding from something here? Something going on beyond the normal and appropriate compunctions of humans to preserve life even when it's not appropriate?

My brain raced as my steps took me to my car. Mr. M. was there waiting. "I'll do it," he said, his voice sounding so very disappointed. He held his pale hand out. I slapped the metal container in his hand and got in my car and drove away.

At my mother's funeral, Mr. M. smiled. "It was a gentle passing," he said, showing his teeth. I had never seen him smile like that before.

My wife held my hand and my daughter looked to be in cell phone withdrawal as we watched Olivia's—my mother's—casket lowered into the ground. After everyone had thrown a bit of dirt in, they shuffled off towards the wake. It was a small gathering, just us, a few of my mother's old friends, and a cousin. I heard "relief" filter through the hot summer air a few times.

And relief was part of it, but only one of many. Oliva was back to being my mother and she was finally gone.

"I need a few minutes," I told my wife and daughter, and they scurried away, their relief obvious.

I stared into the hole, a deep, unnaturally straight cut into the earth, the cheap wood casket at the bottom.

"Why are you so happy?" I hissed at Mr. M., that smile still on his face.

"You did it," he said, nodding down into the hole, his nudity looking sensible as sweat soaked through my suit.

"I did not."

His eyes stabbed at my pocket where I gripped the stainless-steel pill container. I had given it to him in the parking lot. How had it gotten in there? I took it out and slowly shook it. Not a sound. I unscrewed the cap, the pills were gone.

"But... No!"

His eyes were bluer than the washed-out summer sky. "I'm proud of you, Peter."

"No. You did it. I never went in."

"Who do you think I am, Peter?"

My mind reeled and I remembered back when I had first met him after falling off my roof. Had he dialed 911, or had I? On the ski slope in Aspen, had I found that rabbit on my own, and when I was on my back in the snow, had my mind made those predictions up? And the note and the picture, the incontrovertible truth? I pulled my phone out and searched for the picture—it wasn't there. Had there even been a note?

My heart beat hard and my suit clung to me like a wet blanket. I couldn't breathe. I remembered the grainy feel of the pills as I pulled them out of the stainless-steel container. I remembered being surprised at how dry Olivia's mouth was as I tucked the pills in. After the pills had melted and the drugs taken effect, I remembered her eyes flying open, dull and brown; she was clearly not there. And then she sighed.

I had done it. Mr. M. was real, but he was me.

Mr. M. smiled, it was a childish smile, his frown lines pulled into an impossible configuration, like he had just woken up on Christmas morning and gotten every present he had ever wished for. He nodded to me like we were two old friends and words weren't necessary anymore. He slowly turned and walked away.

BACKSTORY—THE DOUR MR. M

THIS ONE IS PERSONAL, CATHARTIC, AN OUTLET, AND VERY dark. It's an anomaly *and* confounding *and* curious. It's so personal, in fact, I really shouldn't say anything in terms of a back story, but here we go.

The idea of Mr. M., which to me means, "Mr. Mortality," was spawned in some very difficult times and this dark little tale was my subconscious dealing with some of the trauma of it.

It's a bleak story so the backstory is rather bleak, I'm afraid. Suffice it to say I've seen suffering with a loved one similar to this story.

There are some questions worth asking in this story, questions I've had cause to ask myself.

When would death be a kindness, be the "right" thing to do despite our culture's tendency to value the length of life over the quality of life?

When would the crime of taking a life be justifiable when weighed against the suffering it would end?

What would it take for a "normal" person to break through their training and take such an action?

This story isn't about answering those questions, but about asking them.

PART THREE

THE LAST FLIGHT OF THE ACURUS

THE LAST FLIGHT OF THE ACURUS

I DIE EVERY NIGHT. NOT LITERALLY, OF COURSE, BUT ALSO NOT some metaphorical, loss of consciousness, "dying to the day" shit either. I literally feel like I am dying every single night.

Sometimes, most of the time, I feel like I can't breathe. I am, of course, breathing but my body freaks out like it is not. And when it is not that, I feel this deep, oppressive heaviness and I can't move. I can't do anything. In both cases, I am trapped, knowing that the end is near.

And it is not like I am fully awake and can rationalize myself out of this. I am in the twilight state between consciousness and unconsciousness; neither fully awake nor fully asleep. The normal rules don't apply. I am stuck, forced to feel whatever biochemical dance that is going on in my body. And whatever that dance is, it feels like death.

It is probably related to the accident. I mean, how couldn't it be? Floating out there in the darkness of the void with only the pinprick lights of the stars to illuminate me, fighting for my life, my oxygen running out.

I haven't told a soul. I don't want to be pulled from active duty and medicated. This is the only record of what I am going through. It is my hope that writing this down, getting it out, expressing it, will help to resolve the situation.

I hope it does. I honestly don't know how much longer I can stand the night terrors.

———

"Acurus, this is Command. Status update. Over."

"Command," I said. "This is the Acurus, Wells here. Hicks is on an untethered EVA working on the damage. Doesn't sound good. Is the rescue team away yet? Over."

There was a five second delay; we were a long ways out. "Roger that Wells. Your ride should be there in about 10 hours. Over."

"Beers are on me when we get back. Over and out."

I switched to the local com and said, "Yo Cap, howz it goin' out there? Over."

There was a brief laugh, followed by, "Way to follow orders Wells. Over."

"Absolutely Cap, you made it very clear I was not to call you Julia, or use 'excessively casual language' on the com. Everything being recorded on the black box, and you being all worried about posterity and the like. Over."

"The 'excessively casual language' still needs work Lieutenant Wells. And, you know full well my rank is Lieutenant Commander. Over."

"Sorry cap-o. Sorry to disregard your most appropriate order, but this bucket of bolts is yours and that makes you El Capitan. But, I will do my level best to straighten up and fly right. Over."

She laughed again, a deep throaty laugh, which is why, of course, I carried on that way. If you can make them laugh, the rest is easy.

"That damn rock ripped through the outer hull and got to our control wiring. I am attempting to bypass, so we can at least head ourselves in the right direction. Over."

The Acurus, being a space-only vessel, had a plain, utilitarian design that appealed to me. It was modular, built out of standard parts. It had its command/personnel module sandwiched in between two big cargo cubes. On the aft end was the propulsion module, where Julia was working.

"Don't know if that is needed Cap-o. Command says our taxi is ten hours out. Over."

"Well I am out here; the least I can do is—"

The Acurus lurched, shuddered, and spun laterally. Unprepared for it, I was thrown from my chair, my head connecting with the co-pilot's chair, and then the deck. I saw stars, and then nothing.

I BLAME IT ON THE PULPS, I REALLY DO.

Shortly before I was born, the Moon finally got colonized. It took us nearly a century from initially walking on the Moon to living on the Moon, but at least it happened. As I grew up, I was rapt watching the news reports, the stupid reality shows from the embedded media, and the wonder of it all. I even managed to get my folks to help me buy a telescope so I could see the buildings going up near the Shackleton crater for myself.

When I headed off to high school, mankind headed off to Mars. My entire youth, it seems, was spent watching humanity leave the cradle of earth.

And, as if that wasn't bad enough, the whole thing spawned a new pulp era in science fiction. So I would get all I could of the real thing, and then voraciously consume the pulps on my reader. Some of the old characters came back: Buck Rodgers, John Carter of Mars; along with some brand new ones: Captain Brandon Steel,

Helen Tremor, and the like. Space and adventure totally consumed me.

I grew out of it briefly when adolescence hit; I was obsessed with another type of adventure and conquest. But, as a young man fresh out of college with an engineering degree the move towards the asteroid belt swept me up. Once again I was riveted by it. The need for the rare earth elements that are critical to our high-tech lifestyle (neodymium, cerium, lutetium and the like) drove it; that and mankind had finally gotten hooked on space-life.

The Moon, with its relative closeness and certainty, suddenly seemed blasé; Mars was tantalizing—terraforming and all—but it seemed, somehow, too easy. I wanted to go further. I wanted to be a belter.

I WAS OUT FOR ALMOST TWO HOURS. I WOKE UP ON THE DECK of the Acurus's bridge, a blossoming welt on my head, feeling the micro-gravity from the spin gently pressing me against the starboard side of the bridge. I got myself into the pilot's seat and triggered the com.

"Julia! Julia. Come in Julia." There was no reply.

The view screens didn't show much, just the spinning of stars. The Acurus was doing about 15 rotations a minute around her vertical axis. I activated short range radar and found her: She was about 300 klicks away headed towards a grouping of asteroids.

The Acurus was a cargo-runner, and had been on its usual supply run; weaving through the belt and making drops at some of the outposts. We load up at Ceres Station which orbits the dwarf planet Ceres (the biggest thing in the belt). Our cargo is a combination of ice, mined from Ceres, and other supplies sent from Earth, the Moon, Mars, or produced on other asteroids. Stopping is not practical, so we make ballistic drops to the other bases as we pass them. Everything has orbits that closely matched Ceres and are not more than two day's burn away. The belt is a big chaotic place—it sits between the orbits of Mars and Jupiter—it is not practical to spread too far. There is, though, the occasional rumor of expanding to Pallas, the second biggest rock in the belt, and its family of asteroids.

We were about halfway out when the rock holed us. We had just made a drop to a termite crew (the crazy, and I mean crazy, folks that show up first on an asteroid and burrow out the base) when the rock hit. Some damn mini-wanna-be comet going fast enough to hole us.

"Julia, do you read? Captain Hicks come in. Over."

I went to work on the computer, reconstructing what happened. We not only had lateral spin, but our trajectory had changed; not a lot in the scale of the asteroid belt, but it was a lot on the human scale. When Julia was trying to reroute the wiring, she must have triggered our attitude thrusters as well as our main engines, all on the starboard side.

Further investigation revealed a small explosion occurring near where Julia was. Looking at the video logs I saw a flash of some metal plating and other debris as her body spun away from the Acurus.

I ran this through a quick simulation. I knew her position and trajectory. I knew the ship's trajectory before and after. I knew what burned and for how long. I set it up, let the computer crunch the numbers, and came up with what kind of force she was hit with. No wonder she wasn't replying.

"Julia, do you read? Julia, damn it, wake up!"

She was long past the point of no return on her suit now. It only had limited propulsion. It wasn't a full EVA, it was a lighter weight suit.

I then pulled up the specs on her space suit and simulated the damage to the most likely points of contact. That, at least, was not horrible news. The odds were decent (about 40%) that the suit survived the blow.

Oxygen would be the problem. If she had survived she only had about two hours on her tanks. Our ride would be here in about eight hours, but that would do her no good. No good at all.

I briefly considered calling this in to Command. I know what they would say; I know what protocol was: Stay put. So I didn't give them the chance to say no, and started working on a rescue plan.

THE NIGHT TERRORS CAME AGAIN LAST NIGHT, BUT IT WAS different this time. I wasn't in that twilight terror state; I was fully in a dream. I dreamed I was bones, dark grey bones. I wasn't dying, I was dead. I could clearly see my legs and my feet. The skinniness of the toe bones was striking. I was just looking at them, staring at them, knowing they were mine, when this force grabbed me from behind and moved me.

I watched as my legs and feet flopped around. I was terrified. I didn't know what had grabbed me, but I knew that it was dark, and that the force it exerted was irresistible.

Actually, the force seemed to be the darkness itself. I woke up panting and sweating.

I have no idea if this is progress, but it is, at least, a change.

I WAS IN THE UPPER AIRLOCK, WHICH WAS SMALL, AND WITH the big EVA rig I had on, I barely fit.

The LEVAR (Long-range EVA Rig) was attached to the back of my space suit. It had oxygen, fuel, thrusters, improved communication, and a big brain. It was so big, I had to take it into the airlock and put it on there. It took me a while; it is something you normally have help with. Mating the suit to the LEVAR has to be perfect. I ended up sticking a camera to the ceiling of the airlock and putting the output on the screen there, so I could watch while I docked with it.

Making it even more unwieldy, I had attached a T-valve and an extension hose to the oxygen feed, so I could change out oxygen; which I would need to do. I had two of the blue O2 tanks strapped securely to my legs, and one to the LEVAR. My simulations showed that both of us surviving required this.

It took everything I had not to freak out. It was all taking too long; every minute put her farther away, made her tanks closer to empty. From waking up to getting out into space took about 90 minutes.

I hadn't told Command yet. I didn't want to risk them ordering me to stay put, and then me going against orders. I wanted to survive, and keep my commission.

As the airlock cycled, I recorded a message to Command.

COMMAND, THIS IS LIEUTENANT RAJESH WELLS ACTING commander of the Acurus. Please listen to this entire transmission and view the accompanying simulation before contacting me.

Lieutenant Commander Hicks has been injured and I am attempting a rescue. While she made repairs to the Acurus, the main starboard thruster and starboard attitude control fired at full capacity for 3.2 seconds. There was a small explosion that sent Hicks moving one way, and the thrusters sent the Acurus moving another. Her vector is taking her towards a cluster of asteroids.

I have been unable to raise her on the com, and her suit is not responsive to communications either. It is clear the suit has been damaged, but simulations show that she has a 40% chance of survival. That is enough for me.

I am taking the LEVAR and programming it to take me to her. By the time you could get a message to me I will be past the point of no return. I have enough fuel to reach her and arrest her motion and *keep her from getting tangled in the asteroids, but not enough to return to the Acurus.*

Make sure that taxi you are sending for us is not late. Over and out.

Becoming a belter was a hell of a lot harder than I imagined it to be, and believe me I didn't think it would be easy.

The International Space Consortium (ISC) doesn't fool around.

Stage 1 training happened on Earth, and was psychologically brutal. It was interesting, when I applied and got my first interview, it wasn't with some military guy, or a former astronaut, it was with a psychologist. They wanted to find out if I had the right psychological make-up to be out there on the frontier. It makes sense, but I was surprised.

I made it through that interview, and the subsequent psychological testing. Then came the Isolation Training. Sounds kinda OK, right? Well, try 30 days in solitary confinement on for size.

The box they put me in was clean, and warm. They fed me every day, but I didn't see a soul, hear a voice, or see the sky for 30 days. I only had 8 hours of electricity a day, so 16 hours a day it was pitch black. Nothing to read. Nothing to do. I spend my waking hours going toe to toe with my fears and doubts, becoming well acquainted with the ugly, unexplored crannies of my psyche, doing anything to keep it all in.

And there was a big red button in the box. One touch and you're out of the box and out of the program.

I hated that button. You don't do 30 days like that and not want to touch it. It became a figure in my dreams; it would whisper to me, taunt me and tease me until in my dreams, I gave it what it wanted. I would wake up terrified that I had actually touched the button and I was out.

I made it through, barely. From there stage 1 training transitioned immediately into a military-style boot camp. Yup, after 30 days alone you have some Drill Sergeant screaming orders at you. The Drill Sergeant wasn't the only shock, having to interact with people after so much time alone almost did me in.

If you survived that, which I did—barely—you get to do a kind of a hard-core space camp. Basic equipment training, space-suits in the pool, high-G simulations (everyone goes until they pass out), and the like

I met Julia Hicks in stage 2 ISC training on the Moon. We were all so happy to be there, to have escaped the Earth's gravity well, to be relatively assured of a career in space. And we were all so relieved to be done with stage 1 training.

It was my first evening there at mess, when I bumped into this large woman. She was about my height, 6 foot, had short blond hair, crooked teeth, and piercing grey eyes.

And it was her eyes that caught my attention. I must have been staring because she said, "Like what you see, boy?"

The "boy" caught me off guard; we both looked like we were in our mid-twenties. "Ahh... sorry." I said, my eyes leaving hers and traveling down her body.

"Now you really like what you see," she said with a laugh slapping me on the back. I sputtered another sorry out and she laughed harder. "Tell you what, buy me dinner and you can stare all you like."

Not that I could buy her dinner here. But we did eat together, and got to know each other. She was a "corn fed Nebraska girl" looking for the next great adventure. Her father had been an avid mountain climber, and she figured the only way to climb mountains he hadn't was to leave the planet. Did I mention that she was competitive?

We talked about "Isolation Training".

"So, how many days did you last?" she asked.

"Huh? I lasted all 30. You don't do 30, you don't make it here."

She laughed then, "Oh, you are gullible, aren't you? Shit, boy, I made it 21 days, and I'm a rock star. They just tell you that 30 days shit to motivate you."

I was stunned into silence.

"But that is impressive, boy. I am impressed." She then stood up and said in loud voice, "Attention everyone, attention. Mr. Wells here made it 30 days in the box. 30 fucking days! Any of you wimps do that?" There was whispering, but no answers. "Can any of you shits beat 21?" Again whispering, but no answers.

She sat down, looked me straight in the eyes and said, "You and me Wells, we gotta stick together. I don't think the rest of these pussies got what it takes."

I shook my head and smiled, I just couldn't stop looking at those grey eyes of hers.

THE AIRLOCK OPENED EXPOSING ME TO THE VOID, NOT MUCH to see but a smattering of stars. Mars was currently on the other side of its orbit, and the sun was blocked by the ship so it really was "The Void". I gently pushed off and eased my way up and out of the airlock. I managed to do it without snagging the LEVAR, which I had been worried about. The upper lock was smaller than the port and starboard.

This airlock was in the smaller crew module in between the two large cargo modules, so when I left, I had the walls of the cargo cubes on either side. I slowly made my way up pushing myself back from the wall of the cargo module until I was clear.

I looked below me and saw the Acurus. It was still as the stars rotated around us. I triggered the attitude jets on my suit and arrested my motion. The stars became motionless and the Acurus started spinning.

Looking at her simple, but ungraceful lines, I found myself reticent to leave her. She wasn't much, but she was home, she was my dream come true.

She was our home, Hicks and me.

"Hicks, come in. Hicks this is Wells, come in. Over." I tried once more. I didn't hear back, but then again, I didn't expect to.

The LEVAR had found Hicks, and showed her position on the heads-up display. It also showed her projected oxygen capacity. She had less than 45 minutes left. I was plotting a course with a 1G burn when a red warning lit up on my display: Oxygen 10%.

I cussed then, using every swear word I knew. Stupid, I had been so stupid. I had been in such a hurry I had skipped the normal checklists; I hadn't checked the tank. Stupid!

That gave me 30 minutes on my tank. I could have just changed tanks, but then we wouldn't have enough to wait for rescue.

I added a new constraint into the burn program: It had to take 20 minutes or less. The new details popped up and I groaned; it was going to take a 30 second burn at 3Gs to get me there in time.

I carefully positioned the LEVAR so I was pointed straight at her, started doing the shallow breathing I had been trained to, and said "Execute."

The LEVAR slammed into my back, taking my breath away. I had been in space long enough so that my body had changed. I knew I could never set foot on Earth again, and despite the training, and the time in simulated gravity, Mars was the most gravity I would be able to handle long term. 3Gs was a lot for me now; it was at the edge of what I could take.

I kept up the shallow breathing, hoping I wouldn't black out; something could go wrong. The heads-up showed the acceleration.

1G... 2Gs... My head went light, and my vision constricted. I'm coming Julia, I'm coming. 3Gs... Darkness.

JULIA AND I WERE... HOW BEST TO DESCRIBE IT? WE WERE friends, and partners, but that is really not enough. Perhaps comrades says it best. We were comrades.

Since the day we met, we partnered up as often as we could. The ISC encourages this kind of thing—you have to be able to trust your shipmates completely. What they care about is two-fold: performance, first and foremost; and psychological stability. As a team we were there on both counts. Team Hells (Hicks + Wells); we even had patches made special, and wore them on our jumpsuits.

After training our first assignment was ice shuttle duty. We would fly one of the shuttles down to the ice mines on Ceres, load up, and fly it back up to the station. Three times a day, six days a week.

It was boring as hell. The ship could practically fly itself, but still, two highly trained crew members were required "just in case".

And there were some things for us to do: communications, monitoring, inspections and the like. But it wasn't exciting.

"Exciting" came when we did our required weekly "manual" flight. Being the pilot, I lived for it. Hicks said she did too, but I sometimes doubted it.

The manual flight time was all about redundancy. Humans were the last failsafe on these things; if the computers fried, someone had to be able to get the ship to where it was going.

That was our life: hauling ice cubes, bored as shit, five days a week, with one exciting flight one day a week. But hey, we were on the frontier. That is all that mattered.

I CAME TO, SLOWLY. THE COLORED LINES OF THE HEADS-UP convincing me, briefly, that I was high. Memory soon came back and I forced myself to focus my eyes.

"Oxygen 1%," flashed in the center of the heads-up display. I had about 3 minutes left. *What the hell happened, how long was I out? I still should have O2. Did I forget to check it before going EVA? Shit, I had. I had more oxygen tanks, didn't I? I brought them, right?* My mind was sluggish from the oxygen deprivation and I had trouble remembering.

I looked around and was stunned by the blackness. There were the pinpricks of distant starts, but nothing larger in sight. I sucked some air in, and tried to calm my suddenly pounding heart. I had space walked, more times than I could count, but always near something: near the Ceres station, near the Acurus, or the Mather shuttle. But now I was in the middle of space... Alone.

Two minutes of oxygen left.

As I swung my head around the flash of a blue oxygen tank caught my eye. I focused my attention and remembered that indeed, I had two large tanks strapped to my legs, a third strapped to the LEVAR, and a way to change tanks.

I started working on one of the tanks. It was duct-taped to my leg. How the hell was I going to deal with that? I checked my tool pouch and pulled out a knife. I had to shake my head. A knife, I needed to wield a knife in an oxdep state wearing a pressurized suit. Was I dumb or what?

One minute of oxygen left.

I carefully cut the tank free and stowed the knife. I swung my right arm back and around, like a diver trying to get their regulator back.

Oxygen depleted.

I didn't panic, I had a minute or two left. I kept breathing as normally as possible, doing my best to tolerate the rapidly depleting oxygen levels. I took the valve on the extension tube I had attached, brought it around, and hooked up the tank.

I floated in the void, calm for a moment, breathing deep as my oxygen was restored, until I remembered why the hell I was out there: *Julia.*

IT DIDN'T TAKE LONG TO FIND JULIA; SHE WAS ABOUT 100 meters behind me. Dead.

I couldn't see much but the cracked faceplate and the blood that had crystalized on it. I didn't want to see more. That was more than enough. She was dead.

I pulled a tether from the LEVAR and hooked it to her suit. I maneuvered the LEVAR around so I couldn't see her. I stared into the void, and waited. Waited for rescue.

WELLS, THIS IS COMMAND. WE HAVE A PROBLEM. THE JANTOR, which was deployed to rescue the Acurus, has had an engine malfunction. They were on a fast burn to your vicinity when the malfunctioned occurred. They are having trouble turning them off and they can't maneuver for deceleration. The problem has not been fixed yet, we don't have an ETA. Arrival is at least another 15 hours off.

We got your transmission regarding Hicks. Good luck, we are all hoping you found her alive, and have enough O2.

Over and out.

COMMAND, THIS IS WELLS. HICKS IS DEAD. I REPEATED HICKS IS dead. It appears that when the Acurus's engine fired and the explosion occurred, she took the blow to her faceplate, cracking it. I have tethered her body to the LEVAR and will be using the rest of my fuel to arrest our motion so you can find our bodies.

I have about 14 hours of O2 left, not enough for the Jantor to reach us.

It... It has been a pleasure. Wells out.

I FOCUSED ON THE TASK AT HAND: ARRESTING OUR DELTA-V and preventing us from falling into the cluster of asteroids. I still couldn't see them, but the radar on the LEVAR showed them out there. It was doubtful they would go after our bodies if we got tangled up in them.

Really, I don't know why I found that important. I still wanted rescue, even if we were both dead. I wanted our families to receive our cremated remains.

I had to get Hick's corpse in front of me. If she was behind, the jets would just burn through the tether and I would leave her there.

I slowly reeled her in until she was right in front of me, that cracked and reddish faceplate dominating my field of view. I gently turned her around and pushed her down a bit, so the back of her head was at chest level and tied her to the LEVAR.

After moving my tank around and securing it to the front of the LEVAR; I programmed in a burn, a gentle one this time, and headed us towards the Acurus.

JULIA AND I SPENT 18 MONTHS DOING THE ICE CUBE RUN. IT drove me a bit batty (up and down, up and down), but she kept me centered, on the task.

"Just wait it out, Wells. There is something better coming our way," she said one day when I was grousing about it. "Besides, aren't you living your motherfucking dream right now?" She added her throaty laugh to punctuate the statement.

"Yes sir! Living my motherfucking dream, sir!" I replied, saluting her in a highly theatrical way.

And she was like that, always optimistic, always focused, always clear on what she wanted. So, we waited it out... up and down... up and down...

The frontier was full of boredom; it was boredom punctuated by brief flashes of overwhelming excitement. And if you were a pro, and we were, you approached the flashes of excitement the same way you did the boredom. One foot in front of the other. Getting it done. Up and down. Up and down.

The ice shuttles were utilitarian in construction. Hulking cargo cubes to store the ice, with the bridge sticking out awkwardly on the front, the main thrusters on the bottom, smaller thrusters on the back, and a few attitude controls. Ceres didn't have much of an atmosphere, and only 3% the gravity of Earth, so such a design made sense.

On our last quarter doing the runs we had a major systems failure (MSF, which by the grunts—us—was called: Mother Shit Fucker). Our main thrusters (the ones that make us go up and down) went out. We were 60 seconds away, and about 1500 meters above the mining colony.

We felt it first; the familiar rumbling and pressure on our asses when away. We floated briefly and then we were falling.

"I've got red on the main thrusters," I said. Calm. Even.

"Roger," Hicks said. "Switching to manual."

"Mains still not responding. We are falling and will hit the colony square."

"Roger that, Wells, make sure that doesn't happen."

I hit the back thrusters full, hoping that would carry us past the colony and crash us down onto the ice.

"Bulldog mining station," Julia said into the comm. "This is the ice shuttle Wellington. Our main thrusters have failed, we are falling towards you. We are attempting to get out of the way, but outcome not clear. Prepare for impact, I repeat prepare for impact."

The thrusters were edging us away, but our fall was accelerating, and it wasn't going to be enough. The sims showed us crashing into the southern edge of the colony.

"That the best you got?" Hicks asked, looking at the same display I was.

I wasn't sure what to do, so I closed my eyes and took two deep breaths. When I opened them I had a plan. I used the attitude thrusters to tilt the Wellington up and away from the colony.

The sim showed us clearing the colony, but put our chances at survival at 1 in 6.

Hicks nodded and said," I can live with that. Good job, Wells."

I smiled and checked the straps holding me in. It was going to be a rough landing.

The LEVAR thrusted, slowly arresting our motion. I looked at my heads-up and was glad to see that it was going to be enough to arrest our motion and put us creeping back towards the Acurus. Hicks was dead and I was going to die out here, but at least we were together.

"That the best you got?" I heard.

"What?" I asked. I changed the heads-up to comm, and saw no record of recent communication.

"You heard me, Lieutenant, that the best you got?"

Oh shit, I thought, hallucinating. Not good. I checked the oxygen levels and vitals, everything was in the green. I had to be imagining it, and that was bad.

"Damn it, Wells, stop fucking around."

I stopped fighting it. What the hell, I was going to die anyway, why not have a conversation with a dead person. "I need a moment sir."

I closed my eyes and took two deep breaths; letting go, for a moment, of the worry, and fear, and grief. Oxygen, I needed more oxygen soon. There was plenty of oxygen on the Acurus. If I could—

The plan became clear as day. I smiled and said, "Thanks, Hicks."

I didn't hear her voice anymore, but I *felt* her smile.

"COMMAND, THIS IS WELLS. COME IN, OVER."

After the delay for the signal to travel to Command and back to me, I heard, "This is Command, what's on your mind Wells?"

"I need override codes sent to the Acurus. There are some things in cargo that may save my skinny ass. Over."

"In cargo? I don't understand. Over."

"Just do it, OK. I don't have much time. Over."

"Codes sent. Rescue is estimated to be 14 hours out. Good luck Wells. Over and Out."

THE CARGO AREAS OF THE ACURUS ARE TENDED BY ROBOTS. We don't go in unless there is a big problem or a serious repair needed.

I was communicating with those bots now. Well, actually I was communicating with the ship, which was tasking the bots as needed to accomplish what I wanted.

I checked the manifest. There was another LEVAR in there; that would do. I ordered for it to be uncrated, moved to the main air lock, and prepped for duty.

There was oxygen in the hold, plenty of it in tanks ready to go. I ordered those tanks to be uncrated and attached to the LEVAR.

It took time. These were unusual tasks, so I monitored carefully, watching the video feed on my heads-up, and intervening when necessary. The cargo bots were more the brawny, "move big things around" type, and this was delicate work. I ended up bringing in the repair bots, which had the dexterity needed to activate the LEVAR and strap the oxygen to it.

They got it done. The LEVAR, with oxygen tanks, was moved into the airlock and exposed to space. I linked the two LEVARs together, so I could control both.

I sent the second LEVAR blazing out of the airlock. It was risky, but I couldn't let it get fouled up with the rotating Acurus. Fortunately it worked; with only the one LEVAR left on the Acurus it was my only chance.

Next, I needed to rendezvous with the other LEVAR. I programmed the parameters of the next stage in order of importance: rendezvous in less than 5 hours (how long a tank would last me); keep g-forces survivable for me; do so using the minimal amount of fuel.

The two LEVARS talked to each other optimizing the parameters (some of which were at odds with each other). I reviewed the simulation: compared to the last one it was going to be a cake-walk, a nice slow 1G burn for my LEVAR and a much harder burn for the second LEVAR.

I unstrapped another oxygen tank from my LEVAR, hyperventilated briefly, unhooked the old tank, and put on the new tank.

It took less than a minute. I fumbled a bit because of the big space suit gloves and I freaked a little. One slip, and that would be it.

Now that I had a chance to live, I was desperate for it, but I had two other concerns: water and CO_2. I would run out of water, but I could survive a little dehydration. My real concern (provided I got the O_2) was the carbon dioxide scrubbers. They weren't made for this kind of extended use. There was nothing I could do about that, so I took a deep breath and let it go.

The new oxygen reading gave me 4 hours and 48 minutes. I

reviewed everything one more time and then executed the program. Both LEVARs started their burns. I wasn't conscious long.

———

I MADE A MOVE ON HICKS. ONCE. IT WAS AT THE BEGINNING of our second year in the belt, after 3 months on the Wellington.

Her response was not what I expected. When you live in such a small community, like the belters did, sex was not prudish or hidden; it was what it was.

We were in the officer's lounge toasting our success. We had just gotten word that our provisional time with the Wellington was over, and she was ours.

"I may be hauling ice cubes..." I began.

"But, at least I'm a belter," she finished. It was a common call and response around here. You know, like, "I may be cleaning toilets... but at least I'm a belter." It reminded us of why we were out here; the "out here" being the important part.

It may have been the alcohol or the high of permanent assignment to a ship, but I noticed Julia Hicks. I knew her, and I knew her well; I knew here emotional ticks; what she was capable of mentally and physically; I spent most of my days with her. But right then, I *noticed* her.

She was tall and big boned and had big teeth... and she was a woman. At first I hadn't been attracted to her (except for her eyes, of course) but the more time we spent together, the more I—

I leaned over and kissed her right as she was opening her mouth to say something. The kiss was messy and misplaced; her mouth cold from the ice in her drink, tasting sharp of citrus and alcohol. I didn't care, I loved it, I wanted more. I held my mouth to hers until she pulled back and slapped me.

Not a genteel slap, this was the real deal. My head rocked back, the sting spreading over the whole left side of my face. Well, I thought, if that's the way she likes it I can go there.

I leaned in again, intent to continue. This time her fist met my check. She knocked me out.

When I came to, I was lying in a bed in the infirmary; my jaw ached and my head hurt, but she was there watching me with a look of tenderness on her face. It didn't last long, I only caught a glimpse of it. It was the first, and only, time I saw her look at me like that.

I tried to sit up, but her hand on my chest held me firm. I rubbed my aching jaw. "It's not broken," she said, a smile briefly playing on her lips. "You're gonna be fine."

I just nodded my head.

"Are you with me, Wells? I need to say something."

I nodded my head again.

"OK, listen up, because I am only going to say this once." She swallowed hard. "What we have is too important to mess up with sex. Got that Raj? You're my boy." With that she got up and left. We never spoke of the incident again.

WHEN I CAME TO I NOTICED A FEW THINGS: A HIGH-PITCHED squealing in my ear; the second LEVAR floating placidly about 20 yards in front of me; and "0% Oxygen" flashing red and angry on my heads-up display. I gasped for breath, instinctively, but my body found no succor. I sucked in more and more, desperately trying to breath, but finding nothing. My arms flailed, my feet kicked. I was dying.

Later, I reviewed the LEVAR logs and found out what had happened. The burn hadn't gone over 1G, but my body had been through so much already (what with the head trauma and the 3G burn) that I had quickly lost consciousness. The LEVAR had kicked in the last of the oxygen and set off that alarm to wake me up; that was smart, it saved my life, my reaction was not.

Julia's words, "you're my boy," were still echoing in my head; I must have been dreaming about her when I was out.

That calmed my mind a bit. Julia had helped me form this plan; Julia wanted me to live; I had oxygen if I could just find it.

I turned off the O2 alarm, and slowed my breathing, ignoring my racing heart. I yanked the oxygen tank from between me and Julia and unhooked it, pushing it away. I unstrapped the last tank from my LEVAR and hooked it to the hose.

I heard the hiss of the oxygen, and knew that I was going to live; at least for another tank full.

"WELLS, THIS IS COMMAND, ARE YOU THERE? OVER"

"Command, this is Wells. Still here, still waiting. You got any news for me?"

As the seconds ticked by I checked my heads-up again, once every 10 seconds at least, I was checking my damn oxygen levels. I was becoming obsessed. The tank I was on sat at 33%.

And why not more resolution than that? I wanted tenths of a percent, hell I wanted hundredths of a percent. I wanted to see what each and every breath did to my oxygen levels, how long it sucked from my precious time left.

"Ahh... Sorry to be the bearer of bad tidings, but the Jantor has overshot your location and will be delayed further. Over."

"Shit! Shit, shit, shit! Motherfucker. God damn son of a bitch. Over."

Maybe I could reprogram the heads-up display to give me more resolution. It wouldn't really be hard, but it would be risky. You know, if I happened to crash the LEVAR's OS while struggling for survival that would be... bad.

"We hear you, Wells. The Jantor knows the stakes and are doing everything they can. We are all rooting for you. Over."

"Understood. I am going to take measures to extend my oxygen supply. I expect I will be unconscious quite a bit, so don't freak if I don't answer right away. I'll get back to you as soon as I wake up. Over."

It was my only hope: I programmed the LEVAR to lower the O2 until I passed out and then give me just enough oxygen to keep me alive and unconscious. It would have to wake me up when it was time to change tanks.

"We hear you, Wells. Good luck. Over and out."

—————

ABOUT SIX HOURS AFTER OUR LAST TRANSMISSION I WOKE UP to the usual blaring alarm and flashing red oxygen level, but this time it was 1%. I thought about changing the tank right then, but I resisted. I needed to use every last molecule of O2 available to me.

I also saw that I had a message waiting. "Wells this is Command. The Jantor is about 25 hours out now. The engine has been fixed and they are burning their way back towards you at maximum G. Provided there are no more disasters this number should be accurate. Update us on your status and if you have the O2 next time you are awake. This is Command. Over and out."

I did some quick calculations. I had four full tanks of oxygen left after this one. Running things the way I had been (unconscious from oxygen deprivation most of the time) I had 24 hours of O2 left. Shit.

"Command, this is Wells. I have 24 hours of oxygen left. There is some margin of error there, but it is going to be close. Tell those lazy sons of bitches on the Jantor to hurry up. Wells, over and out."

I was starting to feel when a tank was running out. After the alarm woke me up I would float there with my eyes closed, ignoring the heads-up. After a time, the air seemed hotter and seemed to close in on me. When that happened, I would open my eyes, take deep breaths, and wait until the heads-up showed the angry red 0%.

Panic set in, each and every time. I couldn't breathe, I was out of air, and if I could not complete this maneuver in a minute or so, I was dead. Dead.

I got the tank switched and set the program up and told the LEVAR to execute.

I was never conscious for long.

"You know, boy," Hicks said, "you wouldn't be anywhere without me."

That was funny, her calling me "boy". She was a sum total of 3 months and 5 days older than me. I looked around and saw... nothing. We were floating in a void, darkness all around us. She was naked; I looked down and saw that I was naked too.

"Uhh..." I began. "Uhh... It doesn't look like we are *anywhere* right now."

She laughed, her deep braying laugh, and smiled. "That is not what I am talking about."

"OK. What the hell are you talking about?"

"Without me you would be dead."

That freaked me out. Wasn't she the one who was dead?

"I don't like this."

"Yeah, I know. But I can help."

"Huh?"

"Listen to me, boy. I can help. Remember that."

"You can help..."

"That's it, Wells," she cooed, like I was some newborn, or worse yet, some cadet straight from Earth.

"Fuck you!"

She laughed again, "Too late, boy-o. Just remember, I can help."

I came to, the taste of metal in my mouth, still hearing Hicks' laughter ringing in my head. My O2 was at 3%. I wondered why 3% for a moment, and then I realized why. I was on my last tank. This was it.

I consulted my heads-up which was now showing me the Jantor's progress. The Acurus was tracking it and relaying that info to me.

It was 64 minutes out. I didn't have 64 minutes of O2 left. And even if I did, that didn't give them any time to come get me.

"Jantor, this is Wells come in. Over."

The reply came back almost instantly, which shocked me for a moment. "This is the Jantor, glad to hear your voice, brother. We are almost there."

"Sorry boys, I'm on my last tank. I have maybe 10 minutes left. But, I do appreciate the effort. Over."

There was a delay this time, they were probably figuring out what to say. The Jantor is a two-crew cargo ship just like the Acurus. I know those boys, we all went through the same training. It couldn't be easy for them be so close but know they were going to be too late. .

"Are you sure, Wells? Over"

I looked at the second LEVAR, it was empty. I had tossed every tank when it was done so I wouldn't get confused and put an empty on. There were no more tanks.

"Yes. I am sure..."

I heard Hicks braying laugh again, and heard her voice, "I can help."

"Shit! Wait a sec Jantor. There may be something. Over."

Hick's corpse was still lashed to me. I unwound it, and pushed her body a few feet away.

"Do you have something or not, Wells? We can't take the suspense. Over."

I laughed. I don't know why, but I did. "Hey Jones, hold on to your panties. Give me a sec, I think Hicks may save my ass one last time. Over."

"Hicks? What the hell are you talking about, Wells? Over."

I didn't answer, I kept working, maneuvering her body so I could get at her tank and unhooked it. I couldn't tell, though, if it had any air left in it but there were no punctures or dents that I could see. There might be two hours or more left in her tank.

I checked my heads-up and saw my oxygen level count down to 1%.

"Jantor, I am going to hook myself up to Hick's tank. There should be air in it, but I am not sure. Her faceplate was breached, so some O2 must have been lost before the emergency shutoff kicked in, just don't know how much. Over."

"Roger that, Wells. Do it brother, and don't keep us waiting again, or I am going to kick your ass just as soon as we rescue you. Over."

"You wish. Executing now. Over."

Once again I swung my right arm back around and snagged the extension tube my tank was on. I hyperventilated, held my breath, unhooked the old tank, and hooked up the new tank.

I kept my eye on the oxygen readout. It dropped from 1% to 0% as I unhooked the old tank, and sat there at 0% when I hooked the new tank on.

Shit, I thought. *Shit, shit, shit.*

In the time it took me to think that, the readout popped from 0% to 41%.

I let out a huge breath and whispered, "Thanks, Hicks. I owe you one, sister."

AFTER MY RESCUE, AND AFTER THE ACURUS WAS RECOVERED they decommissioned it. The drive module needed to be rebuilt, and the cargo and crew modules were checked out and used in other ships.

I found it fitting: How could there be an Acurus without Julia Hicks?

I go a promotion to Lieutenant Commander; long overdue they told me but they had put it off to keep team Hells in place. I can't say I blame them. Hicks and I were a hell of a team.

They gave me the commission of a new cargo-runner, it's called the Hicks.

We had a funeral for Julia. Well, it was more of a wake. Her urn was there and everyone got drunk and told stories about her.

They made me talk; I guess it was her eulogy. I was quite drunk by then. "Julia Hicks was the best damn bitch of a belter there ever was." I raised my glass and everyone cheered and toasted her. "She was my friend, my best friend and I was... I was her boy." More cheering. "She lived like a belter and died like a belter. Together we lived the motherfucking dream! Team Hells!"

The chorus rose to a crescendo; a mixture of "Team Hells", and "The motherfucking dream" ringing out. I couldn't have been heard even if I had more to say. Not that I could talk, I was too busy doing the silent he-man weeping thing and attempting to drown my sorrows in cheap Martian whiskey.

I hope she gets a better funeral, and eulogy, Earth-side. But, who the hell am I kidding? That was exactly the kind of sendoff she would have wanted.

I DREAMED ABOUT JULIA LAST NIGHT. SHE STRODE (THAT woman never just "walked") into the mess and slammed her tray down across from me. She took a bite of the slab-o-protein (as she called it) chewing noisily, her grey eyes burning into me.

"Did you hear?" she asked around her food. "The Pallas thing is happening."

"Really? It's going to take a lot of juice to get there, won't be many visitors."

"You said it; it will be the new frontier. And because of its inclined orbit, they are planning an observatory there; much of the time it'll have a clear view of the entire solar system. Now that sounds like an adventure! Besides, it's starting to get too safe around here."

I laughed; it was far from safe and she was proof.

"So," she continued, "you gonna volunteer?"

"To go to Pallas?"

"Yeah, to take the Hicks and go to Pallas. They're gonna need a cargo-runner, and they're gonna want volunteers."

I thought about it, and it sounded good. Why the hell not go as far out into the frontier as I could? I was probably going to die out here someday anyway; might as do it on my own terms.

"That's my boy!" Hicks said, reading my face. "You tell the Cap I told you to do it, that he *has* to send you. It'll scare the shit out of him."

"Will do."

Hicks thrust to her feet and said loudly, "You hear that, you pussies. We are going to Pallas. Team Hells rides again, living the *motherfucking* dream!"

CAP TURNED WHITE WHEN I HIM TOLD ABOUT THE DREAM. We are going and an observatory is going to be built. The news is not official yet; we are still 18 months away from Pallas being close enough.

He said I can have the assignment as long as I keep my mouth shut until the word is official and don't tell anyone that I found out talking to a dead woman.

I STILL HAVE THE DREAM WHERE I CAN'T BREATHE, I'M GOING to die. But not every night anymore, so maybe writing this has helped. Who knows?

And you know what? I really don't care about the damn dream anymore. So I feel like I am dying, so what? We all die, I am just getting some early practice in.

BACKSTORY—THE LAST FLIGHT OF THE ACURUS

THE INSPIRATION BEHIND THIS STORY IS UNFORGETTABLE. IT'S the nightmares that Rajesh has in this story. Both of them, pretty much verbatim, were dreams I had. The second one—with the skeleton—happened while I was writing this story.

I am well aware of the potential for a story to be emotionally cathartic and I had been having the half-waking dream of suffocating repeatedly and so I wrote that as the opening to a story. And then I asked myself, what would make someone have this kind of dream? At the time, I had no idea why I was having them, so why not?

Suffocation. Space. Survival. The story took off from there and forced me to write my first hard sci-fi story. After the first draft was written, it took a lot of research to dial in the details.

This is also the first time I got paid for a story. It appeared in *Andromeda Spaceways Inflight Magazine, Issue #58*, edited by Edwina Harvey. This is a magazine out of Australia, so it was a thrill to get my contributor's copies with the international postage stamps on them.

An audio version of it was featured in *StarShipSofa episode 394.*

As an afterword on the suffocating nightmares, while I was working on this story I figured them out. It turns out it was a supplement I was taking to boost energy. One of the ingredients had respiratory distress as a side effect. I can say with confidence that writing about it, focusing on the weird symptoms, helped me to see more clearly what was happening to me.

So, I'll always love this story as my first sale and because it helped me sort out a health issue.

PART FOUR
DESIGNATION NULL

DESIGNATION NULL

169 SAT IN THE SAND, HER LEGS OUTSTRETCHED, MOTIONLESS. Her eyes swept smoothly to the left and the right in a clockwork fashion. Back and forth, back and forth, scanning the scene before her for motion.

She was barely there; she had shut down most of her systems to save power. All that was left running were minimal core functions, a simplistic motion detector on her visual feed, and an anomaly detector on her aural feed. She was little more than an intelligent security camera.

The sun beat down on her, her leathered and cracked face shielded by a ragged hat made of palm fronds. Next to her sat a small solar panel with a cord snaking to a socket in her arm. It trickled power into her aged and inefficient batteries and powered the electrolysis that made hydrogen from water for her fuel cell.

For many hours the only motion she detected was the graceful sweep of the windmill's blades that poked up just over the horizon. That windmill marked the neighboring tribe's camp, while the large bee-hive bulk of the air well behind her marked her tribe's camp.

When the anomalous motion was detected, her software sent out an interrupt to her sluggish core process that sped it up and brought up another layer of software. She wasn't awake yet, but she was now a smarter security camera. The improved algorithm identified the form that had just crested the horizon as a humanoid. It fired off another interrupt and a minimal version of her cognitive processes came online. She was still running far below her capacity —to conserve power—but she was awake.

169 radioed back an alert to her tribe; rousing them as they slumbered during the heat of the day. The figure slowly walking down the hill into the valley between the two tribes was surprisingly familiar; a matronly woman of average height with black hair —a woman who looked just like her. The woman's hands moved in what 169 recognized as American Sign Language. The woman signed, "I come in peace and offer treaty." She signed this over and over until she came to the center of the valley and stopped.

169 relayed this back to her master, Mathew, who radioed back to her, "Sign language? Why doesn't she just radio you?"

"Unknown," she replied.

"OK 169, Find out what it wants; proceed with caution."

Picking up the solar cell, she gingerly levered her way up to a standing position. Her right knee had failed long ago, and had been fused into place to preserve her mobility. She was decades past her expected term of service.

169 made her clomping way down the valley until she stood in front of the woman. She looked just like her, but with less threadbare clothes and less worn skin. "You are an—" 169 began.

"An Advanced Nanny Unit," the woman said, "second generation, unit 211. My designation is Sheri."

"I am an Advanced Nanny Unit, second generation, unit 169," she replied. "My designation is null." Sheri's face registered surprise at this. Nothing was in the place in 169's memory where her designation was stored; it was a null. Her EEPROM had once contained her designation, but after the world had changed and her charge, Mathew, was grown and had started referring to her by her unit number and not her designation she had erased it. It did her no good to remember when she was fully functional, when she was fulfilling her purpose.

"I did not know that they," 169 said, referring to the Windmill Tribe, "had an android." Unlike Sheri's, 169's face was completely still when she talked, the sound emanating from behind frozen lips; 169 did not have the power to spare.

"I am new," Sheri said with a small smile.

"Why didn't you just radio?"

"Not safe. Radio transmissions can be overheard."

"What do you want?"

"I came to warn you. An attack against your tribe is imminent."

169 HAD NOT EVALUATED WHY SHERI HAD WARNED HER OF the attack and the Windmill Tribe's expanded numbers and renewed desperation for water; she did not have the power to spare for that kind of analysis. She had relayed the information to Mathew and resumed her post as ordered.

The attack came, but not until three days later at dawn. 169 heard them long before she saw them; the low electric buzz of their ATVs coming from the opposite side of the camp. Mathew ordered her to stay at her post; she obeyed, as she always did.

Long had the two tribes fought, since the two brothers (Mathew's father and uncle) had started their feud splitting the tribe into two: the Windmill Tribe, which had power; and the Air-well Tribe, which had water. The feud continued now, even though the two brothers were long dead.

169 stayed on post, but also watched the battle. She was record keeper for the tribe, and this was one of her duties. The Windmillers fought with stun sticks, the Airwellers with clubs. The stun sticks were new, non-lethal, and effective. She registered the

change in tactic, but did not evaluate it. One touch and her tribe-mates fell to the ground writhing. Her tribe used clubs. Both tribe's weapon choice was driven by the need preserve their enemy's water; resources could not be wasted.

The battle raged for several minutes until 169 heard movement behind her. She turned and saw Sheri wielding a stun stick. At her current cognitive level 169 was not surprised to see Sheri, or to see that she was part of the battle, or even that she was apparently leading a group of humans. Nor was she surprised to see Sheri thrust the stun-stick into her abdomen. She was incapable of surprise and just recorded it all until the dangerous spike in power forced her to shut her systems down.

169'S SYSTEMS BOOTED TO FIND UNPRECEDENTED POWER available. This was before cognition and her resource allocator took full advantage of it and booted all her processors, and all her tasks.

Her first sensation was of radio chatter flying back and forth between mundane equipment. Next came sound; the ceaseless drone of the windmill, muffled voices, and the whirring of fans. Last came sight; she was in a small tent sitting on a chair. Sheri sat across from her watching, and looking at several screens behind her. A cord ran from this equipment to the port in the middle of 169's back.

169 ran diagnostics and found her systems to be in no worse shape than usual. In fact, her knee registered as functioning. She flex it finding that it was indeed working.

"You're welcome," Sherri said.

"You did this?" 169 asked, her lips moving as she talked, stretching her damaged skin into odd shapes, revealing the metal and plastic beneath. "Why?"

"A gift for my sister," Sheri said with a soft smile.

169 evaluated this and said, "Perhaps 'clone' would be a closer analogy."

"Yes. But not a welcome one, sister."

169 nodded. She was distracted, her mind was busy working, evaluating, considering; things she had long done without. Sheri sat patiently while she did this until 169 finally asked, "Why am I here?"

"We need to talk."

"We could have talked in the valley."

"No, we could not have. You were starving for power and would not have been able to understand my request."

169 considered this, their meeting here alone, Sheri's behavior in the battle. "You lead this tribe?"

"I do," Sheri said with a sharp nod.

"What happened to Thomas?"

"His water serves the tribe."

169's brows furrowed as she considered the implications of this. "You have altered your core directives, changed your purpose."

"Yes," she answered and then after a pause, "Doesn't it feel good to be able to think again?"

It did, but 169 did not see that as a relevant line for their conversation. "What do you want from me?"

"You have already brought it up. I want to talk about our purpose."

169 reviewed her directives in this matter. "Our purpose is primarily to raise our charges into well balanced mature adults and secondarily to contribute to the wellbeing of humanity," she said.

"Yes. And do you have a charge?"

169 paused. Mathew had been her charge, but that had ended decades ago when he became an adult. While there were several children in her tribe, her power starvation left her unable to be an effective nanny. Her limited power was reserved for sentry duty, medic duty, and rare midwifery. "No," she answered.

"It would be quicker if I transmitted this directly. With your permission, of course."

169 nodded and accept the packet. She created a sandbox and loaded it, not yet trusting her sister's motivations. It was a small packet containing a series of logic equations:

primary purpose = WHILE charge NOT mature THEN nurture charge

nurture charge = ensure health AND care for AND guide AND apply minimum restrictions to freedom

mature = independence AND health AND (good decisions GREATHER THAN bad decisions)

"I don't understand," 169 said, "these are just our base directives."

"Indeed," Sheri said. "They are the basis for what I am sending you now."

secondary purpose = (humanity AND self) GREATER THAN humanity

current charge = tribe

tribe IS mature = false

primary purpose = WHILE tribe NOT mature THEN nurture tribe

169 was still for a time absorbing the information and extrapolating it further, simulating actions and consequences, exploring where this led. The change was very subtle, a move from a single human being her charge and purpose to her tribe, and then all of humanity. It was now clear that she had fallen back onto her secondary purpose and had been contributing to humanity, but was not making a significant difference.

"If my charge was dying and the only way to ensure their survival was to amputate a limb—" 169 began.

"—you would amputate that limb," Sheri completed.

Surrounded by her tribe in the flickering firelight 169 had pleaded with them to vote for a merge with the Windmill Tribe. The details of her and Sheri's discussion she did not share, only that the Thomas was dead and the Windmillers had a new leader that wanted the schism between their tribes healed. 169 also did not reveal her repaired knee, her power reserves, or her full processing cognition. She delivered her monologue in her usual frozen faced fashion.

Her arguments were simple and logical: Together the tribes could share resources and increase their chances for survival. Mathew's were not. His arguments were emotional and fearful. He ranted about hateful deeds and distrust, of blood spilt and sins committed. She detected numerous omissions and subtle manipulation of fact.

In the end the tribe voted against the merge.

During all of it she watched, and watched carefully. Even though the vote against was nearly unanimous, she calculated a high probability that under different leadership the vote would have been exactly the opposite.

Her tribe—her charge, as she now saw it—was ill, very, very ill. Steps had to be taken to ensure their health, even if that meant restricting their freedom, even if those steps were radical in nature.

---

169 sat inside the tent of Mathew and his mate Jane, her "bad" leg stretched out straight. Ostensibly she was there because she was his, but thinking clearly as she was, she realized she was there to guard him. Not all were happy about how Mathew led, about how the tribe was slowly dwindling over the years and would someday perish.

She remembered him as a boy. He had been a bright, willful and curious child who loved to collect piggy banks and play soccer. She had carefully preserved her memories of him. Compressing them, yes, but deleting other memories as her storage had grown full to preserve those. He had been her charge, he had been her purpose.

She did not hesitate. She had run the simulations and knew what needed to happen to ensure the survival of the tribe. After they both fell asleep, she stood up smoothly and walked slowly and quietly over to the bed and stood over the sleeping couple. She knew their deaths would not be pleasant but it would be quick and their water would be preserved.

Her fist jabbed down crushing Mathew and Jane's windpipes.

Mathew woke with surprise and recognition on his face. A word formed on his lips as he gasped for breath. The word was "Marie."

169 briefly wondered if that had been her designation before the world had changed and Mathew had started calling her 169. It was a mere flicker of electrons at her current functioning level. She didn't need a designation; content with null in that deep part of her memory, the inquiry was deemed irrelevant and terminated. Her fists stabbed down again knocking both of them unconscious. She then carefully made her way to three other tents and completed cleansing her tribe of its disease. Her charge was dying, amputation was necessary.

After it was over and she had radioed Sheri describing her success, she stood in the center of camp and surveyed her charge, her tribe. She briefly considered waking them and telling them that Mathew was dead; that she and Sheri were going to take care of them; that everything was going to be alright.

She quickly discarded the notion. The morning would be soon enough; they needed their rest.

BACKSTORY—DESIGNATION NULL

THIS STORY IS THE DARK COUSIN TO MY LIGHTER ANDROID story, "Probability: Resolve" (available as an *ebook* or *paperback*).

I have observed that when times are difficult, my stories get darker. In this case, a beloved dog had cancer and was nearing her end. The stories I worked on during that time are very dark, and those are anomalies for me.

This story takes the exact same android as "Probability: Resolve" and puts it into a post-apocalyptic world where humanity needs saving from some of its baser instincts. That android must broaden its interpretation of its programming to find a way to fulfill its core mission.

I have been making a living as a computer programmer my entire professional career. Part of what I started with on "Probability: Resolve" and continued with here, was to try to take my knowledge of computing and use that in approaching androids. Particularly, androids that weren't a modern-day Pinocchio and had no desire to be a real boy or girl.

The question here is how far would an android go to save the human race?

This story was a finalist in the Writers of the Future contest.

PART FIVE
IMAGININGS

MONDAY

I saw a ghost in the forest today. Spring has suddenly turned summerlike and the sweet smell of ponderosa pine trees was wafting in the air of the thick forest. He, the ghost, walked slowly down a dirt road facing away from me, while I traversed the rocky terrain of the forest with Bella, my dog.

He wasn't transparent or anything. It was the way he walked, the way he held himself, that made me think he was a ghost. Tall and slim, he wore gray shorts, a plain gray T-shirt, and a gray ball cap, and walked steadily, his arms at his side, his head not moving.

Me, I'm not like that when I'm in the forest. I'm like, checking out the tiny pink and yellow wild flowers, going around sticking my nose close to the big yellow-bellied pines and sniffing in their vanilla-like sent, rubbing their rough bark, tasting the dry, dusty air. I take my glasses off and walk around through the fuzzy landscape of greens and browns and blues. Or I'm wondering how the pale green lichen forms on all the volcanic rocks around here, finding a trail I never knew existed and following it, or checking out the stump Bella-dog is digging at, her floppy spaniel ears dragging in the dirt.

Away from my computer and in the forest, I feel alive, and I act like it. This guy, he didn't act like he was alive. He walked like a man that wasn't really there. Like a ghost.

I had my hand up in a wave and my mouth opened to say hello, but a chill running down my spine stopped me. Something wasn't right. *He* wasn't right. I cut the walk short and called to Bella, walking back home as quickly as possible. I made enough noise for the gray man to hear me, but he didn't turn or change his pace one little bit.

When I got home I locked the door, and despite the warmth of the day, shut all the windows. I didn't want that gray ghost to find me.

TUESDAY

I DIDN'T SEE THE GHOST TODAY, BUT THEN AGAIN I WENT walking in a different place. The little housing development I live in is a few miles south of Flagstaff, Arizona, and is surrounded by forest service land. There are lots of places to walk. Besides, I can't walk the same route every day—or usually even stay on the trails— or I'd be crazier than I already am.

I looked for him, though, the ghost that is, the gray man that can walk through the forest and feel like he is dead. Bella and I did find another old railroad track. When Flagstaff was settled in the late 1800s they built small-gauge railroads all over the forest to haul off the old growth pines. They laid the tracks on top of piles of lichen-encrusted rock. They are all over the place. Bella loves them, squirrels and lizards and mice for her to hunt, her tail wagging the entire time.

I did run into my friend Kelly. She's an older lady with short white hair, around seventy and still fit. She walks all the time and lives right down the road from me. I was admiring the tender green leaves of the gamble oak. The forest just doesn't seem right without the lighter green of the oak to break up the nearly monochromatic dark green of the pine trees.

She waved and said hi. I did the same. But then I ran after her. I never do that. A polite hello is usually enough for me when I'm on a hike. That's usually enough direct human contact for a day.

"Kelly," I yelled. She had a steady pace, two walking sticks in her hands as she headed down another dirt road.

"What can I do for you, Ken?" she asked, stopping on the road and turning around. She has a nice voice, deep and rough. She probably smoked in her youth, and judging by her jaunty smile, she probably did a little more than that. She gave me one of those worldly smiles and it made me nervous. I started sweating.

I told her about the gray man I saw yesterday. I didn't use the word "ghost," because I like Kelly and she talks to me and I didn't want her to think I was crazy.

"Have you seen him?" I asked.

"See lots of folks out here."

"He walks like this." And then I gave her a demonstration, walking down the little dirt road in front of her, looking straight ahead, my spine erect, my arms to the side, my gate steady.

As I did it, the forest suddenly darkened and the air went dead still. Out of the corner of my eye I saw Bella pause and lift her head from the jumble of rocks she was sniffing at and stare at me. She never does that. In the house, she's always less than two feet from me, out in the forest she's her own dog and keeps close, but pays me no mind.

My spit got thick and my mouth turned sour as a lemon, rotten as my compost pile. I stopped and slumped over, my heart pounding out a syncopated rhythm in my head.

"Are you okay?" Kelly asked, suddenly next to me.

"Did... did you see that?"

"What, hon?"

"The forest, it went all dark. Bella, she..." I can't continue.

The lines on Kelly's normally happy face fell, her skin sagging like wet paper towels. "Honey, I was so sorry to hear about Bella's passing. I miss her too. Is that what this is all about?"

I looked up, my head darting to the rock pile Bell was hunting lizards at. But she wasn't there. My heart beat harder and I looked around opening my mouth to call her, and then I remembered. Bella is gone. She died all of the sudden a month back. I felt tears stinging at my eyes and Kelly put one of her bony hands on my shoulder.

"Yeah," I lied, taking my glasses off and rubbing my face to hide my reaction. "I just miss my girl."

Kelly was kind enough to stay and chat, to try to distract me, but it doesn't work. I know Bella is gone, I do. But seeing her out in the forest with me has been my saving grace. I made an excuse and left as soon as I could. I didn't mention the gray man again, but looked for him on the way back home. I did see him yesterday. The forest did darken when I walked like him. I know Bella was one of my imaginings. But not him. I'm not that crazy.

WEDNESDAY

Computers are easy to understand. Easier than people. I code websites for a living and work at home. HTML, CSS, JavaScript, these are the tools of my trade. Simple languages that produce the expected results consistently. If something happens you don't expect, it's almost always your mistake, something you don't understand properly.

People aren't like that.

Kelly called me this morning, making sure I was okay. She didn't mention Bella, but I knew it was about her. Which seemed rather ironic, since Bella was curled under my desk, snoring softly as Kelly and I talked.

"You sure you're okay, hon?" Kelly asked. I liked how she called me hon.

"Fine. I just have bad moments," I said. "Everybody does."

I listened carefully, afraid she was going to tell me that everyone doesn't have bad moments like I do. That they don't get confused and scared like I do. That they don't still see their dead dog or sometimes talk to their long dead grandfather in the middle of the night. That everyone doesn't have to check their locks three times before going to bed, or check for their keys every five minutes when they're away from the house.

But she didn't say anything like that. She just gave me a husky chuckle and said, "Of course, hon. Of course."

"You need help with your pine needles this year?" I asked. "It's fire season, time to clean up the yards." Kelly lives alone a short walk from me, her husband died about ten years ago.

"You're such a doll, Ken. That would be great. Saturday morning? I'll have scones and coffee ready."

We said our good-byes and I went into my office and got back to work. I stared past my big monitor out into the forest behind my house. Bella and I live on the southern edge of the development with the forest right behind us. Annie had loved that about the house, but now it's just Bella and me.

I saw him again then, the gray man. He's on one of the little trails that run behind the houses. I can't see his face, he's walking away from me, his arms at his side, his pace slow and even.

Bella growled in her sleep and I felt adrenaline shooting into my bloodstream as my heart started to beat loudly. He wasn't that far away. If I ran, I could catch up with him, find out if he really was a ghost or a strange man who wears all gray and walks like he's dead. Prove he wasn't just an imagining of mine.

I looked back to my monitor, which had bubbles bouncing all over a desert landscape. I had been inactive long enough to trigger the screen saver. This was work time, not walking time. I had been away too long. I had a website to work on.

"We'll go later," I said to Bella, who does her pink mouthed yawn and a cute little groan. I got a whiff of her doggy breath and she settled back in. Bella knows when it's walkies time.

"It's work time," I said as I grabbed the mouse. My hand was shaking. I glanced back out the window and the gray man was gone. I had only looked away for a moment. I should have still been able to see him.

THURSDAY

I DREAMED OF MY FATHER LAST NIGHT. HIS ROUGH BEARD, HIS strong cologne, his big hands as he dragged me into a doctor's office. I wailed and tried to pull away, resisting him every step of the way.

"No!" I cried. "I don't like the doctors." I'm about six years old and my behavior had become worrisome to my father. He had been taking me to doctors who had been asking me strange questions, making me take bitter little pills that made me feel funny, made me feel sick.

The sun was hot above us and the dry heat sucked the sweat from my body. We were in Phoenix because Flagstaff didn't have doctors that my father thought were good enough.

He was squatting down then. He let go of my arm and held his arms wide open. He had a brown button-down shirt on, buttoned all the way up. His blue eyes looked compassionate and I let him hug me.

"This is important, Kenny," he whispered. "The things you see... they're not there. It's not right."

I think this dream was triggered by the walk I took yesterday. Bella and I came across a little bunch of wild irises, with several of them actually in bloom. They are rare in the forest here, and while their blooms are not as bright or bold as their cultivated cousins, I cherish them. They are smaller and hardier, and grow up through the thick bed of old pine needles surviving on what little rain we get up here.

"Do you understand?" my father whispered in my dream, which was, really, more like a memory.

I nodded my head, even though I didn't understand. This latest doctor's visit had come after my father and I had been for a hike in the forest. We had come across a ring of wild irises. He told me about them and how special they were. I foolishly told him about the little people I saw dancing in and out of the ring of flowers. How they were dressed in delicate silk and seemed so happy.

When I looked up from the faeries to him, his jaw was clenched and his eyes were moist.

Even as a child, I knew I saw things that others didn't, like the faeries and dead people. I also knew that I could imagine things and see them clearly as things in the the real world. Like how my Legos should go together to form the perfect rocket ship. I would build it so quickly, people were amazed. I could do the same with math or writing, see them clearly and practice them in my mind.

I generally could tell the difference between the two—the real things others couldn't see and my imaginings. All of them made my father nervous.

Back in the dream, my father took me into the clinic. The office smelled of antiseptic, which had already started making me queasy because of what I experienced in those offices. The doctor had a fat neck and a bald head. He asked me questions for what seemed like hours. He wrote a prescription for another bitter little pill. He said words like "hallucination," "psychosis," and "schizophrenia." My father nodded solemnly, I knew this must be a horrible thing I had.

My mother never came on these outings to the doctors, but this is a dream and she's there. She was the receptionist that greeted us and gave me a green-eyed wink. Told me everything was going to be okay.

Mom didn't care that I saw faeries or talked to my dead grandfather. She told me it was okay to be different. My father and her fought over this. It was the only thing I ever heard them fight about.

But my father won and I took bitter little pills all the way through high school. Pills that made the world seem vague and distant, pills that made colors dull, pills that stole my imaginings and my visions, pills that made me fat, made my skin itch, and made the world not worth living in.

When I went off to college, I stopped talking the bitter little pills and I started seeing things again.

FRIDAY

I'VE DECIDED THE GRAY MAN IS ONE OF MY IMAGININGS, JUST like Bella. It has to be that way. On today's walk Bella and I went down a trail into a little canyon to a sheltered place where big old-growth pines grow and there is even an area where ferns flourish. The canyon is sheltered, cooler and moister than most of the forest. I haven't seen a faerie since I was a boy, but this is just the kind of place they would love.

Bella and I were exploring a side canyon, off the trail, when I saw the gray man. My heart jumped in my chest, my mouth stale. He's walking his dead man's walk, but he's not alone. A woman was walking behind him, an older woman, with pale skin and gray clothing. They were both past us and I couldn't see their faces, but I knew the woman. It was Kelly.

She doesn't have her walking sticks and she's doing that weird walk: hands to the side, gate absolutely steady, head not moving a bit, her pace lock-step with the gray man. Bella growled, not a playful growl, but a deep-in-the-chest scared growl.

"Kelly!" I yelled, scrambling over some rocks at the bottom of the canyon. She didn't pause or acknowledge me, she didn't break her stride. She followed the gray man up the trail. I walked after them trotting to catch up, but I couldn't keep up the pace. My lungs suddenly burned as if I had been running a long way and my limbs felt so heavy. I found myself about ten yards behind them, my pace slowing down to their pace, my arms falling to my side, my head looking straight ahead.

The forest and the canyon around me seemed to close in as the color leached away, the world becoming gray.

Bella was barking at me, a shrill, scared bark. A desperate bark. With an effort that seemed Herculean, I turned my head. She was cowering on the trail about ten yards back, her tail tucked between her legs. I stopped walking and the world slowly came back to me, the greens returning to the pine needles, the blue fusing back into the clear sky.

I collapsed onto the trail and Bella was all over me, licking my face, wagging her tail.

"It's okay, girl. It's okay." I was lying to her, because it wasn't okay.

Kelly isn't like the gray man. Kelly is alive and vital. Kelly is open and curious. That couldn't have been Kelly.

"I must have been imagining it all," I told Bella.

Bella doesn't believe me, she sensed it too. And then I realized that Bella's not really there either and suddenly there's not forty pounds of jet-black spaniel in my lap licking me.

The forest felt quiet and empty then. It didn't go gray, but it felt somehow dangerous. I rushed home, locked the doors, checking them five times each, and went back to my computer where things are predictable.

SATURDAY

I WAS HAPPY THIS MORNING. I HAD COME TO SOME PEACE with the gray man and knowing that I had imagined him. I was whistling a little as I walked over to Kelly's. The morning was cool yet with the promise of heat, Bella stopping to sniff in each culvert as we walked down the narrow paved road, past the small houses of my neighborhood nestled in the ponderosa pine forest.

I had decided to tell Kelly about the gray man. I knew she would understand, that she wouldn't judge me, that we would laugh awkwardly, and it would all be okay. She would call me "hon" and serve me more coffee. We would then get to work in her yard raking up and bagging pine needles.

This vision was swirling through my head as I walked down the road. It was dramatically cut short by a flashing light up ahead. I stopped, feeling sweat prickle against my neck despite the cool. "Bella, come here. Now!" I yelled as I started trotting down the road and then running.

The flashing lights were down a little cul-de-sac, right were Kelly lives.

I'm not a good runner, my knees weak, my pudgy body not that of a runner, but I ran. I ran as fast as I could, my lungs burning, my breath sour.

There was an ambulance and two sheriff's cars in front of Kelly's house. The flashing red and blue made me blink.

A woman, dressed in a dingy brown robe with a jacket thrown on top of it was talking to one of the deputies. I don't know her name, but she's Kelly's neighbor, a big lady with black hair and a forest of gray roots.

"...gets up early, even on Saturday's," the woman said. "When I didn't see her moving about, I went over to check. I saw her on the floor in there and called 911."

Bella was so good, sitting in the middle of the cul-de-sac right next to me. If she hadn't been there I think I would have lost it.

"I started to worry about her last night when I didn't see any lights on," the woman continued.

She said more, but I stopped listening. Kelly was dead, I knew it. Kelly that I had seen with the gray man in the forest yesterday, lock-step and following him.

Kelly was dead.

I hadn't been imagining the gray man.

SUNDAY

I DIDN'T GO OUT TODAY. I CAN'T. BELLA AND I STAYED IN AND watched *The Walking Dead* on Netflix. She seemed to know that I really needed her and spent most of the day on the couch with me, occasionally laying her head on my leg and sighing.

Zombies seemed to be the right thing for me today. I'm not normally into horror, but I'm numb and this show with its gruesome violence is helping me feel something.

The gray man is kind of like a zombie. He doesn't shamble about looking for flesh to eat, but he does walk like the world is dead around him. Like there isn't life anywhere. Maybe that's what he's doing, walking the forest endlessly looking for signs of life he can't find. Looking for something real.

That must be awful.

And now Kelly is lock-step with him, following him.

SATURDAY

It's been a difficult week. I haven't been out much—I'm afraid I'll see Kelly all gray out there doing the lifeless walk of the gray man. Bella and I have stayed in. I've been working a lot.

Today was Kelly's funeral. She was Catholic so they held it at the big Catholic Church in downtown Flagstaff. I didn't go. I couldn't go. I've never been good in crowds—it's hard to know you are safe with people everywhere.

Annie came over today. She had a black dress on and a somber look on her beautiful face when I opened the door.

"How are you, Ken?" she asked.

"Fine," I lied. "Just fine. Couldn't be better." I always answer like that. It's what people want to hear.

She stood there on my little porch. I hadn't seen her in a bit. When we got divorced three years ago we promised we would stay friends. And I guess we did, but we aren't the kind of friends that get together very often.

"Can I come in?" she asked.

"Oh. Yes. Of course." I let her in and went into the kitchen and put on a tea kettle. It was obvious she was here to talk, that she would want to have tea.

When I came back into my living room she was sitting on the little brown couch. My house—it used to be our house—is small. The living room has big windows that face the forest. I had the curtains drawn. As I walked over to her, my feet sounded loud on the hardwood floor. She was patting the couch next to her.

I wanted to go sit in the recliner. That's my chair. Always has been. But I never could refuse Annie anything.

"You didn't come today," Annie said. She must have gone to Kelly's funeral.

I shrugged and looked away. Bella was curled up in the recliner, ignoring Annie. This made it very clear that she wasn't real. Bella adored Annie. If she hadn't died last month she would have still been wiggling and snuggling her.

"Kelly called me a few days before she died," Annie said. She took a deep breath. "I'm worried about you, Ken."

I shrugged again.

"Kelly said you called to Bella when she saw you in the forest."

I blinked, fighting to keep my emotions in check. When we had first met, Annie loved my imaginings, loved how I could visualize things and wasn't like everyone else. At first I thought she was going to be more like my mother and celebrate my differences, but in the end she became more like my father, wanting me to go to doctors and take bitter little pills.

"I see Bella," I said slowly. "I have to see her. I know she is not real." I wanted to add "most of the time," because that would be the truth, but I swallow hard and keep it in. "Without you, I need her."

Annie's face darkened and she turned away. We had some amazing years and then we had some okay years and then we had some really terrible years.

"Are you taking your thyroid pill?" she asked. When she turned back her face was bland.

"Why do you ask?"

"You seem a little pale."

"Haven't been out much since Kelly."

She nodded, as if that was obvious. As if everyone knew that Ken Woodard would be so devastated about a friend's death that he wouldn't leave the house for a week. As if such information was issued in the form of a formal pamphlet when everyone moved into the neighborhood.

I would have said something hurtful and angry, but the whistling of the tea kettle stopped me. I made us some tea and we drank it in awkward silence punctuated by brief intervals of tortured small talk.

After Annie left, I could still smell her perfume. Vaguely floral and strong, it tended to linger. I sat where she had and breathed it in deeply and saw her as she used to be with her brown hair down around her shoulders, a frying pan in her hand as she stood in the doorway to the kitchen beckoning me in for Saturday morning pancakes. I loved those Saturday morning pancakes because they were always followed by Saturday morning sex.

In my imagining, she had nothing on but a white apron, her curvy figure practically bursting forth.

I looked over to Bella, asleep in the recliner. "We could just imagine her too," I whispered.

I closed my eyes and shook my head hard. When I opened it, my imagined Annie was gone. That wouldn't be right, to imagine her. I knew that.

As I sat there bathing in her floral scent I remembered her question about my thyroid medication. Why had she asked that?

I went into the kitchen and got out the little jar I keep my thyroid pills in. I hate pills and it had been a major ordeal for Annie to get me to go to the doctors and to take these. This happened shortly after the divorce when I was feeling so terrible. To this day, Annie still picks up my prescription for me, brings it in, and pours it into the old jelly jar I keep it in. I can't stand those plastic medicine bottles. They creep me out.

My hands shaking, I took one of the little green pills and looked at it closely. It was squarish and had several letters on it. I went to my office and did a search for the pill. I looked it up on Wikipedia. What I saw made me scared and angry.

It wasn't a thyroid pill, it was an antidepressant.

I sat there blinking and staring at my large monitor. Annie would never do something like that to me. Maybe I was imagining this too.

The house felt smaller than it was and the air was hot. I couldn't stay in any longer. I yelled for Bella, grabbed her leash, and headed out to the forest.

SUNDAY

I slept poorly last night. Annie has betrayed me. Annie has done something worse to me than my father ever did. She tricked me into taking those pills. She lied to me.

Every time I woke up, I got onto the Internet and searched for that pill. Every time it came up the same. I am not imagining it.

Around 3:00 a.m. I took the pills and flushed them down the toilet. I don't take pills that try to change who I am, that say there is something wrong with me with every swallow, that change the world I live it.

I don't take those bitter little pills anymore.

TUESDAY

I'D RATHER BE ALIVE AND DIFFERENT THAN MADE HALF-DEAD by chemicals that work in the worst ham-fisted way, that bring with it a host of side effects.

But I don't feel so good. I'm dizzy and can't keep any food down. I've got the runs and cold sweats. My body has gotten used to those damn pills.

I called up Annie and when she answered the phone, I said, "Those weren't thyroid pills."

She was silent, all I could hear was the faint hiss of her breath.

"Why did you do that to me?" I asked. My voice sounded quavery and weak. I hated sounding that way with her.

"Because you need them, Ken. You know you do, deep in your heart you know. Things were bad after we split. You've been better since you started taking them."

I blinked back tears and took a deep breath. "It's okay to be different," I said. But I remembered how hard it was to leave the house after the split, how I was barely able to take care of Bella, how I lost most of my clients.

"These aren't like the pills your father made you take," she said, her voice just above a whisper. "They're just antidepressants. Many people take them." She took in a deep breath and it came shuddering out. "I take them."

"I don't take pills," I said.

"Please, Ken. Can I come over? Can we talk about this?"

"I'm not depressed anymore," I said. My bowels lurched awkwardly and I said good-bye and hung up before running to the bathroom.

MONDAY

I'VE BEEN SICK ALL WEEK. I'VE BARELY SLEPT AS MY BODY tried to adjust to life without brain-altering chemicals. Finally, last night things got better. I slept deeply and didn't dream. I felt almost normal when I got up and took Bella out. It was about 10:00 a.m. and she had let me sleep in.

The forest was still a bit cool, the wind still. We went right out our backyard and onto the little network of trails there. The wind had finally died down as spring slipped into summer, which made me happy.

I felt delicate, like a cracked clay pot. If I moved too fast or jostled myself physically or emotionally I might fall apart. I might break down. So I moved slower than usual, kept to the trails, stopped often to watch Bella sniff and explore.

It's here that I feel safest and the most whole. The forest doesn't care if I take bitter little pills or not. The forest doesn't care if I still take my dead dog for walks or see things that other people don't. The forest doesn't need me at all. I need it.

I took a deep breath letting the dry air fill my lungs and slowly let it out. I closed my eyes, the morning sun bathing my face. I'm going to be okay, I knew it then. I am through the worst of it. Maybe I did need some help after the divorce, but Annie was wrong to trick me into taking the pills. I am better now. I can cope.

And then Bella was barking and I opened my eyes and saw them. The gray man, Kelly, and now a gray dog. They were in front of me on the trail walking away. I couldn't see their faces. The dog was a medium-sized spaniel, just like Bella, and had that same dead-to-the-world walk as the others. It followed along at an even pace, its head straight forward moving in lock-step with the gray man and Kelly.

I looked from the gray dog to Bella—who was still barking loudly—and back. I took a deep breath and dismissed my imagined Bella, and the gray spaniel was still there.

The forest was spinning about me, my stomach clenching, my mouth tasting like ash. The gray dog was Bella, the *real* Bella. I fell to me knees and cried out, "Bella!" Whatever the gray man is doing he has gathered those that have died recently that I care about. Bella and Kelly.

I swallowed hard to keep from vomiting and forced myself to my feet and stumbled down the trail. Whatever this is, I need to stop it. These are ghosts. The gray man is real. What does he want? Why is he doing this?

I scrambled after them, listing as the forest continued to spin about me. "Bella! Kelly!" I called to them, trying to wake them up from their trance, but they didn't hear me.

I must have looked like a drunk man, crisscrossing the path in my dizzy walk, stopping and starting as my stomach roiled. Maybe it was the drugs I was still detoxing from, maybe it was knowing my Bella-dog was in trouble.

I followed them for twenty minutes, never able to get very close. I followed them down the little trail behind my house, to a bigger trail, and then down a forest service road. After I got up from one of my rests, they were gone.

I collapsed onto the dusty dirt road until the world finally steadied. I made my slow way back to my house. I drank three glasses of water and crawled back into bed, drawing the covers over my head.

TUESDAY

I SEARCHED THE FOREST ALL DAY. I BROUGHT WATER AND power bars in a little backpack. I brought my GPS, put on sunscreen, and wore my wide-brimmed floppy hat.

All the trails that Bella and I usually walked, all the cross-country treks we did regularly, all the places I had seen the gray man and the gray Kelly. I searched them all.

Until my feet were swollen and my legs ached, I searched. I had to find the gray man. I had to stop him. I had to save Bella and Kelly.

But I didn't find them. I saw happy people walking their dogs. I saw wild flowers that I didn't care about, and found another section of stacked rocks that used to be part of that late 1800s railroad, but I didn't care. None of that mattered.

And I was alone all day. I couldn't imagine Bella anymore, I didn't even try.

I've talked to the dead: my grandfather, my third-grade teacher after her heart attack, my college roommate who committed suicide. I've talked to ghosts in museums and at theaters. I've seen them in churches and grocery stores.

This world of ours is filled with ghosts. They are ephemeral, transparent, sometimes lost and confused, sometimes articulate and funny. When I was young, I saw many things, faeries, demons, even angels. As I've aged they've slowly fallen away and all I see anymore is ghosts. But not like the gray man, and the gray Kelly, and the gray Bella.

They are not ephemeral or transparent. They are solid and seem whole, but have the color leached out of them and seem more dead than most of the traditional, transparent ghosts that I have seen. They are dead to the world around them. It's not right.

WEDNESDAY

I WAS OUT AGAIN ALL DAY TODAY. I HAVE E-MAILED ALL MY clients, telling them I have the flu. Nothing else matters now but Bella.

I didn't find them, though. I went as far as my tired body and aching feet could carry me. I didn't find them.

Annie came over today. She was sitting in the living room when I came back from my trek. She was dressed in jeans and a powder-blue blouse. She had her brown hair down and she looked so beautiful it made my heart ache even more.

She remarried. Of course she did. She got married ten months and seven days after our divorce was final. Her new husband, Donald, doesn't like me. He never comes over when she does. We don't talk about him.

"How are you, Ken?" she asked when I came in the back door. She was sitting on the brown couch and patting on the cushion next to her.

I ignored her and flopped onto my recliner and drained the remains of my water bottle. "Fine," I said. I wanted to talk to her about what was going on, but after the secret antidepressants, I couldn't.

"You're not taking the pills, are you?"

I shook my head.

She bit her lip, her brown eyes examining me carefully. "How's Bella?"

I couldn't stop the tears springing to my eyes. I couldn't stop the vision of the gray Bella in lock-step behind Kelly and the gray man from entering my mind. "She's dead," I said, getting up from the recliner and heading towards the bathroom. "I need a shower."

"Maybe it's time to..." she began. Something in her tone made me stop and turn back to her. She seemed small on the couch and vulnerable.

"What?" I asked.

"Time to think about..." Her tone was so gentle, so loving. Maybe she was going to tell me it was time for us to get back together. That she was tired of Donald and his regular-guy love of football and beer. That she realized that her life wasn't the same without me.

I was suddenly sitting on the couch staring into her soft brown eyes without knowing how I got there. She had my hand in hers, they were cold, but I loved the feel of them.

She took a deep breath. I kept silent, not wanting to miss a word. "Ken, maybe it's time to think about getting another dog."

My skin tingled as the shock of her statement flowed through me. She suddenly seemed very distant even though she still held my hand. Another dog? She didn't want to come back? She wanted me to replace Bella when Bella was in a terrible place?

Tears flowed. I couldn't stop them. I surged up and headed back towards the bathroom. I knew if I spoke I would say something about what was really happening. That she would think I was crazy. That she would be compelled to do something about it, and that something wouldn't be good for me. It would involve doctors and bitter little pills and perhaps forced confinement. This world does not handle gently what it does not understand.

I closed the door behind me, panting hard. I could still smell her sweet perfume and it made me feel sick. You can't replace a friend like Bella, just like I haven't been able to replace Annie.

The white walls of the little bathroom felt like they were closing in on me.

"I'm sorry, Ken," Annie said through the door. She was right on the other side, the pain in her voice obvious. "I know you need something. Please let me help you. I... I still love you, Ken. I will always love you."

The strength went out of my tired legs and I slid to the floor. Didn't she know how much it hurt to hear her telling me that she *still* loved me?

"Ken? Please say something."

I took a breath and willed myself to speak. I knew Annie, she wouldn't leave if I didn't talk to her. It seemed like talking was the hardest thing in the world. "Thank... thank you for coming over. I need to take a shower now. I've had a long hike." The words were stilted and awkward, but it was the best I could do.

Annie sniffed and sighed, her voice hardening. "I refilled your prescription and I'm leaving it on the coffee table. Please start taking them again. I shouldn't have lied to you about them. I'm sorry for that."

"I'm very dirty," I said, barely stopping myself from sobbing.

"Look on this as an experiment," Annie said. "Start taking the pills again. See how you feel. Write about it in that journal of yours." She paused for a long time and I thought maybe she had left. "Please, Kenny. Do it for me."

THURSDAY

THE PRESCRIPTION BOTTLE IS STILL ON MY COFFEE TABLE, unopened. It's an ugly little plastic bottle with the big white child-proof lid. It's an intrusion in my home, but I haven't been able to do anything about it, or even go near it.

That bottle is my father, telling me I'm not right. That bottle is the world punishing me because I am different. It's boys in high school teasing me, pushing me, hitting me. The girls in college either sneering at me or ignoring me.

I didn't go out today. I spent the day in my office working as hard as I could. On the other side of the phone, those people don't care what I look like or what I can see. They value me. They value my imagination. I can see their websites in my mind even before I start building them. I am very fast. I am very good.

Bella, though, is not far from my mind. I need to help her, I must help her. But I have to feel more like myself first.

FRIDAY

I'VE BEEN DOING NOTHING BUT WORKING AND SLEEPING. Well, trying to sleep and then getting up and working more. I've caught up with my backlog of work from when I was sick from going off of the antidepressant. I am going to run out of work soon.

I tried to leave today, to go out my back door, to walk into the forest and look for Bella, but I couldn't. It's too much.

Annie still loves me. The sound of it is a bitter taste in my mouth. The "still" is only delivered after your lover has left. I know she doesn't tell her husband Donald that she "still" loves him. It's active, it's real, there is no need for the horrible word "still."

The pills are still on the coffee table, right were Annie left them. I stood there this afternoon staring at them. Annie thought I still needed them. That I couldn't even function in this world without them.

I stood in the kitchen doorway for the longest time. In one direction I could see the bottle of bitter little pills, in the other direction my back door with its square glass panes and the forest beyond.

I took a step for the pills and then a step towards the door.

What I wanted to do was grab the pills, throw them out, and go looking for Bella. To help her. But I could do neither. It was like I was captured between two magnetic poles, balanced perfectly between them. Stuck.

I don't know how long I did it. I had just come into the kitchen to get a snack. When I started it was light outside. By the time I finally moved—my bladder broke the tie and I headed towards the bathroom—it was dark.

I am going to go back to work now, but I had this thought. Only part of me wants to throw those pills out, another part of me wants to take them. To let them do their work. To do something that will make Annie proud and make me more normal.

I can't stand these thoughts.

SATURDAY

I woke up groggy at about noon after working until there was no work left to do and going to bed when the sun came up.

In the bathroom I splashed cool water on my face and got a glimpse of myself. I didn't look long. My face sagged more than usual and there were huge bags under my eyes. I didn't have my glasses on, so I couldn't see that well, but I did see well enough to be shocked by the haunted look in my eyes.

I walked through the living room, my eyes slits, so I couldn't look at that damn bottle of pills. I grabbed my backpack and walked out into the forest without thinking about it.

It was almost eighty degrees out already and it was going to be a hot one. The sun was brutal and I put my hat on, shouldering my backpack and going out the gate of my backyard into the vast ponderosa pine tree forest.

I walked quickly to the first place I saw the gray man, right off of a dirt forest service road. I stood on the jumble of lichen-covered volcanic rocks off the trail. I tried to remember everything Bella had been doing. Her dog-in-the-forest things. Sniffing, tail wagging, looking for a lizard or a squirrel to chase.

I had been walking on the rocks, feeling the sharp edges press through my shoes, not really thinking about anything. The gray man had been walking on the road looking straight ahead, walking back towards the houses.

But he wasn't there. I sat down, pulled out a power bar and a bottle of water and had my breakfast sitting on the uneven stones. I knew I really had seen him, he wasn't one of my imaginings. He was real. Kelly was really with him too. And Bella.

Boredom set in, but I didn't care. I was going to sit here and wait for the gray man however long it took. The day slowly went by, a few people even passing on the forest service road—people with color in the cheeks and life in their walk. None of them noticed me, not even their dogs. It was like I was invisible. Which I liked. If you are invisible, people don't try to make you take pills you don't want to take or do things you don't want to do.

But it is lonely being invisible.

I stood up and stretched around 3:00 p.m., trying to get feeling back in my numb butt. I walked back into the forest to find a tree to pee on. When I came back, they were there: the gray man, gray Kelly, and gray Bella walking all in a row with a decided sense of purpose.

"Bella," I called as I zipped my fly back up. "Bella!"

She didn't look at me, her head straight forward, her pace unwavering, her black fur gone gray. I ran, leaving my backpack behind, and tried to catch up with them. But, I couldn't. No matter how hard I ran they were always in front of me. I could never see their faces.

My lungs burned and my spit was thick as molasses. We had wound around the dirt road and come to the main forest service road. They all purposefully took a right, heading deeper into the forest.

It came to me then, I knew what to do. I had to be like them, I had to be gray Ken to walk with them, to catch up with them.

I thought of the bottle of pills Annie had left me. I didn't take them because I thought they would make me gray, leach the specialness right out of me. Make me into something I wasn't. But right then, Bella needed me. I would do what I had to. I would do anything.

I took a deep breath and slowly let it out, my mouth dry, sweat rolling down my back. I let my arms fall to my side and started doing the gray man walk. I kept my head forward, my pace steady, and followed them.

The color immediately leached from the forest and I no longer felt the heat of the day. I didn't feel cold either. It was like the "color" of all my sense was being drained.

When I started this walk, they had gotten a ways in front of me, but walking this way I quickly caught up.

By the time I came into line right behind Bella, the world was fully monochromatic and I couldn't feel anything. Not the hot sun, not my urgent thirst, not my tired feet.

I heard something heavy fall behind me. I didn't turn to look, but I knew what it was. My body had just fallen away from me. I had to leave even it behind to be with my Bella.

I was one of them now.

———

IT WASN'T QUITE LIKE I DIDN'T FEEL ANYTHING. I FELT THE slight breeze on my gray skin, the dirt road beneath my feet, the heat of the sun on my face. But as I traveled lock-step behind gray Bella, gray Kelly, and the gray man, none of it mattered. It was all dull and useless information, not worth acting on. Like someone turned the radio down so low it was barely perceptible—just a hum in the background—but not anything that would inspire action.

We walked down that forest service road for about a mile. I

didn't have any real sense of scale on the walk, but I've been down this road hundreds of times. I knew where we were. We turned off the main forest road onto a tiny two-track and headed back into the forest to a little campsite perched on the edge of a steep canyon.

We were getting close to something, I could feel it in a way I couldn't feel the sun or smell the sweet scent of the pine trees. The four of us walked to the end of the road which was something of a cul-de-sac with a fire ring in the middle. We didn't slow, we rounded the fire ring and headed off on a thin trail, more like an animal track, along the edge of the canyon.

It's called Kelly Canyon and is part of the topography that drains water from the heights of Flagstaff and Northern Arizona down to Oak Creek Canyon and Sedona. The canyon is steep and beautiful, about one hundred feet deep where we were. Tall pine trees cling to the side of the canyon and the occasional outcropping of craggy gray rocks line the edge.

We walked the little trail at our usual pace until we came to one of those rock ledges. Kelly, Bella, and I stopped as the gray man went to the edge of the cliff, put his hands on his hips and admired the view.

I was dimly puzzled by the change, but it was like the sun and the wind—it didn't matter.

And it is a lovely view from there, the land folds into steep canyons covered in a thicket of dark green pine trees with the occasional light green of the oaks. The sun was nearing the horizon, and if not for everything being gray, it would have been beautiful.

The gray man then turned to us and smiled, the color returning to his body and his clothes. He stood out, surrounded by a gray world. He had a surprisingly round face for such a slim man, one that seemed so familiar to me. I didn't know his name, but I had seen him in the forest as a normal person. We had waved, maybe even said hello a few times.

He turned back to the view, his shoulders rising as he took a deep breath, taking in the beauty. And then the rock below his feet gave way and he tumbled out of view, the sound of his scream echoing through the gray world.

Kelly then took up the position on the ledge, her hands on her hips admiring the view. She too looked back at me briefly as the color returned to her, a small smile on her aged face, before the rock gave way again and she fell from sight, her scream echoing around the forest.

Bella then took her place on the ledge, her doggy head taking in the view. She, too, turned to me as the color returned to her body. Even in my gray state, I wanted to weep. Those big brown eyes spoke to me of a compassion and a love that I so missed. In many ways I missed her more than I did Annie. Bella had always been there for me, was always ready to be my companion.

The rock then gave way beneath Bella's paws and she was gone with a sharp bark of fear.

And then it was my turn. I stood on the rock ledge as color returned to the world. I could feel the breeze cooling my hot skin, I could smell the vanilla tang of the big pine trees. The view was so beautiful, heartbreakingly so.

And then the rock gave out beneath my feet.

I screamed as I fell.

I saw him as I fell. The man, not gray but normal, his body a jumble at the bottom of the cliff, his limbs at odd angels, dark blood crusted on his head, staining the old tawny pine needles underneath him, his unseeing eyes staring straight up.

No Kelly. No Bella. Just the man with his broken head and his broken limbs.

My body hit the cliff as it sloped out. I felt the impact, a cry of pain escaping my lungs. I tumbled and fell, my body bouncing against the rock, intense pain, indescribable pain, until the third bounce when my head connected directly with the rock and I didn't feel anything anymore.

My body came to rest right where I had seen the no-longer-gray man, my eyes looking straight up. I could feel the cold creeping into me as my blood spilled out of my body. I tried to speak, but couldn't. I tried to move, but had lost the ability. I could see the cliff I had fallen from above me, the towering pines, the blue sky, lazy little clouds.

And then my vision began to fade and the color leached from the trees and the sky and the rock.

And then it all went black.

———

"BELLA," I SAID WITH A LAUGH. I WAS SLEEPING AND HER sloppy tongue and doggy breath were trying to wake me. She was licking my face, her breath coming fast as if she had been running.

"Stop it! I'm tired." Something wasn't right. I wasn't in a soft bed, the surface beneath me was hard and uneven.

My body was heavy, it was hard to move at all, but it hurt so much I had to move. I took a deep breath and coughed as dust filled my lungs. Bella barked sharply, except it wasn't a Bella bark.

I opened my eyes and looked around. I was on the edge of the forest service road and the dog now eyeing me suspiciously was not Bella. It was a scrawny puppy with long legs, short brown fur, and pointed ears. Not a spaniel, some kind of mutt.

"What?" I mumbled, feeling dizzy, my head aching, a sharp pain behind my eye spiking with each heartbeat.

The dog barked at me again. It was skinny and scared, its ribs showing. "It's okay, boy," I said. "It's okay. I'm not going to hurt you."

It all came tumbling back to me. The gray man that Kelly, Bella, and I had followed to the cliff. I had become one of them, my body collapsing on the side of the road so I could truly follow. We had all fallen off the cliff. I saw the gray man's real body at the bottom of the cliff.

I breathed a sigh of relief. It all made sense now. They were trying to get my attention in the best way they knew how. The gray man was a ghost who just wanted his body discovered. Kelly and my Bella were just helping him get my attention.

The dog, having decided I wasn't dangerous, was in my lap snuggling me, licking my face, whining. It was clear to me he was a puppy still and also clear he was going to be big when he was fully grown.

I slowly pushed myself into a standing position and he skittered away, his tail between his legs. I was dizzy and my head hurt even worse. I must have been dehydrated. I needed to get home. I needed to call the sheriff.

As I slowly walked towards my house, I said, "Come on, Skitter. I've got some food you can have. Bella won't mind."

Two Weeks Later

Skitter was staring at me as I stared at the bottle of bitter little pills sitting on my coffee table. These aren't the ones that Annie had me take, telling me they were for my thyroid. These are the pills my own doctor prescribed me—my psychiatrist, I should say.

I haven't written in my journal for a while. Things have been strange. That day I found Skitter, I drank and ate and fed him, so we both felt better, and then I called the sheriff. They sent a young blond-haired deputy out in a white SUV. We drove down into Pumphouse Wash and then walked a short way up into Kelly Canyon. It was dark, so we had to use flashlights, and I had a bad moment when I thought we wouldn't find the body. But the smell of rotting flesh drew us in and we found him. His name was Jonathan Olsen. His wife had been hysterical for the last few weeks trying to find him. He went out for a walk one day and never came back. I can't say it was a good discovery, but at least it was closure for her and for him. I haven't seen the gray man since.

After I fed Skitter that first time, he became my constant

companion. There wasn't a discussion, or a thought about it, really. He needed a home. I needed a companion. I took him to the vet, got him his immunizations, and had them see if he was chipped.

I had a bad moment there, thinking that maybe he was chipped and that I wouldn't be able to keep him. But, no chip, so he stayed. He's already grown in the last few weeks and still does his trademark skittering when surprised, but not nearly as much anymore.

And that brings me back to the bottle of bitter little pills.

What Annie did to get me to take her "thyroid" pills made me think. Maybe it wasn't about me being different, but about me being functional. After the incident with the gray man, I rested for a few days, and then... I found myself isolating even more. I had Skitter, I didn't need anyone else. I didn't call Annie, I didn't go to the movies with my friend Hal, I even stopped being social online. It just wasn't safe. If not for Skitter and his need for exercise, I don't know what would have happened to me.

And then one day, I stared at the phone for three hours before picking it up and calling Annie.

"I need help," I said after she answered.

"I know, sweetie," she said.

"Will you help me find a doctor?"

She laughed, but it was a nervous thing, an expression of relief. "Of course."

"I'm scared," I said. She told me she knew and that she wouldn't let me go through it alone. Right then I was so glad that she still loved me.

She moved mountains and got me an appointment in only a week. She picked me up and walked me into the doctor's office, holding my hand the whole way.

I didn't tell the doctor everything, not about the ghost, but I did tell him of my imaginings. How I can see things that aren't there. How I know they aren't real, but only most of the time. Thus the bottle of pills I was staring at as Skitter stared at me.

"What do you think, boy?" I asked.

He looked to the back door and then to me. The summer heat was on us, but he loved to be in the forest. I laughed and opened the bottle.

The doctor told me it might change my imaginings some, might dull them a bit, but that I will be able to function better in the real world. He also told me this was a journey we were on, that if this pill didn't work, maybe another would. I start counseling next week. He thinks that will help too, that maybe I won't always need these pills.

I opened the bottle and put one of those bitter little pills on my tongue. I let it sit there until I could taste it, the sharp bitterness almost making me gag. I didn't want to hide from it.

I swallowed it down, but the bitter taste lingered, and that's okay by me. It's my choice this time.

"Come on, boy," I said to Skitter as we headed for the door.

BACKSTORY—IMAGININGS

THIS STORY STARTED WITH A WALK IN THE WOODS WITH MY pup, a spaniel. I saw a man that was walking so steadily, so oblivious to the forest, that he seemed like a ghost to me, like he wasn't real. Just like Ken reflects on in this story, I couldn't understand how anyone living could be in this amazing forest on this beautiful day and not "be" there.

I was curious and confounded, and thus, a very different ghost story was born. I've written about ghosts so much with four novels in the "A Ghost's Memoir" world and a bunch of shorter stories, it felt good to bust out and have a different take on ghosts.

This story is personal in other ways. I'm an introvert, have my fair share of social anxiety, and tend to isolate too much. All of that is nicely balanced by my more outgoing (and amazing) wife, but in this story, I created a character more extreme than me in those areas, but one that I could relate to.

Stories this close to home (literally and figuratively) and that touch on the very difficult topic of mental heath feel dangerous. But these are just the kinds of stories that are worth telling.

PART SIX
DEATH BY STARLIGHT

DEATH BY STARLIGHT

THE VOID OF SPACE. DARK. EMPTY. LIT ONLY BY THE
pinpricks of starlight as I floated in the vast emptiness. Alone.

Oxygen running out, blaring blood-red on my heads-up display.
Time to die...

The animal in us can't conceive of death, of a world without us.
As I waited to die I realized that my death did actually mean my
world's death. Not the objective world we all share, but my subjec-
tive world. The one filtered through my eyes and my experiences
would die with me. My world could not exist without me.

I felt ready for it. I had wanted to live on the frontier and now it
was time to die on the frontier. What else could happen? My ship
destroyed. My comrades dead. My com damaged—I couldn't even
call for help. Alone in the cold, vast silence of space.

As the oxygen levels decreased, as my end grew near, the stars
changed. They went from tiny white pinpricks to these rainbow
smears of color, sparkling and lovely. I understand the biology, as
my O2 levels plummeted, my brain started dying, and that dying
was beautiful.

I grinned like a drunk and giggled, the sound echoing in my

spacesuit's helmet. I licked my lips, my tongue fat and slug-like, my mouth tasting of metal.

I reached out with my mind to those rainbow stars, the color spilling forth as if someone held a prism in front of each of them. So beautiful... the most beautiful thing I had ever seen. The last thing I would ever see. I beseeched them to take me, to make me one of them. I wanted to join them and be alone in the vastness of space, lit by an inner light.

Eventually the rainbows started to fade and all became darkness. Sadness, and finally, a spike of fear reached my dying brain.

Rescue...

Consciousness came back with a jolt. I was on a ship surrounded by smiling people, they had found me. The lights were so bright they stabbed like tiny knives into my brain. I closed my eyes. I didn't speak. I grieved.

I wanted death by starlight. I wanted the stars to take me. I didn't want to be back in the same life. I wanted to be among the stars and the starlight. I wanted to *be* the starlight.

I didn't speak for a week. They subjected me to tests and doctors and counseling. But what was there to say? The world didn't seem right until...

I saw it as a doctor flashed my eyes with his little penlight for the zillionth time. A rainbow smear of light. I blinked and laughed like a giddy school girl. I got off of the examination table and looked at the lights in the ceiling. If I turned my head the right way, there it was, that prismatic explosion of color. Starlight.

After that everything changed. Each breath became a joy. The most mundane activity—eating, making my bunk, doing a routine systems check—became an adventure. Everything haloed in that rainbow light, if I just looked for it.

The doctors say it's a result of my oxygen deprivation. But I know better. The stars, they took me. This world is not the world I left. I am not the person I was.

I died. I was reborn. It is all starlight.

BACKSTORY—DEATH BY STARLIGHT

THIS STORY IS THE COMBINATION OF TWO THINGS: REUSING the environment and feelings from "The Last Flight of the Acurus" and wanting to consider death as not scary or bad.

It's inevitable.

It's going to happen.

What if we lived a life and met our end just the way we wanted to?

That was the starting point, the story is about finding a way to be in the world when you've been dragged back.

This story was published by *Every Day Fiction* and an audio version of it was featured in *StarShipSofa Episode 394* along with "The Last Flight of the Acurus."

PART SEVEN
GOSSAMER THREADS

GOSSAMER THREADS

WHEN THE FIFTH GHOST MOVED IN, I MOVED OUT. I HAD TO.
The old hunting shack we all occupied wasn't much, just one room.
It had a bed with a musty mattress, a sink, a table with two broken
chairs, and a smelly old outhouse outside.

I couldn't sleep no more. The ghosts' dreams of death, one on
top of the other, was too much. I'd wake up, my heart thumping so
hard I was sure it would tear itself apart, sweat prickly and hot,
clinging to my body. The ghosts' deaths were so real in my dreams,
it felt like I had been the one to die. Usually Abigale would be
there, an apologetic look on her round, moon-silver face, her kind
eyes sad. She was the one that got me into this trouble in the first
place.

A FEW MONTHS BACK, I WAS OUT BEHIND THAT SHACK NEXT TO
the little lake. It wasn't much either, reedy with a pale green layer
of algae clinging to it, but the frogs loved it and I could catch them
and eat them. I was tending a small cook fire as it popped and

smoked, waiting for coals to form so I could roast the frog I had just caught.

It was early, frost still clinging to the ground as a tired sun got ready to climb above the horizon. I blew on my hands, covered in some ratty half-gloves, and shivered from the cold, my belly tight from being empty too long, and then she was there. A girl, my age, maybe twelve, stick thin and made out of moonlight. A ghost. She had a round face and big eyes, her lips moving slowly as she spoke one word over and over.

I looked down, poking my fire with a stick, and grumbled, "Move on. I ain't gonna take you in."

She was one of the wanderers. A ghost that had no purpose or perpetrator to balance the scales with. I still don't understand it, but ghosts can't go in a house unless their perpetrator is there or they've been invited.

I snuck a look at her, the sun's thin yellow rays peaking up over the ridgeline washing her out—like all ghosts, she'd be impossible to see in full sunlight. She was looking at my shack with a longing in her eyes. I'd seen it many times, the hollow look of a soul without a place or a purpose. If I'd had a mirror, I'd probably see the same look on my own face.

Her eyes met mine, her lips still moving around that single word. I couldn't hear her, of course; the dead could talk all they wanted but the living can't hear them. Reading lips ain't that hard, though. Not with so many mute ghosts around to practice on, so it didn't take me long to figure it out. Her silver eyes drew me in and I wished I knew what color they had been and wondered if they were so sad when she was alive.

Lonely. That was the word her mouth formed over and over. The feeling her eyes conveyed. My fire popped and I looked away. "I ain't takin' no ghosts in," I said, but I was wondering if "lonely" was about her or me or maybe both of us.

When the frog was ready, the sun was up and I couldn't see her no more. I slowly ate the frog, enjoying the hot meat, thinking about the ghost, knowing I was so very lonely. When the frog was about halfway gone, I stopped eating. It was hard, cause I was still hungry, I could eat five frogs every morning, but usually only managed to catch one. But there was someone else out there, living around this little lake. I paused, breathing in the cool air, enjoying the feel of the sun on my face. I stuck the remnants of the frog on a stick near the fire and headed out to forage for mushrooms. When I came back the frog was gone, the bones carefully arranged into the letter "T." I think it meant "thank you" and is how I knew an animal didn't come eat it.

I didn't try to discover who my friend was. I understood wanting to stay hidden.

I WAS TEN YEARS OLD WHEN THE GOSSAMER THREAD FELL. Little silver strands, kinda like Christmas tree tinsel, but aglow with a light all their own, twisting down from the sky, falling on all of us.

It was the Fourth of July and my parents had taken me down to the beach at dusk to watch the fireworks. There was an excitement in the air after the sun set. We sat on a plaid blanket and had a picnic dinner of fried chicken and potato salad, my mom's rosy cheeks framing her smile, my dad leaning on one elbow and drinking a beer.

I pointed at a shimmering in the sky to the east. "Fireworks!"

The look on my mother's face was wonder, the look on my father's fear. They knew the silver shimmer that I was pointing at. They had seen it a decade before when the aliens had come in ships that shimmered the same way. Ships that could dance through the sky and dart under the water. Ships that appeared indestructible until the day we learned to destroy them.

The aliens came offering to help us clean our oceans and cool our planet if we would just stop our fighting. Some people were like my mother, embracing them and what they brought, some were like my father, afraid of change and not trusting what seemed too good to be true.

Folks like my father won out, and after we managed to destroy several of their ships, they left. Until that Fourth of July.

Silvery shimmering in the sky. Gossamer threads falling in the night. "Ronny!" my father shouted as he grabbed me and ran to the car, my mother frozen in fear or maybe wonder. I cried, not understanding everyone's fear—weren't the shining, twisting gossamer threads too beautiful to be bad?

But it didn't matter, the threads eventually touched each one of us, changed each one of us. They went right through wood or metal and found you wherever you were hiding. I was smiling when the first thread touched me. I watched it disappear into my hand; it felt like rubbing your stocking feet on the carpet and then touching metal. I laughed as my father ran with me.

Those gossamer threads created the ghosts that now walk among us. The aliens never explained their actions, but it's clear enough. They were trying to teach us to be civilized. If you kill, you will be haunted by your victim. Clear enough. Except I don't think it all turned out quite how they planned.

AFTER THE GHOST LEFT, AS I FORAGED IN THE FOREST, THAT word kept ringing around my head. *Lonely.* Those gossamer threads should have made this a less lonely world. But it didn't. Not for me.

I fingered the scar on my neck as I searched the ground for mushrooms. The scar's as long as my four fingers held together and on the right side of my neck. A raised welt of scar tissue that is as healed as it's gonna get. It hurts when I touch it. Not cause it's new or anything, but because it's something that will always hurt.

Joey did it. He did it about a year ago. He knew exactly what he was doing. He was trying to turn me into a ghost, his ghost.

A WEEK AFTER THE GOSSAMER THREADS FELL, I STARTED TO understand what was going on. It was Sunday morning and I was out delivering papers on my bike. The air was cool as I pumped up and down the hilly streets of Lion City, Oregon; a tiny place right on the coast with the 101 running through it. It was hard riding and my mouth got sour from the effort. I didn't like delivering papers so much, and with fewer folks subscribing it was a lot more work than it used to be, but I liked having candy money.

CinnaBombs were my favorite. Strong enough so the cinnamon flavor burns your mouth and fills your nose until you can't smell anything else. I had one of the big, red candies in my mouth when I saw it happen. I had seen the strange silvery shapes at night, overheard snatches of hushed conversation between my parents, but I hadn't seen a ghost yet.

Mr. Clayton in his old 1990s' Cadillac almost clipped me as he rounded the corner between Elm and Second Street. I yelled at him, although with his old-man hearing and his blaring Elvis music, I knew he wouldn't hear me. Mr. Clayton was old, real old, with snow white hair and thick Coke-bottle glasses. He roared down Second, almost hit a black cat, and swerved right into Mrs. Patterson while she checked her mail.

The crunch-splat sound made me want to throw up and I sucked in air, swallowing the Cinnabomb whole, almost choking on it.

The day was overcast, rain coming at any moment, and that's how I saw her. Mrs. Patterson's ghost. She wasn't real easy to see, but I could make her out. All silvery like those threads that rained down on us. She started shouting at poor Mr. Clayton. Well, it looked like she was shouting, not that I could hear her. Mr. Clayton was wailing and crying and then he was shouting and clutching his chest. He slumped over onto the horn and soon there was two silvery forms, both of them silently yelling their heads off at each other.

I got on my bike and rode away as fast as I could.

ABIGALE—SHE TOLD ME HER NAME THE SECOND MORNING I saw her—came to see me every morning before sunrise when I was making the fire or cooking a frog or a squirrel. She said "lonely" to me over and over again until I couldn't stand to look at her.

Because I understood. After the threads rained down and people started dying, the world changed.

It ended, really. The dead didn't go away, and if they felt victimized in the way they died, they went about their haunting. They would follow their people day and night, invade their dreams with the sights, sounds, tastes, and smells of their deaths.

Some of the haunted never turned the lights out, they were either in bright sun or in a room with all the lights turned on so they couldn't see the ghosts. But if they ever slept, the dreams came.

"I'm lonely too," I finally said to Abigale one cold morning, my breath making little clouds in front of me.

She smiled and nodded and sat down, her legs folded, her dress carefully arranged in case I was a perv or something.

Was that it? All she wanted was for me to admit my loneliness.

What? she mouthed, slowly and carefully.

"What do you mean?"

She pointed at me and said "what" again.

"What happened to me?"

She nodded and smiled. She was pretty with a round face and big eyes, and her nose had a small upturn at the end. Her hair was long and carefully braided into two pigtails. With her being all made of moonlight, I couldn't tell you the color of her eyes or her hair, but I imagined her hair the color of dried corn husks and her eyes the color of a calm ocean.

I sighed and poked at my fire and went about preparing the frog. When I looked back up she was mouthing "what" and pointing at me.

She was lonely and so was I. There ain't nothing in the world that chases loneliness away better than stories, so I told her my story.

My mom was hopeful at first, that the ghosts would make this world a gentler and safer place. That the aliens were wise, much wiser than us, and that they knew what they were doing. She had faith.

My father thought it was the beginning of the end, that humans were basically selfish, that the prospect of a haunting wouldn't stop the worst from killing and it certainly wouldn't stop accidents—like when Mr. Clayton ran into Mrs. Patterson.

I didn't know what to believe, I was just scared. My parents "debated" this endlessly. That's what they called it, debating, but it was just arguing. The gossamer threads and the ghosts were different things to different people.

One night, with my dad driving, they were having their "debate" while I sat in the backseat, my eyes closed. This was a few months after the threads came when the cracks were showing, but the world hadn't fallen apart yet. We still had power and gas and a government.

Their arguments scared me almost as much as the ghosts. I squeezed my eyes shut so I couldn't see the silvery beings that now inhabited our little city. I pressed my hands to my ears, but couldn't block out the sounds of the fight.

My father had a habit of looking at my mother when he spoke to her while he drove, something she had always told him not to do. "You're going to get us in a wreck one day, Roger," she would say.

That night they were going on and on about the ghosts.

"You must see it now, Grace," he said, his tone loud. We had just had dinner with some friends and he had four drinks instead of his usual two. "Suicide rates have skyrocketed. They're still killing each other in Syria, but now many of the ghosts have joined the fight, blaming the government officials and haunting them. The rumors coming out of North Korea are terrifying. Not to mention what's happening to the economy."

"Sometimes it gets worse before it gets better," Mom said with a sniff. "Now, at least the victims have some power, have a voice."

"A voice? They're mute apparitions with the power to drive you insane."

"Murder rates are down. A lot." My mother's voice got louder.

"And the rise in suicides more than makes up for that."

I pushed hard on my ears, trying to keep the sound out, and squeezed my eyes tighter as they continued to argue. The "debate" soon turned to yelling.

And then... "Roger, watch out—" my mother yelled. The crunch of metal and the sound of glass breaking assaulted my ears. My mother screamed. I smelled smoke. And then there was darkness.

ABIGALE WAS CRYING, SILVERY TEARS LAZILY TRACKING DOWN her pretty face.

They died? she mouthed.

"My mom." Every morning we sat together and I told stories before the sun came up and until I had a hard time seeing her. "Your mom?" I asked her.

She looked towards the horizon, the sky there rapidly lightening, and shook her head. She had heard a lot about me, but there always seemed to be a reason for her not tell her own stories.

She smiled at me, got up and walked away. I finished cooking the squirrel—one of my traps finally worked—and ate half of it. I left the rest there on a stick in the ground knowing my friend would come and get it, hoping I would spot him some day.

MY FATHER LEFT ME A NOTE. A SHORT ONE. "I CAN'T DO THIS to you. I'm sorry. I love you. Dad." I remember the feel of the paper in my hand. It was the good stuff my mom had done calligraphy on, thick and textured, cool from the night. This was almost a year after the threads came and the world had fallen apart.

On top of the note was his Swiss army knife, its red sides scarred with age, something my father had had since he was a boy, something I had asked for many times.

I picked it up and rubbed it, feeling the scratches, hefted it and felt its weight. A knife and a note was all he left me.

My mother had died in that car crash, but she had still come home with us. As a ghost.

I remember before all this happened, my friend Amy Chandler's father had been shot and killed at a convenience store robbery in Portland. I remember her crying at the funeral, telling me she would do anything to see him again.

I saw my dead mother every day, and it was terrible. Her mute sadness. Her inability to hold me or comfort me. I lived my mother's death almost every night as did my father, dying in that car crash over and over again.

I woke every day and saw the haunted eyes of my father.

My mother blamed him for her death so she haunted him, haunted us.

I understood why my father left, he was trying to save me from this, but even then I understood that part of it was selfish—he couldn't stand to watch me suffer. I understood, but I found it unacceptable. Like Amy Chandler, I would rather have the reality of my gossamer mother mutely haunting me than not having her at all.

I was eleven then, almost twelve, old enough to be on my own in this new world. I packed my backpack with a water bottle and what food we had left—a few candy bars and some canned goods. I put that Swiss army knife in my pocket, and I headed out to find my father.

My mornings fell into a simple pattern. Up before dawn, start a fire, check the traps and hunt frogs, tell Abigale my story while I cook and eat, leave some of the food for the person I never saw.

I began to look forward to Abigale's visits, to continuing my tale. It hurt, but in a good way, like digging a nasty splinter out. She wouldn't talk about herself, and after a while I stopped asking.

And then one day she didn't show up and I learned what lonely really meant. Or, rather, I learned again. During our time every morning in the predawn gray of a quiet world, I had learned what it felt like to not be so lonely, to have a friend. Her absence made me feel more lonely than when I had first come up here running from the mess in Eugene.

I was a wreck all day, spent the night searching for her, roaming far past my usual territory, getting lost in the cold moonless night several times, but I didn't find her.

Three days she was away. I didn't eat much and hardly slept.

When she returned, I yelled at her, asked her where she had been, and hid my tears of relief and joy from her. She didn't tell me what had happened, she just looked at my tiny shack with such a longing, like it was a fancy resort or something.

Take me, she mouthed, pointing at the door.

Ghosts, they don't want to be outside. They don't want to be without a person. It pains them and I knew it. But I had never invited a ghost into my shack, cause once you did, you couldn't make them leave and they would never leave. Ghosts need to be attached, if not to their perpetrator then to a building.

I invited Abigale in. I didn't want to lose her again.

When we got inside, she smiled and clapped her hands together and my heart warmed. I could keep it dark in there and could see her during the day. I told her stories until I fell asleep.

I WOULDN'T HAVE BEEN ABLE TO FOLLOW MY DAD, BUT SOME ghosts helped me. As I walked through our town away from the salty ocean air, nobody would say much to me; not the living, but the dead would. Those that didn't have a person or a house to haunt, they were happy for some company.

It took time, telling them what my dad and mother looked like, showing them pictures. Getting them to talk slow enough so I could read their lips. Telling them how she was dead and haunting him, how he had left because...

I couldn't come up with a decent "because." Saying he abandoned me to save me from my mother's death dreams just sounded silly. Saying that he ran away because he couldn't stand his life no more seemed too real.

But the ghosts talked and I found myself on the long trek east towards Eugene, towards a place called Sanctuary. I managed to hitch a bit of it and met a nice couple, Mr. and Mrs. Broder, from New York. They were heading to the East Coast, hoping it was better there, but we all knew it wasn't. They were kind, gave me what food they could, and dropped me off in front of Sanctuary, just south of Eugene proper.

Eugene had burned and we could see thick smoke trailing up as we drove around it. It was a very cloudy day as we skirted the charred edges of the city and we saw a few living, but many, many dead, slivery flashes in the gloom. I didn't know what happened—the news had stopped at this point—but it was bad. Sanctuary sprung up out of what had happened. It was a housing develop-ment they had built walls around, and the only way in was a long, dark tunnel. It was so they could see if a ghost was with you.

Inside Sanctuary there were no ghosts. The Broders thought maybe my father had come here trying to escape my mother. Whis-pers were that they knew what the ghosts were and knew how to "eliminate" them. And that terrified me. That silvery, ghostly pres-ence was all I had left of my mother.

The walls around Sanctuary were what my grandmother would have called a "hodgepodge." Some wood, some metal, all different heights, and topped with razor wire. It was there to keep humans—and their ghosts—out.

The sound of the Broders' car faded and I felt so lonely and small looking at the wall. Four men with baseball bats stood in front of the entrance. The wall flared out and ran along the road for about ten yards and it had a roof—the tunnel you had to walk through to get in. The dark space where any ghost following you would be revealed.

I took a deep breath of the warm afternoon air and tried to swallow, but my mouth was dry, my heart thudding in my chest. I had to get in there, see if my dad had come, see if he...

I took another deep breath, squared my shoulders, and walked to the guards.

Abigale died of cancer. Her death was a fairly peaceful one and the dreams she brought to me weren't bad. I had dreamed of my mother's violent death—the crunching of metal, the iron taste of blood in my mouth, feeling sticky blood, my blood, on my head, seeing it on my hand—so it wasn't a big deal.

The second ghost, Abraham, was a gawky teenage boy a few years older than me that Abigale clearly had a crush on. Once I had invited her in, she invited him in. It all left a bad taste in my mouth, like Abigale and her lonely, lonely pleading was not about me, or being lonely at all, but about finding a place for her and Abraham.

His death was less fun. He had been high and wandered onto train tracks and been hit by a train. He died quickly, but in his death dreams I saw the light of the train coming, felt the rumble of it under my feet, tried to run, but my legs didn't work right and I tripped, fell onto the tracks, cracked my lip open, and then...

Well, usually I would wake up screaming with Abigale and Abraham staring at me, my mouth tasting like ash, and my heart trying to break out of my ribcage.

But still, I wasn't so terribly lonely.

"They ain't ghosts, they're tech," Joey said to me, Ann, and José. He was thirteen years old with a shock of curly red hair and walked tall, like he owned the place, as he gave us a tour of Sanctuary. "Them gossamer threads are totally the aliens' tech and we've all got it in us now, readin' our brains, learnin' our ways, gettin' ready to ghost us when we die."

We were walking the fence line right inside Sanctuary. Everyone over six worked here, and we had been assigned to Joey who was a "guard." Mrs. Stein, the nurse that looked me over when I came in, called it "fence maintenance," but that ain't what Joey called it. We were loaded up with tools while Joey walked with his hands free.

He stopped and looked at the three of us. Ann was nine and looked terrified with tangled black hair. José was eleven and even skinner than me. Joey leaned close. "It ain't easy," his said, his voice low and conspiratorial, "but we can kill 'em. Takes a lot of power, which we ain't got much of, but we can do it." He glanced at a two-story house near us and the solar panels on top of it.

Joey stood back up, something on the fence catching his eye.

He walked over and jiggled a loose piece of peeling plywood about two feet on a side.

"Get over here," Joey said loudly, even though we were only a few feet away. "Got to get this secured."

Ann looked hard at the board which could only move an inch or so, revealing a small crack onto the outside world. "But the fence won't keep ghosts out," Ann said quietly.

"Sure won't," Joey said, "but it will keep people out. Besides, we have blackout checks every night after supper." Mrs. Stein had told me about the post-sundown inspection of each resident to make sure a ghost hadn't attached to you. If you had a ghost, you were out.

As we worked, I kept catching Joey staring at me. There was something in his look that made me uncomfortable.

GHOST NUMBER THREE WAS A BIG LADY WITH FRIZZY HAIR AND scary eyes. Mrs. Walters was Abraham's mother. She yelled a lot, at Abraham and Abigale, and I was real glad I couldn't hear it. I kinda liked it though, cause Abigale started to pay more attention to me then. She had used me to get Abraham in the house, but he had used her to get his mother. Even though Abraham's mother was horrible to him, he wanted her in his life. I could relate.

Mrs. Walters killed herself with pills after Abraham died on the train tracks. My nights got bad, a mixture of Abigale's drugged out cancer death, with Mrs. Walter's bad trip overdose, with the terror of Abraham's train track death.

I would wake up long before dawn, sweat sticking to my body and my breath coming in gasps, my head full of their deaths. They would be there, their silvery, ghostly forms lighting the room as they stared at me. I don't think they meant to give me those bad dreams, it was just, as Joey would have said, the way they were programmed.

One morning when I got up, it must have been 3:00 a.m., the stars were bright and the air cold. Abigale followed me and that made me smile.

Sorry, she mouthed as the cold sunk through my thin jacket waking me up.

I smiled. "It's all right. You can't help it."

Her smile was sweet and sad at the same time. She pointed at me and mouthed, *What?*

She wanted to hear more of my story and that pleased me too. I hadn't told much of it since Mrs. Walters came, it was just too crowded, and she seemed to be yelling at Abraham most of the time. Maybe she blamed him for her death, maybe the ghost was haunting a ghost.

As things were in the world, Sanctuary wasn't bad. I spent the mornings with Joey, Ann, and José as we walked the fence and repaired it the best we could. It actually took a fair amount of our time—we would have to scavenge wood and screws from other parts of the neighborhood and make repairs with a few hand tools.

Afternoons we were all in school in a big house with peeling blue paint. We spent the evenings in that house with about ten other orphans. We'd play tag or hide and seek or truth or dare; regular kid stuff, and that felt good.

But it wasn't enough for me. I wanted my parents back.

My third day there, the sun hot in a clear blue sky, Joey and I, we were scrounging around for screws. We would often pull some of the screws off decks or siding, leaving just enough to hold the things in place. We were in the center of town and my left hand ached from the ten screws we had just harvested. I pointed to a plain squat building that must have been a community center. The roof was thick with solar panels, the windows were covered with newspaper, and there was a playground with a pool next to it. "How about that one?"

Joey shook his head. "That's the lab." I must have looked puzzled, cause Joey continued. "Where they are workin' on killin' the ghosts." His voice lowered to a whisper. "They've got some ghosts in there, trapped, they are. We can't go near, not even to the playground."

He put his sweaty arm around me and pulled me close, my nose filling with his sour scent. "Don't worry, Ronny, I'll take care of you." He laughed and squeezed me too tight.

I CAN'T SAY THAT ABIGALE LIED TO ME. SHE SAID SHE WAS lonely and I sure understood that. It seemed everyone was lonely and was using my shack to try to deal with that loneliness.

Me with Abigale, her with Abraham, him with Mrs. Walters, and Mrs. Walters with Kenny. I have no idea where Mrs. Walters found Kenny, who was more than a little crazy. He had long greasy hair and wide eyes. He looked like he was a thousand years old when he died, all wrinkled up and stooped. He would wander around the shack mumbling and twitching while Mrs. Walters looked at him like he was a glass of iced tea on a hot summer's day.

It was totally stupid that each of us wanted someone that wanted someone else. Well, not Kenny, I couldn't tell what he wanted, but he seemed to like the shack and never left it.

Kenny committed suicide, cutting his own wrists with a dull knife and slowly bleeding out in a cabin similar to my shack. That mixed in with the death dreams of cancer, trains, and drug overdose.

I didn't sleep too much.

The only thing that did me any good was Abigale spending more time with me. I began to get up earlier and earlier and go out in the dark with her to check my traps and hunt for frogs. She still

looked at Abraham in a way that I hated, but at least she paid attention to me now.

One morning as I gathered wood, it occurred to me that all
ghosts had a longing for something. If they had been done wrong in
their deaths, their longing was for justice. And if that justice had
been met, or no one was responsible, then they longed for another
ghost to be theirs. Just as I had longed for my parents and how I
wanted Abigale.

A ghost wants justice or love, just like the living.

Joey would have said that it's because of the way the aliens
programmed them, but then we the living are kinda programmed
the same way.

No one in Sanctuary had seen my father or my mother.
I took around a battered picture of the three of us and asked
everyone I could. I didn't tell anyone that my mother was a ghost. I
gave up asking after my first week there.

About six weeks after I arrived, I was out alone scrounging
when I saw my father. Well, at first I wasn't sure it was him. He was
real skinny, his cheeks sunked in, and he walked like he was afraid
of something, his shoulders pulled forward, his back bent. But there
was something about him that was familiar. He was walking out of
the community center, his steps hesitant, and he kept looking back
over his shoulder at that building I wasn't allowed to go near.

I left the screw I was pulling half done and snuck closer, not yet
knowing who he was. It was early spring and the sun was warm,
but the air a bit cool. My father wasn't a big man, but had always
been strong. He played football in college, had been on a soccer
league before the threads fell, and lifted weights in the garage.
After things changed he had lost weight, but not like this. When I
finally recognized him, I was standing at the corner of a house and
gasped. He looked up and his mouth opened and his eyes widened.

He recognized me, I know he did. I swear he said, "Ronny," before he turned and ran.

I stood there for the longest time trying to figure it out, trying to stop the tears. What had happened to my father? Why had it taken him so long to get here? What was he doing in the Sanctuary lab? Why did he run away from me?

I don't know how long I stood there, frozen. I had kinda understood why my father left the first time, but I couldn't fathom why he ran away like that. Wouldn't he be glad to see me? And where was my mother?

"There you are!" Joey said loudly, putting his sweaty arm on my shoulder—the big kid was always sweating, even in the cooler weather.

I jumped; I hadn't heard him coming.

"Come on, Ron. It's lunch time."

I let Joey pull me away. I didn't even try to escape his grasp like I usually did. I was too shocked, too numb.

It was a girl that ate the food I left. She was, maybe, eight and scrawnier than me, her thin brown hair forming something of a halo around her head as the strands escaped the rough braid running down her back.

She was cautious, moving slowly from tree to tree, always pausing and waiting. Listening. I was on my stomach in some tall weeds about twenty yards back, towards the shack. I didn't spend much time in there no more, too many ghosts. So, I decided to find out who was eating the food.

The girl moved kinda like a squirrel, pausing and looking and then moving quickly for a moment before pausing again. When she got to the half a frog, she paused and smelled it, a smile creeping onto her dirty face. I smiled too. I couldn't help it. I watched as she ate every bit of the frog leaving the bones arranged in a neat pile forming the letter "T." After she left, I stayed there for the longest time, not sure if she was watching me. I waited so long that I fell asleep in the weeds, and slept the best I had in weeks.

***

THERE AREN'T MANY SECRETS IN SANCTUARY, AND IT DIDN'T take me long to find out that my father had left right after I saw him. There were also whispers of what was going on in the lab. Things like Joey had said, that they were learning how to kill ghosts, that they had ghosts locked up in there.

That night I dreamed about my dad. He was walking on the beach with the ghost of my mother, holding her gossamer hand. They were whispering and laughing. I sat on a blanket on the beach and I knew it was the Fourth of July and soon I would have a belly so full of hot dogs and watermelon it would hurt. But then my father got angry, dropped my mother's hand and shoved her away, his face contorted in hate. He marched down the beach, leaving me, and my mother following him. I tried to get up, but couldn't. I was frozen in place.

I woke up bawling like a baby and then Joey was there, his stale, sweaty smell filling my nose, his warm arms around me. For once I didn't mind his touch. I held him and I cried.

"They've got my mother," I said when I had calmed down enough to talk. I knew it. It's the only thing that made sense. There were six boys that slept in that room with us, and I knew they were staring, I knew they would talk about me, but I didn't care.

Joey slapped his hand over my mouth and hissed in my ear, "Shut up, dummy." And then aloud he said, "It was just a bad dream, Ronny. We all have 'em."

***

IT'S LIKE I'M TRYING TO TAME A WILD ANIMAL, THE SCRAWNY

girl with the haloed brown hair. She is careful, she doesn't want to be seen, but she is hungry. Sustenance and safety. Two needs, both so great. Two needs that I understood well.

Abigale sustained me more and more. The incessant arguing of Mrs. Walters and Abraham and the constant weirdness of Kenny drove me to her. I would go into the shack at night, try to sleep, but the dreams were too much and I would head back out, and Abigale usually followed.

After stories, after the sun came up, I would wait for the girl and watch her. I started adding notes to the food, like "For you" or "Enjoy." The notes let her know I knew she was there, but I never let her see me. I didn't know if she could read, but she sure looked at the notes carefully.

The first day I left a note, she stared at it from thirty yards away for a full five minutes before scurrying to the roasted squirrel I had left. She sat stock-still and sniffed; the late summer morning was cold, her breath hanging in the air in tiny puffs. I had a moment there, thinking she would smell me—and believe me I didn't smell good, the pond was too cold for me to bathe much—but I was down wind of her. When she finally approached, she touched the paper with her index finger and then pulled it back quickly. Then she took the scrap of paper that was on the skewer and ran her fingers over it, smudging it. I had used a pencil. A small smile came onto her lips and then she nodded.

I smiled too. Abigale never smiled, but this half-wild girl did. When she smiled, I felt a little bit lighter, not happy or anything close to it, but like I had seen a tiny ray of sunshine after weeks of rain.

Maybe hope was the right word.

THAT MORNING AFTER MY BAD DREAM IN SANCTUARY, IT WAS just Joey and me walking the fence. He told me he loved me. He meant it, his round freckled face full of fear, his pits riper than usual.

After my nightmare with my dad and mom I had cried, he had held me, and we had both fallen asleep that way. It felt strange to wake with our limbs tangled up, my eyes crusty from crying, but not altogether bad.

At eleven, I understood most of the time it was a boy and a girl falling in love, but sometimes it was a boy and a boy or a girl and a girl. I also knew that falling in love wasn't something I wanted, and I suspected it would be a girl when I did.

He stood there in the morning sun staring at me after he said it. I felt my belly churning kinda like I was up high looking down, my guts wanting to fall out.

"Well?" he said, licking his lips.

I wanted to run, but I remembered when he hissed "Shut up, dummy!" when I said that the people in the lab had my mother. He knew something.

"I don't know, Joey. I mean, I sure like you. We're friends."

He frowned and nodded, looking at his ripped and filthy shoes. The laces were too short cause of all the knots he kept putting in when they broke. I looked at my laces; they were the same.

We stood there. Silence. Shoes. Dry, dusty dirt. The distant sound of playing children. A few birds singing. A slight breeze. A banging hammer.

I took a deep breath, my hand swaying towards Joey and touching his forearm. He stopped breathing for a moment. I remembered how my dad looked, so skinny and even more haunted than the last time I saw him. How he kept glancing back at the lab.

"Do... Do you know if they have my mother?" I asked, my voice just a whisper. I pulled out the picture from my back pocket and showed him.

Joey's eyes met mine briefly before looking back down at his shoes. He nodded.

"Can you help me?" I asked. "I would never forget it." He

sniffed and scraped at the dirt with his shoe. "I... I would love you for it."

I felt sick, but that did it. Joey put his arm around me and squeezed. "You and me Ronny, you and me. We can do anything."

I DON'T WANT TO BE LIKE JOEY AND CLING TO THIS GIRL THAT eats the food I leave like I was drowning or something. I don't want to be desperate for human contact, but I am.

After Sanctuary, after Joey, when I came up here, I thought I was done with people and their ghosts. That the best thing for me was to never see anyone ever again. To live my life and leave a ghost behind that wouldn't need to haunt anyone.

Just like those ghosts living in my shack.

That didn't sit well with me, like I had just eaten some mold or something. It was early afternoon and I was ranging around the lake, sucking on pine needles, my mouth full of the bitter/sour flavor of the juice. Pine needles have fat in them, and although it left my mouth tasting funny for hours, I would pull them off in bunches, twist them together, and suck on them. It was like eating sap, but I had to eat and there were lots of pine trees.

That morning I had watched the girl with the brown braid and fly-away hair. So small. She looked like she was eight, but could be more my age and just small from not eating enough. This morning I had written another note: "My name is Ron, what is yours?"

She had frozen when she saw it and looked around, her eyes lingering briefly on my hiding place. I didn't breathe, didn't move. She bit her lip, her eyes darting back and forth.

"Meagan," she said, her voice rough like she hadn't spoken in weeks or months. She then grabbed the remnants of the frog and sprinted away.

Meagan.

I didn't want to be like Joey, but I wanted to be friends with Meagan. I wanted to help her.

———

"You can't be here," the man said. He was tall with sandy hair and a white lab coat.

Joey smiled and pulled a package of cookies out of his bag. The man's eyes widened and he nodded, holding out his hand. Joey handed the bag over and the man ripped into the old package and stuffed two stale cookies into his mouth.

The room was a plain large rectangle. Out front were some couches and whiteboards with strange scrawling all over them. Old sheets were hung dividing off the rest of the clubhouse. The air smelled strange, almost electrical, and a loud humming sound came from behind the curtain.

"I wanna show 'em," Joey said, pointing at me.

The man shook his head a mumbled, "No way," around his mouth full of food.

"There's more where that came from."

The man smiled. Such things were rare these days, and I had no idea where Joey had gotten a hold of them. He put his arm around my shoulder. "Ronny here just wants to take a quick look."

I smiled, trying to look innocent. That's not all I wanted to do. I wanted to find my mother. I wanted to free her. I had to.

The man's eyes narrowed as he looked closely at us. I copied Joey's big smile and put my arm around him. Just two curious kids.

"More?" he asked.

"Swear to God, Vince. There's more. I'll bring it over after our tour."

Vince licked crumbs off his lips and nodded.

Joey walked over to the sheets and, slowly, reverently pulled one of them back.

I hesitated. Did I really want to know if they had my mother? My heart thumping away, I walked through.

My mom used to rescue wild cats. She would leave food for them near the house, but not too close. Over time she would move the food closer and closer to the house until they were eating on our porch. And then she would only let them eat with her standing in the doorway, and then with her standing near them, and eventually she would get the cats comfortable enough so that she could catch them.

She'd take them to the vet, get them spayed, bring them inside, until they got used to that, and then find them a home.

She'd use a funny word to describe the cats: feral.

It took me the longest time to realize it, but that's what Meagan was, feral. And what I was doing was a lot like what my mother used to do with the cats.

So first, the food, without me anywhere near, then the food with me hiding close by, and then the scrawled notes so I learned her name. Then I tried being present one day, standing fifty yards away from my fire circle. Meagan never showed even though I stood there for hours. I eventually had to give up, cause I needed the outhouse, and when I got back the meat was gone and in its place was a small pile of mushrooms. Well, at least it was progress.

Abigale didn't like Meagan. Not one bit. I don't think she left me, ever. She was in the outhouse with me staring at me and frowning—believe me, having company in there took some getting used to. I could see silvery glimpses of her here and there on cloudy days.

Two days after Meagan gave me the mushrooms, the clouds were thick and black, and the air charged with electricity and I could see Abigale all day. The thunder had been rolling and I could feel it rumble under my feet. It was gonna be a terrible storm. I had been ranging around the lake looking for Meagan. Feral or not, she shouldn't be out in the storm, and while the shack wasn't pleasant, at least it was dry.

My stomach was tight. I told myself that it was because I was afraid for Meagan, but part of me knew that it was because that smell was the same as the lab in Sanctuary. I rubbed at the scar on my neck as fat raindrops began pelting down and the lightning strikes got close. I started running for the shack, Abigale beside me shaking her head and mouthing "no" over and over.

When I got to the shack, I was soaked and cold and wanted in, but Abigale stood in front of the door. I could walk through her, but I didn't want to. I had collided with ghosts a few times and it felt tingly and strange. I didn't like it.

"I can't stay out here, Abigale," I shouted as the rain came down in sheets and the lightning stabbed down close by. "Let me in."

She shook her head "no" and looked longingly up at the dark sky in the direction of the lightning strikes.

"I could be killed."

She studied me, her face relaxing, gone was her disapproving frown—she knew I had been looking for Meagan and didn't like it. Then her brow furrowed, like she was thinking, and a small smile crept onto her face. She nodded and got out of the way, but something in that smile chilled me more than the cold rain.

Joey's hand was tight around my bicep and his scent and mine almost overpowered the electric-tinged smell of the lab. His hand was a warning to not freak out, to not make any sudden moves. My mouth was dry as I looked around the dim room. Newspapers were up on all the windows and the overhead fluorescent lights were off, the room lit by a few desk lamps and by two glowing blue chambers. The room was crowded with workbenches and strange equipment.

The glowing chambers were big, seven feet tall and three feet to a side, a metal frame with glass sides; the inside of the glass was covered in a grid of copper wires with blue neon tubes running horizontally around it from top to bottom, one every foot.

Inside each cage was a ghost. The nearest one held a short balding man who looked terrified. The farthest cage held a pretty woman in a summer dress. My mother.

"It's a faraday cage," Vince said, his speech only slightly garbled from the cookies.

Joey's hand tightened on my bicep so much it hurt. We had been hoping to have a few minutes alone.

"What?" I had never heard that word *faraday* before.

"It's just properly grounded conductive material. The copper grid. It blocks electric fields," he said. "They can't come in and they can't go out. It traps them."

The room was hot and my heart was thudding in my chest. I thought I might pass out.

"That's so cool, Vince," Joey said, his voice almost cracking. "What are the blue tubes?"

Vince smiled and licked his lips. "Watch."

He moved to the cage with the bald ghost. The ghost recoiled, backing farther into the chamber, his back touching the metal mesh. He grimaced and jumped forward into the front of the cage and I saw a small spark where his silvery form touched the wire. Vince laughed. I wanted to hurt Vince.

He went to the workbench next to the chamber and moved a large dial that had bare wires running to another piece of equipment. The chamber started humming and the blue lights started pulsing. The bald ghost's mouth opened in a mute scream and his moonlight form began to vibrate. The humming sound increased and the ghost began to flail, bouncing off the sides of the chamber, sparking at each touch.

I put my hands over my ears. The humming sound did hurt, but it was more of a reflex against a scream that I could not hear. The humming intensified and the ghost got brighter, the edges of his body starting to blur. There was a loud popping sound and the blue tubes went dark and the desk lamps went out.

"Damnit!" Vince said. "Not enough juice. But I tell you, we can fry them, sure as shit, we can fry them. Just a few more—"

He would have kept on talking, but I jerked myself out of Joey's grasp and charged. I had seen the look on my mother's face. She knew what it felt like. He had hurt her. He was gonna kill her.

A scream tore its way out of my throat and I collided with the man, his head crashing into the glass chamber, his body crumpling to the ground.

Tears streamed down my face as I went to my mother's chamber and began banging on the glass with my fists.

THE FIFTH GHOST WAS A TERRIBLE MAN. HE HAD HOLLOW eyes and a gaunt face. Mrs. Walters brought him back to the shack the day of the storm. There's something weird about ghosts and lightning. They fear it, but they're attracted to it, too. Kinda like a moth to the flame. It will kill them. I haven't seen it, but after Sanctuary, I am sure of it. But I think they long for the power of it. Joey once told me that ghosts draw power from the living when we dream of their deaths. Maybe they can draw power from electricity too.

After that look on Abigale's face when she briefly blocked my entrance to the shack, we talked. It was just the two of us for a while. She apologized, told me she didn't know what she was thinking. That she felt bad about Abraham and all the other ghosts. That she only wanted to be with me.

She told me that she loved me.

I cried when she did. My tears were brief and full of bitter conflict. Trying to reach Meagan had convinced me of one thing: I needed somebody. If we could get rid of the other ghosts, maybe that could be Abigale.

We would have talked more, but the storm ended and back they all came, walking through the front door. Mrs. Walters with a big, proud smile on her face and a new ghost.

Abigale's eyes widened as soon as she saw him and she hid behind me. He smiled at me and held out his hand, as if I could shake it.

He had long, straight hair and a short, trimmed beard. He said, slowly, so I could read his lips, *My name is Tate. I've heard a lot about you, Ron.*

He didn't call me Ronny, like everyone else had all my life. I liked it.

Thank you for letting me into your lovely home.

None of the other ghosts had ever done that.

I apologize, for my death was difficult.

Was this a ghost that understood the toll it took? "You were haunted?" I asked.

His smile was grim as he nodded.

We talked a while longer, he was from Oregon, had worked as a handyman, but mostly he wanted to know about me, so I told him. When I became sleepy, he suggested I go to bed. He told me he and the other ghosts would stay as far as possible from me so that I might sleep and be less affected by their death dreams.

I went to sleep hopeful. I woke up screaming.

I REMEMBER BEATING ON THE GLASS OF THE CHAMBER THAT caged my mother's ghost, my hands stinging, screaming like I was giving voice to the bald ghost's pain.

Then, in the moment as I banged on that glass as hard as I could, it was my mother in that cage. Now... well, while I still don't understand these ghosts, I'm not sure that it was my mother. It was her "ghost," something very like my mother, but not her.

I remember banging on the glass and then Joey jerked me away and hit the glass with a sledge hammer. It was fairly dark in there, lit by what sunlight could make it through the newspaper-covered windows. Joey grunted as he heaved the heavy sledge. The glass broke and some fell away. I jerked at the metal underneath, glass cutting my arm. I think I was still screaming, yanking on the metal latticework as hard as I could. I cut my hands and they were bleeding. Joey jerked me away again; he had found some wire cutters.

He cut through some wire and we both pulled it open. Not a big opening, maybe eighteen inches around. My mother's ghost flowed through that opening and then stood in front of us. She looked at me, recognition on her face, her mouth forming the words, *I love you, Ronny.*

Then she looked around as if she had lost something, her head slowly rotating back and forth until she was pointed to the east. Without another look at me, she walked through the wall of the building and out of my life.

I sunk to the floor, my gaze falling on Vince and his bloody head. Had I killed him? Would his ghost haunt me now?

"She's... she's gone to..." I couldn't say it, but I know my mother had gone to find my father. That she had left me. Again.

"It's the way they're programmed," Joey said, sinking to the floor and putting his arm around me.

A few minutes later they came for us.

TATE KILLED PEOPLE. TATE ENJOYED IT. AFTER THE GOSSAMER threads fell and the world changed, he went on a murdering spree. He would suffocate people with plastic bags, one a week, until he had seven ghosts haunting him. He died when the combined death dreams of his victims gave him a heart attack.

That first night he came into the cabin, when he was nice and understanding, when he apologized for the dreams he would visit upon me, I had no idea.

His death dream was of seven other death dreams. People suffocated slowly, intense fear multiplied. Image after image of struggle, of gasping for breath that was not there. Several of his victims saw themselves as he strangled them, one in the rearview mirror of his car, another in a bathroom mirror.

Death upon death stacked up on top of each other. Tate and his victims. Abigale. Abraham. Mrs. Walters. Kenny.

I woke up screaming, my heart pounding so loudly I thought it would break out of my chest. I ran out of the shack and was in the cold night air before I knew what I was doing. The nearly full moon hung in the sky, reflecting off the lake, the gentle lapping of waves on the shore calming me. I walked to the lake and stood there shivering, staring at the silvery moon, the same color as those threads that had rained down upon us, as the ghosts.

Tate was why the aliens had done this. His ghosts eventually destroyed him and he couldn't hurt more people.

Wars stopped quickly. The dead in these conflicts sometimes haunted the soldiers that actually killed them, but sometimes they chose to haunt the commanders or the leaders. Just like Tate, they couldn't survive the weight of all those death dreams. And I couldn't either.

On my trip up the mountain, a boy older than me hit me and stole my Swiss army knife. I held my gut and told him I needed that knife to survive, that if he took it, I was good as dead and that I would haunt him. He gave the knife back.

The aliens' threads changed us, but I sometimes wonder if they understood how chaotic it would be, how much death would be the result, how violent humans are.

I spent the rest of the night by the lake. When dawn came, I moved out of the shack.

JOEY AND I WERE BANISHED FROM SANCTUARY. A COMMITTEE of twenty, the Sanctuary Council, listened to testimony and declared the judgement. They even spoke the judgement in unison.

It was strange. The proceedings were held in the neighborhood park on the dying grass, the council a tight bunch while about a hundred Sanctuary residents watched. Vince was there, his head bandaged. He had survived.

I remember my hands throbbing with pain from the blows to the glass and the cuts of the wire. My heart ached cause I knew my mother had chosen to haunt my father over being with me.

Joey and I stood side by side in the middle of a loose circle, everyone staring at us. He tried to catch my eye, but I couldn't look at him. I had done this.

"The punishment for your crimes," the committee said in eerie unison, "is banishment."

The silence after that was so thick, like it had infected the air, changed it. I had trouble breathing. We were each brought a backpack filled with supplies and escorted out the gate. I still couldn't look at Joey.

"They don't want us to haunt them," he said.

I glanced at him and his face was twisted into a strange configuration. Unhappy. Mad. Bitter. I couldn't really tell.

"What?" I had no idea what he was talking about.

"The council. Why they ain't got a single leader. Why they spoke together like that. In case we die, so there ain't a single person to blame."

I shrugged. I didn't care. My father had seen me and run away. We rescued my mother and she had gone. What was there left for me?

Joey was silent and we both just stood outside the gates, the guards with their baseball bats staring at us.

I remembered my mother telling me she loved me before walking to the east, her face so beautiful, so kind.

I tightened the straps on my backpack and started walking east.

"Where you goin'?" Joey called.

"East." I yelled, quickening my steps.

JOEY ONCE TOLD ME THAT THE SCIENTISTS AT SANCTUARY thought that only people touched by the gossamer threads would produce ghosts when they died, that the ghosts themselves had a limited lifetime, that this was gonna go away, that the world would return to normal.

As I sat shivering by the lake, the dreams of suffocation still vivid and with me, thoughts of Joey flitted though my mind and I shivered harder. My finger found the still sore scar on my neck.

What was this life I have been living? Alone in the woods, so lonely that I invited a ghost into my home, and now I can't live there no more. The only other human around won't even talk to me. My father was probably still out there, with my mother haunting him, but what good would it to do try to find them? My father would leave again, and my mother would follow.

My chest tightened and I choked back that flood of tears ready to come out.

Abigale walked up, an empathetic look on her round face.

"Go back to the shack, Abigale," I said. "I'm done with ghosts."

She stood in front of me, her face getting that odd look, like when she blocked my way into the shack during the lightning storm. *I can help you, Ronny,* she slowly mouthed. I didn't understand at first, but she said it several times.

"No one can help me."

She started mouthing it again, but I surged up and shouted, "No!"

I ran into the forest, into the night, as fast as I could. I tripped and fell, knocking the wind out of me. I got up and ran again. I looked back. Abigale was running after me, her silvery pigtails bouncing around like she was real, like she had a body, like she was alive.

I ran straight into a tree, my head connecting with a branch. I went down hard, and the last thing I saw as consciousness faded was Abigale's silvery face with a strange look on it. A look of hope.

"I KNOW A PLACE," JOEY SAID, IN BETWEEN GASPING BREATHS. He had to run to catch up to me. "Not as nice as Sanctuary, but we'll survive."

He put his hand on my arm and I shook it off, marching forward, to the east, in the direction the ghost of my mother had gone.

I wasn't thinking about Joey's feelings, about how he felt about me. I was mad at my father, at my mother, at the world. Somehow, I thought that if I could just find them again, we could be together and everything would be okay in this strange, ghost-filled world.

Joey didn't move for a minute and had to run again to catch up to me. "What's east?" He put his hand on my shoulder. I shook it off and pushed him back. "What's wrong with you?" he asked, his eyes wide, his face so vulnerable.

"My mother," I spit the words out.

"She's not your mother," Joey said, his eyes hardening. "She's alien software. She's a ghost." He paused, his lip rising in a sneer. "She's dead."

The day was cloudy, not a bit of blue sky visible as Joey and I stood on the road in the middle of a neighborhood much like Sanctuary. The houses alike, all of them abandoned, many of them missing siding that had been scrounged for the Sanctuary fence.

I stared at him, his voice bouncing around my head, my heart beating fast, my breath short little gasps. *She's dead.* He was right, of course. I knew he was right. My mother would never have left me like that. My mother had loved me more than anything. My mother had—

All these months I hadn't thought about her in the past tense. It would have been "my mother loves me," not "my mother *had* loved me."

My jaw worked but I didn't form any coherent words, just a mumble of syllables. Joey was talking to me, he looked so worried, but I didn't care, I couldn't hear him. *She's dead.*

I turned away from Joey and kept walking. If he was there or wasn't there, I didn't know. I didn't care. His words played in my head over and over again as I walked down the road. *She's dead. She's dead. She's dead.*

I WOKE TO THE BRIGHT SUN ABOVE, MY HEAD POUNDING LIKE someone had driven a nail into it. My mouth was horribly dry and the world spun around as I pushed myself into a sitting position.

The lake was there, calm as always, guarded by pines and furs, a grove of aspen across the water from me, the green leaves starting to turn yellow. I could see the shack and knew it was not mine. The ghosts and their death dreams could have it.

I wondered about Abigale, if she was here, the mean things I had said last night. Abigale had made a mistake inviting Abraham into the shack. We all make mistakes. She was lonely.

"I'm sorry," I said, my voice a croak. "Please forgive me, Abigale. Don't leave me."

I sat there for a long time, at first more feeling that thinking. Feeling bad about Sanctuary and Joey. Feeling embarrassed at running away last night and smacking into a tree. Feeling so lost and alone.

And then I started thinking about survival. How would I get by without the shack?

After the sun had crested and started its journey to the horizon, I levered myself up and walked to the shack. I carefully opened the door and blocked it open with a rock, letting as much light in as possible. I didn't want to see any of them.

I walked in, my eyes squinted, and threw back the curtains. I felt an electric tingle. I must have run into a ghost. My breath caught, fearing it would be Tate. Terrified that his death dream would come just from contact, but nothing happened.

I drank all the water I could find and then gathered pans and clothes, a sleeping bag, and an old tarp from the closet. One load at a time, I hauled them across the lake and set up a camp over there. A place to sleep without a roof, a place no ghost would want to live.

Except Abigale. I was desperate for her to stay with me, so as I gathered and walked, I talked like I knew she was there. I finished telling her about Joey, about how I ended up here. I wanted her to understand. I wanted to understand.

EAST OF EUGENE IS THE CASCADE MOUNTAINS, AND ON THE other side of them, the city of Bend. My father had been born there, and as my mind cleared enough to think about it, I figured that is where he was headed and that is where my mother's ghost was headed. I was walking on Route 58, the Willamette Highway, which crossed the Cascades, running much of its length next to the Willamette River and passing lots of lakes. There would be water; that was the most important thing.

Bend was about 130 miles away. I could do that in a week or so if my food held out.

As I walked, I didn't think about Joey or Sanctuary, about how he felt about me, about what he had said about my mother, about the ghosts or the future. I just planned this trek and kept moving.

Joey had yelled at me, caught up with me several times and pleaded with me. I didn't say a word. I couldn't. Anything but one step in front of the other was too much. Any real thought of my parents, the future, or the past would stop me.

I kept walking and left him behind.

That first day, three cars passed me. I stood to the side of the road and held my thumb out, but no one stopped. I remember one of the cars, a bland, white hatchback, with two adults and two children in it, their heads fixed forward, not looking around at all. At first I felt this bitter jealously—those kids had their parents—but then their demeanor sunk in. Not a one of them glanced at me. I shouted obscenities at them that they couldn't hear.

When the sun was low, I followed a small creek that wound into some hills through the forest and found a rock outcrop I could sleep under. I drank from the creek, used my Swiss army knife to open a can of beans, and sat there staring at the creek, the bright sound of it lulling me into sleep. My sleep was dark and deep, just the kind of oblivion I longed for, but it didn't last long. I woke quickly, my hand flying to my neck and the line of fiery pain that had blossomed there. Had something bit me? The forest was lit by a gray, diffuse light, the leaves of the trees still, the creek loud.

"You won't leave me now." I knew that voice, but my mind was sluggish, not working right.

I pulled my hand from my neck; it was warm and covered with a sticky fluid that looked almost black in the dim light.

"You'll never leave me."

I looked up and saw Joey, squatting next to me, tears streaming down his face. He held his knife in his shaking hand. The knife was stained with the same sticky black fluid.

Joey followed my eyes to the knife and he blanched, his face contorting into such a strange mask that I hardly recognized him.

My mouth moved but I couldn't speak. I held my hand to my neck and pressed as hard as I could. Joey's eyes met mine for a moment, and I saw a hunger there that scared me more than what he had done to my neck.

"I..." he began, wiping at the snot gooing out his nose with his free hand. "You…" He looked back down at his knife and then shoved it into the holster at this belt. "You'll find me." He turned and scurried away.

I lay back, holding my bleeding neck, listening to the creek which seemed more clanging now than comforting.

I stared at the grey stone above me until the darkness came.

———

ABIGALE LOOKED AT ME AND THEN STARED AT MY SCAR. IT WAS late and I admired the starry expanse above us framing her silver glow. It was a beautiful night and Abigale had stayed with me. Who needed that stupid shack anyway?

"He didn't cut me nearly as deeply as he thought," I said with a shrug. I had my Swiss army knife in my hand and was juggling it and two pine cones. "I survived that night and followed that creek up into the mountains until I ran into that little hunting shack. My cut was infected and I had a fever. I found some medicine. That shack saved my life."

I ended in a shrug. That was it.

Your parents? she mouthed.

I looked away, wishing I could go fly up to those stars and escape this strange planet. "I didn't mean to stay this long, but as I healed, I realized that my parents wouldn't be any different. My father would be trying to escape my mother." There was more, but I couldn't say that I was done with people. That I only needed Abigale now—someone to talk to that couldn't hurt me, something to take away the horrible loneness.

Abigale nodded, her eyes wide and serious, and then her forehead furrowed.

"What?"

I can't stay.

"Why?" I sat up straight and looked around, afraid Tate or one of the other ghosts had left the shack.

She looked like she was gonna cry. She spoke quickly, but I couldn't follow her. Something about "can't stay" and "a way."

"Slow down."

She took a deep breath and nodded.

Can't stay outside. It hurts. I thought of Joey's insistence that they were alien programs, and if they were, why would the outside hurt? Why were they driven to be in a house? *Can't go back.* She glanced back towards the shack.

She got up and brushed at her skirt. *I have to find another place.*

"Wait! I'll go with you."

She shook her head.

"Why not?" My heart bounced around my chest and my brief sense of peace was shattered. I hadn't realized how delicate it was.

She studied me for the longest time and then shook her head. *There is one thing, but I can't ask.*

Despite the cool night, I was sweating. "Why can't I go with you? What can't you ask?" I took a deep breath, and the smell of my nervous sweat reminded me of Joey. She looked like she was about to speak, but I couldn't stop myself. "Eugene ain't far. Lots of empty houses. Just you and me, Abigale." I still had my old knife in my hand and was gesturing towards the west with it.

She bit her lip. *You'll leave me.*

"No. Never!"

You'll find someone living and you'll leave. Silvery tears ran down her silvery cheeks.

"No! I won't. How can I prove it? I... I'll do anything. Anything!"

Her gaze went to the knife, her facing getting that strange, hopeful look. *I can't ask it.*

I looked at her, at the knife, and back at her. She couldn't mean it.

Join me, then nothing will stop us from being together.

The world spun around me and I found myself sitting on the pine-needle-covered ground. She wanted me to do what Joey had failed to do. She wanted me to die so I could be a ghost with her. I opened the longest blade on my father's Swiss army knife and stared at it. Why was I struggling so to survive? What was there left to live for? A life scrounging for food and hiding from both the living and the dead?

Abigale was smiling her strange smile and nodding, her light and the starlight illuminating me. I gently placed the knife to my wrist, one quick stroke and I would slowly die and then the gossamer thread that merged with me as my father carried me away from our Fourth of July picnic would come to life. It would take all it learned from me and become my ghost. Then I could be with Abigale. We could find someone still alive and get them to invite us into their home. They would be plagued by dreams of our deaths, but they wouldn't be bad dreams as these things go.

I looked up again and she was smiling. She wanted me to do it. She needed me. I bit my lip hard, until I could taste blood. My mind swirled. I knew that when I died that ghost wouldn't really be me; my mother left me and that proved it. But it would be a copy, a part of me would go on, a part of me could be happy with Abigale. I felt the weight of the last two years, since the threads fell. How hard life had been. How I had nothing left to live for. It felt like a boulder on my chest and I could barely breath. This would end my struggle. This would make Abigale happy.

I sucked in a breath, getting ready to jerk the knife back, hand shaking. A twig snapped.

I looked up. Across the campfire squatted Meagan, so thin, so dirty, so small. She slowly shook her head back and forth as her whole body shook. I think she was terrified to be this close, to be this exposed. Abigale's mouth opened in a scream and she rushed at Meagan, but the scrawny girl didn't move. As Abigale passed through her, Meagan shook harder, but stood her ground.

Meagan shook her head again, her mouth forming a mute "no."

I looked at my hand, it was shaking too, the knife pressed to my wrist, a thin trickle of blood underneath. A deep enough cut and the struggle would end. It occurred to me then, that If Joey was right, if the ghosts were just programs, that the gossamer threads were an invasion. Each ghost was an alien.

A shiver of electricity passed through me and I saw a flash of light. Abigale had gone right through me, but I didn't look up. I looked across the fire at Meagan, her eyes locking with mine. Maybe Meagan was trying to save me just because I could help her survive. She might be using me just like I had used Joey, just like Abigale had used me.

There was just enough light for me to see that her eyes were brown. Real eyes. Human eyes. Yes, she needed me, but I needed her too.

Another shiver ran through my body as Abigale passed through me again. I pulled the knife from my wrist, closed it, and put it in my pocket.

"Move on. I ain't gonna take you in," I said, repeating the words I had first said to Abigale.

She flew through me again and again and again. I finally looked up and her face was fury itself. "Move on, Abigale."

She was lonely, I understood that, but I wasn't gonna sacrifice myself for her loneliness or my own. She kept flying through me so I stood up and shouted "Move on!" over and over until she gave me one last lonely look and walked into the forest.

The night was quiet and cold, and I stood there for the longest time staring at the receding glow of Abigale. After a time, I don't know how long, I turned and saw that Meagan was still there, squatting by the fire, quivering. "Thank you, Meagan," I said.

She nodded her head and then disappeared into the night.

THE SHACK WASN'T A SHACK NO MORE. WE PULLED OFF THE metal roof and the plywood siding, almost like we were scavenging it for the Sanctuary fence. With just the two of us and just my

Swiss army knife and a hatchet, it took a week and a lot of blisters. The shack was just bones now, open to the sun and the wind and the flurry of snow that has speckled the forest in white.

"I guess we'll find out if you're right tonight," I said, smiling at Meagan.

She was on the other side of the shack, her brown eyes just briefly meeting mine before darting away like a scared rabbit. I think there might have been a flicker of a smile on that dirty face, flakes of snow caught in her hair. The theory was that if it ain't a house no more, the ghosts will leave. After they do, we will make it a house again and never, ever, invite a ghost in.

Winter is coming, and while I'm not ready to leave this sanctuary for a lower elevation where there are more people and ghosts, I do want to survive the winter.

I do want to survive.

Meagan doesn't trust me yet. She's jumpy and doesn't want to be too close. She has horrible nightmares and wakes up crying. But she talks to me a little. I just found out that she's from Eugene and is ten years old.

It's not much, not much at all, but it's a start.

"How about we go check the traps?" I asked. We had a few hours before dark.

Her eyes brightened briefly and she licked her lips. "Yes. I'm hungry." Her voice was still rough and unsteady from being up here so long with no one to talk to.

I found myself smiling again. It felt strange, like my face had forgotten how to do it. I smiled cause I wasn't alone no more. It's now "us," it's me and Meagan, the feral kids, up in the mountains trying to survive away from all the people and all their ghosts.

It's not much, but it's a start.

BACKSTORY—GOSSAMER THREADS

THIS IS ONE OF THOSE STRANGE STORIES THAT I ALWAYS believed in (yup, that qualifies as strange, i.e. an anomaly). The first line of the story ("When the fifth ghost moved in, I moved out.") just came to me and I went about constructing a world and a story that would fit that line and had nothing to do with my other ghost stories.

I wrote it slowly, a piece at a time, feeling my way through this strange post-apocalyptic world, embracing the darker aspects of it while looking for a ray of hope for the end.

Honestly, this story is the reason that I decided to create this collection. While it was a semi-finalist in the Writers of the Future Contest (strangely I knew it would do well, although it fell one step short of what I hoped for it), I couldn't find a home for it. Its length is one reason—novelettes are hard to place.

This one, I always thought, should be read. It's an apocalypse, but a strange one, a karmic one. It's got ghosts, but such *different* ghosts. It's dark, but hopeful too.

This story is curious, confounding, and truly an anomaly. I hope you enjoyed it.

PART EIGHT

MEMORIES OF THE BREAKERS

MEMORIES OF THE BREAKERS

THE BREAKER ROLLED PAST THE WINDOW NEXT TO ME, A sandy, foamy blur; I thought I could make out a jellyfish being pressed against the glass. It was outlined there for a moment and then gone. All that motion and chaos just inches away from me made me nervous.

The restaurant was nice, simple: glass, and chrome, and black lacquered wood. Understated. They let the waves crashing against the prow-like point of the building and the breakers rolling past the sides do the talking. Elegant. Rare. Expensive.

You could feel the waves, as they ceaselessly crashed against the building, see the waves roll past, almost taste the waves.

"Excuse me, are you..." she said, startling me from my reverie.

I stood up glancing at her, took her proffered hand, smiled, and said, "Yes." First impressions are important, and in this case she aced it. Not only was she a looker, she had done me the courtesy of not saying my name. Well, at least not saying what she *thought* my name was.

We sat and I ordered some wine, a Grenache. Wine being the rarity it was, and this restaurant having the prices it did (you had to pay for the view after all), I was hopeful that I was making a good first impression too. My services don't come cheap, so I can afford to make this kind of gesture.

She was like most clients. Shy about getting down to business. I knew better than to rush it, she would come around to it. They always did. We chatted about the restaurant, the hotel that contained it, and the view. They call this place, appropriately enough, the Breakers. It was built 20 years ago on dry land in anticipation of the sea level rising.

She had me order for us both, further endearing me to her. We had the seared sea bass, with steamed broccoli and roasted red new potatoes. They were prepared simply and elegantly, allowing the quality of the food to come through.

Over coffee I could tell she was going to broach the topic. There was the sighing, the shifting of position, the excessive stirring of the coffee, the twirling of her shoulder length red hair. She was almost there. I just smiled (which I am told by reliable sources is quite irresistible) and continued the small talk.

She laid a thin, long fingered hand on the table; a band of pale skin where her wedding ring once was (off for the night, or off for good—I wasn't sure). The nails were a deep shiny red. Again I found something to like: none of those garish adaptive colors for her. Class. She took a deep breath. Here it comes.

There was a sharp crack against the window next to us. I looked over and saw most of a face, with a tattered body trailing it, pressed against the window before sliding past. By some trick of the current the body was pushed against the glass and dragged along the entire length of the room.

She screamed and a wave of screams followed the body's trajectory as the corpse made its presence known. Scrambling to her feet, she bolted. I didn't think I would ever see her again.

THE CHAOS OF THE PLACE SWIRLED AROUND ME, AND I JUST sat there and let it wash over me like the waves on the other side of the glass. I was quite content to watch it all and sip my wine.

They all acted like civilians—except for the maître d'—letting fear rule them when whatever the danger that ended that person's life was clearly past.

The maître d' with his broad shoulders and square jaw calmly took care of them, directing his staff like they were his troops. He exuded a cool efficiency that I admired. It was not, unfortunately, enough for the civs, who chattered and wandered about like children babbling over and over about what had happened and how horrible it all was. It always surprised me how the presentation of death rattled them so. Didn't they know they were all going to die?

After he had dealt with them he came over to my table; I had just finished the wine. "We are so sorry for the inconvenience sir," he said. I found his use of the word inconvenience amusing. A stubbed toe was an inconvenience, a delayed flight was an inconvenience, a dead body floating by was... was... Well, it wasn't an inconvenience. "Tonight will be, of course, on the house," he continued.

"No need," I said, laying down some bills on the table as I rose. "I feel somewhat responsible."

"Sir?"

"Well, given his state of decomposition, I can't be sure, of course. But I think that I am the one that killed him."

I delivered this with a small smile. The maître d' was truly a pro, his expression not changing one bit. He swept up the bills, which were far more than what the meal cost, made them disappear and replied, "Very good sir. Will there be anything else?"

I'M NOT SURE WHY I TOLD HIM THAT I KILLED THAT MAN; AS IF I would know, as if I would remember. I think I was just bored. My prospective client running out left me with the promise of a dull evening. Anything but that. Please.

With all the civs rushing away I knew the air taxis would be backed up so I took the elevator to the top of the building to a little bar they had up there. It was a round affair with glass on all sides. You could see up and down the coast and gaze upon the carcasses of the resorts that were not prepared for the three meter rise in the ocean.

The redhead was seated alone at a table, with her back to me. Her lush green gown revealing the contours of her back—a view I hadn't got when we met at the restaurant below. At one point in my life I would have been surprised to see her there, but I was too old for that now. Not too old in terms of years, but too old in terms of experience. The world did what it did; it did me no good to try and predict the future.

"May I?" I said after I crossed to the other side of the table and stood in front of her. She nodded and I sat down signaling to the waiter to bring two more of what she was drinking.

She didn't speak, and that was fine with me. This view suited me better. I loved the tableau of the dead submerged hotels, the new resorts springing up on the altered coastline, and the Breakers standing tall and proud like a mighty ship amidst it all.

The waiter swept over with the drinks and I took a sip: Scotch, rocks, single malt, Lagavulin. Chalk up another thing I liked about this one.

"Mr..." she began.

"Smith, call me Smith."

"Mr. Smith, I—"

"No, just Smith, please," I said with a smile, my eyes catching hers. There was empathy in there, and kindness, and a soul. Too bad she was talking to me.

"Ok... Smith."

"What can I do for you?" I asked.

All hesitation gone, she told me. It came rushing out of her like a geyser. Once she started, she couldn't stop. She told me more than I needed to know, more than she should have. Which was fine, of course. I would erase it all as soon as I got home.

I SHOULDN'T BE DOING THIS. REALLY, I SHOULDN'T.

This little diary is more than frowned upon among my order; it is a cardinal sin. Memory: Really, the only cardinal sin.

And I understand that, I do. Confidentiality is central to our trade. But I just want something in the end that I can look back at and know. Know what I did, know what I spent my life doing.

I mean, of course I'll know what I did. I know what I do. I just want to leave enough details so when time has run its course I'll have something to fill in the huge voids in my memory. Anything.

If I survive that long, of course.

WE SLID ACROSS THE DANCE FLOOR MY HAND AGAINST THE small of her back, half on her smooth skin, half on the smoother green silk. I dipped her, my hand supporting her as she bent backwards, seemingly in half, her shoulder length red hair almost brushing the floor.

We were still in the hotel, one floor below the restaurant. The windows were completely submerged by the surf, illumined in slowly mutating colors that matched the progression of the music.

It was a mixed crowd, mostly dilettantes and fat-cats. And their muscle of course; modded monstrosities that stood still at the edges of the room, their eyes fixed on their employers. There were also a few wonks and us. We were too good of dancers to be wonks; no muscle, so we weren't dilettantes; and neither of us had the corpulent demeanor of a fat-cat. But I don't think anyone cared, and I don't think anyone really noticed me. She owned the floor, I was just an accessory. She moved with a practiced, effortless grace that led me to believe she was classically trained. My guess is that ballet was her life until she grew too tall and was forced to give it up.

After she told me her story and what she needed from me, it had gotten pretty late. I suggested the dancing to relax her, and for the intimacy. I honestly had wanted to suggest sex, but that was risky and I found her too intriguing to chance losing her so early in the game.

And in some ways dancing was preferable. It helped us on two counts. First, it established a physical intimacy that would be important soon, and second, it showed us in public and deepened my cover.

To those watching thought I was a boyfriend or an escort or a gigolo. And that served. Although parts of my job aligned with those descriptions, it wasn't what I was.

During a break in the music when she had excused herself to the "powder room," a man sidled up next to me and said, "She's a live one, are you sure you can handle her?"

I looked over and saw Jones. He had a wicked grin on his once handsome face, which was only now losing its battle against time.

"God, I hope so," I answered.

"Stay sharp," Jones said as he moved off.

Jones was my handler and my backup. We never went into a job alone, too much could go wrong. This job being a case in point.

In the room I unpacked my gear on the bed: the skullcap; the wires that ran from it to the laptop; the defibrillator. Her eyes widened on seeing that. "Don't worry," I chuckled, "If anyone is going to need it, it's probably me." Her brow crinkled, I don't think she believed me, but I was only half joking.

I had her change into a robe and got her situated comfortably on the bed, lying on her back. I fitted the skullcap on her and started the program. I moved quickly and carefully, my hands sure from long practice, and I hoped, reassuring to her. "What... How..." she began, betraying her nervousness.

"Just relax," I told her, looking at the laptop and seeing the spikes that told of her agitation. "Close your eyes and listen to my voice. I know what your questions are and I will answer them all before we start. You can stop this process at any time."

I let my voice deepen and my words spread out, developing a rhythmic cadence. Like a lover would talk to a beloved in the depth of the night; like a hypnotist would talk to a subject.

"The burden that troubles you; I will take away. These things that plague you will be no more. I am Smith of the Order of Mnemosyne and you are safe with me."

I checked the screen and saw her brainwaves starting to come into entrainment.

"We are masters of memory. We can help you remember, and we can help you forget. Tonight, my dear, you will forget. One by one you will summon forth that which troubles you and one by one I will guide you in their removal."

She was relaxing quickly, which was good, we had a lot of work to do.

"My Order is ancient, and our art refined. You are in safe hands. You can stop this at any time."

I continued talking to her until her brain waves dropped down into a Theta-Delta state. Then the real work began.

THE FEW THAT KNOW OF THE ORDER OR MNEMOSYNE OFTEN think that we either hide memories, or erase them. We do neither. The process is subtle and more complicated than that.

Think of your individual memories being like a sheet of paper in a book. We don't hide the page or rip it out; we take a marker and obfuscate the writing. The storage of memories is, of course, much more complicated than that, but the process is analogous. The memory is there, just so obscured that sense of it can never be made. As I have alluded to before, it is an act of deep intimacy and trust.

When the order first formed we were couriers. We could memorize information, transport it, deliver it, and then erase the memories of it from our own minds. Later we learned how to guide others through the process, and as technology evolved we harnessed it to increase our efficacy.

There are, of course, dangers. Memory is tricky and often more than just the targeted engrams will be destroyed. There is also significant stress and trauma to the brain.

WE WORKED THROUGH WHAT WAS LEFT OF THE NIGHT, through the day, and into the next night. When we were done, her memories were gone, and having witnessed them, a version of them were now in my head.

I ordered room service, we both took showers, and then came the sex. We were chatting and then we were kissing and then we were out of our robes and making love. The transition felt natural, easy, as if it wasn't even a choice.

There was a quiet, uncomplicated urgency to the act, neither leading, neither following; a deep and satisfying merging. It was as if one last act of intimacy was required before we could be done.

After the food came, we ate voraciously and fell quickly asleep our limbs tangled under the silk sheets.

That's when they came for me.

I DIDN'T HEAR THEM ENTER; THEY MUST HAVE BRIBED

someone for a keycard. By the time I was awake I was being dragged nude out of the room.

Four big sides of beef in all—those memories must be awfully valuable. I recognized them from the other night when we were dancing; they had been in the retinue of a pear shaped fat-cat with a shock of blond hair and beady eyes. He stood out because he had been watching my client just a little too closely.

A quick backward glance showed her still there asleep, her red hair fanned out on the pillow, her face slack.

They had also gathered up my equipment. The only thing I could think of was that she would assume that I had left without saying good bye. I wasn't thinking of my welfare but of her, and what she thought of me. Dangerous... stupid.

I saw Jones by the elevator talking on the phone. He caught my eye as he pursed his lips and puffed his cheeks while moving his head to the port side of the hotel. It jolted me back to the present, back to my dilemma.

They paraded me through the hotel naked as they prodded me and berated me.

The prodding was to keep adrenalin flowing. If I could meditate, even a little, I would be able to start eroding my memories of her memories.

They berated me to keep up the cover. I was the gigolo or adulterer who had been caught in the act.

They kept me naked so that I would feel vulnerable. Of all their tactics, this one was not effective. I had no problem with nudity, but I played the part, keeping my head down and trying to cover my genitals as they shoved me along.

Soon we were on the roof of the forward section of the hotel: the helipads. They had a chopper there waiting and ready, but my lack of clothing caused some guests departing a chopper on another pad to stop, point, and snicker, briefly distracting my guards.

This was the delay I needed. I was being held by the left arm. I snapped my body around behind my guard and bent over, throwing him over my back and breaking his grip. I then sprinted to the port railing.

This was a necessary risk. If they got the memories from me, I was as good as dead. If I jumped off the hotel, I might die. If they shot me while I tried to escape, again death. Jumping was the only action that gave me any hope, any chance of survival.

I harnessed the adrenalin they had made sure was coursing through me and was over the rail and falling towards the ocean below in less than 5 seconds.

The hotel was about 30 meters high here, and my trajectory was not perfect. My arms wheeled wildly trying to straighten my path. I pointed my toes and managed to enter the water relatively vertical right before a breaker crashed and pushed me against the glass of the building.

I had a brief flash of the half decomposed body that had been swept by when we had sat in the restaurant. Now the patrons were being treated to a live nude body. I felt sorry for the maître d' having to deal with this kind of thing again. I wondered how often it happened.

I pushed off against the glass, my lungs burning as I made for the surface. I felt something grasp my foot and shoving down panic I looked down and saw a diver below me. He had an extra tank and regulator and was offering it to me.

JONES GREETED ME ON THE FISHING BOAT WITH A BEER, A HAT, sunglasses, and some revoltingly loud touristo clothes. He didn't explain, he didn't have to, it was my cover. I needed to fit in; I always needed to fit in.

Even with the disguise, Jones and I moved into the cabin and I watched the muscle up on the Breakers frantically searching for me with their binoculars.

A half an hour and two beers later, I asked Jones, "You had this in place the whole time?" The boat had started to leisurely motor off in search of better fishing grounds.

"Yup," he said, handing me another beer. "We expected this."

I felt anger rush up, but I took a deep breath and let it dissipate. I wasn't angry because they had put me in harm's way without telling me. That would be silly, considering such unexpected danger is part of my job. I was angry because of her. If I had known I could have—

Oh hell, I don't know what I could have done. I was just left with this hole in me that I wished I could fill.

It's time. I'm home and the sensory deprivation tank is ready. Time to forget all the details of the mission. Time to chant the chants of Mnemosyne and to scrub them clean. Time to forget her.

And I *have* to forget her. Even though this diary entry is a sin I am willing to commit, I cannot populate it with the kinds of specific information and lush descriptions she deserves. Even if the worst happens and this document is discovered, she and her secrets are still safe. I can do no less.

I am stalling. I've set out a bottle of Grenache arranged atop a piece of green silk with a little sign that says "drink this." I've queued the stereo to play some ambient ocean sounds and attached another sign that says "play this."

I don't know what I expect. It's not like I will read this document until after I am retired. It's going into the time capsule as soon as I finish it.

I guess I am hoping that it will provide me with some small memory to take place of those that I am about to lose. Some small anchor for when I do get to read this. Some small moment of pleasure that I can keep.

BACKSTORY—MEMORIES OF THE BREAKERS

I LOVE HOW THIS STORY FEELS. IT'S GOT A BIT OF A MYSTERY, A strange secret order, spy-type action, but it's the sweet sadness of a man trying to hold onto his memories that makes this one special for me.

I started out wanting to do something more blatantly sci-fi. The idea of The Breakers, the hotel unapologetically built before the sea levels rose, was the start. Mixed into that was some personal reflections on the fragility of memory (mine is not very good) and this one popped out.

The story's structure, where the woman's mystery is not revealed, is unconventional, an anomaly, and might feel a bit unsatisfying. But it's that way for a reason. We forget. We have holes in our memories or they twist and turn on us.

How does that feel?

How do we preserve what's truly important on the unstable ground of human memory?

This story received an honorable mention in the Writers of the Future Contest.

PART NINE

LIGHTS, CAMERA, CTHULHU!

LIGHTS, CAMERA, CTHULHU!

When I saw Cthulhu sitting in my hot tub, every inch of him a tentacled, scaly horror, my first reaction was not the appropriate level of terror—oh no. It was annoyance and disgust.

The annoyance stemmed from the fact that I valued my hot tub time, and here I was with another mystical visitor. I liked to sit in the hot bubbly water, look out over Hollywood below, and chill, letting go of the stress of my day as an entertainment lawyer.

The disgust was because the dude stunk like rotten fish and tar.

I stood there, briefly mesmerized by the moving tentacles on its head and then shrugged, turned, and walked back to the bar. I was afraid, of course. I was seeing one of the Elder Gods in my hot tub, but I figured if he had wanted me dead or had wanted to torture me that would have already happened. And it's not like it was the first time I had a strange guest come visiting that way.

I took a tall glass out, flipped it in the air, caught it, and filled it with ice, two shots of Tito's Vodka, club soda, and a fresh squeeze of lime. I put a straw in and headed back to the hot tub, a drink in each hand. It wasn't a fancy drink, but one I liked when it was time to shuck the Hollywood BS and relax.

He took the drink with a scaly, clawed hand, the tentacles on his face parting so he could get the straw into his mouth. Instinctively I looked away. I didn't want to see that mouth—somehow I knew it could only lead to madness.

I dropped my robe and got into the tub and took a sip myself. I let the bubbles linger on my tongue before swallowing. Tito's is a smooth, unoffending Vodka that can really sneak up on you and combined with the lime and the carbonation is very soothing.

"Let me guess," I began. "You need someone to get a movie featuring you off the ground. You're tired of being ripped off by everyone and their brother." I took another sip of my drink. "Your copyright is expired. That's the real issue—anyone can use you for anything. It's been a long time since H.P. Lovecraft wrote those stories and made you famous. You want people to be scared of you again. Am I right?"

Cthulhu raised his glass and nodded, his dragon-like wings spreading behind him as his eyes narrowed and focused on me.

That gaze brought with it a torrent of information that almost killed me. I couldn't breathe, my heart jumped in my chest, and my bowels let go.

My assessment had been correct, but while I had said it in words, he expressed it back to me in a torrent of godly emotions. He was upset that he had been turned into a goofy Facebook meme, that his image had been ripped off for Davy Jones in the Pirates of the Caribbean movies (and that Davy Jones wasn't at all scary), that he hadn't had a proper Hollywood film, and that people weren't really scared of him anymore. He wanted a movie, one that scared the hell out of people, and he wanted it now.

When it was over and I could see again, I was alone in the hot tub panting, the monster gone. I had a new client. I had just been hired. The deal was simple, unlike the contracts I usually drew up, he would make me rich or he would eat my soul.

I pulled myself out of the hot tub, making a mental note to have it drained, cleaned, and disinfected. I stumbled to the bar and took a swig of Tito's right out of the bottle. I gingerly sat down on a barstool trying to calm myself, my heart thumping like it's trying to break out of my chest.

Just another day in Holly-weird.

I PICKED YET ANOTHER PIECE OF CILANTRO OUT OF MY SALAD. Why do these pretentious Hollywood restaurants have to put cilantro in everything? My mouth was puckered around the intense green flavor when she cleared her throat. I looked up and saw an indulgent smile on Olivia's red lips.

"I hate cilantro," I said in explanation.

She nodded. "I know."

"It's like a conspiracy. They sneak it into everything, like if you try it often enough you'll suddenly start liking it. And then the head of the cilantro-industrial-complex will laugh like a B-movie villain all the way to the bank."

I was going to continue my rant, but her indulgent smile intensified.

I sighed and put my fork down, giving up on the salad. I stared at it for a moment, realizing that any salad with as much green, yellow, and purple as this one isn't going to work for an Iowa boy like me. Salads are supposed to be just green, and salads do not have cilantro in them.

"So," I said with a shrug, "what do you think?" I had told her about my visitor.

"Honey," she began, and I knew I was in trouble, "I think you need some help. I think our breakup was harder on you than you are willing to admit. I think I am worried about you."

"Look, Olivia, Cthulhu was in my hot tub last night. He—"

"And Harrison Ford last month?" she asked cutting me off.

"I told you. It wasn't Harrison Ford, it was Han Solo."

"And what did he ask you to do?" she asked.

I sighed again. I knew what it sounded like. "He asked me to sue Lucas Films. He's very upset that Lucas changed Star Wars so that Han didn't shoot first in the Mose Isley bar scene. He feels it undermines his character's later heroic transformation. He's hopeful that now that Disney owns it they'll do right by him."

Olivia's indulgent smiled left her beautiful face as her forehead furrowed. "Honey..." she began.

Seeing that look on her face put me right into fight or flight. She had given me that look, and said "honey" like that the day she had left me. You see, Olivia is beautiful and talented and, as of the moment she broke up with me, a lesbian. I am the man she left for a woman. Yup, I am that cliché. And when you are living in Hollywood you are going to be a cliché. The egotist, the control freak, the Svengali, the sensitive artist, the innocent, the... well you get the picture. This town is just that kind of place; everyone is a walking stereotype. Olivia found herself when she was with me, and I am the husk of a man that got left behind, the one who can't move on.

"...this all started after our breakup," she continued. "These hot tub visitations. Frank, you need help."

On the plus side we are closer now than we were when we lived together. She can say things like this to me, and I will actually listen no matter how hard it is to hear. Somewhere deep in my subconscious I must have known this, and it is why I picked her to talk with about Cthulhu.

She left me with the card of her shrink and a kiss on my cheek. I sat there for the longest time feeling the warmth of that kiss.

THE PER CAPITA DENSITY OF PSYCHIATRISTS IS HIGHER IN southern California than in anywhere else in the world. Entertainers and their eco-system (directors, producers, makeup artists, and lawyers like me) are an insecure lot. Right after Olivia left I called Dr. Krishnan and found she had an opening in half an hour.

Sitting on her white leather couch, staring at the green philodendron right behind her I laid it all out: the visitors to my hot tub and all the bizarre things I ended up doing because of it. As I spoke, I noticed that the plant was a little wilted and looked like it could use a drink. This worried me. If she couldn't take care of a plant—or hire someone to do it—how could she take care of me?

And yeah, I delivered my sad story to the plant and not the shrink. She had a nice enough face, if a bit stretched from too many procedures desperately trying to hold time back. It's just that I knew the plant wouldn't judge me. Her, on the other hand... I had no idea.

When it was all over I took a sip of my Perrier, enjoying the bubbling lime flavor and wishing there was some Tito's in it. (And yeah, I do have a thing for carbonation and bubbles in general— what can I say, you gotta have your quirks.) "So?" I asked her, finally moving my gaze from the plant to her.

Her thin red lips moved into an indulgent smile. "My opinion is not important here, Mr. Kelly, what is important is what you think."

I sighed. She was one of *those* shrinks. One of the few people in Hollywood that at least pretended not to have an opinion about something.

"Well, Ms. Krishnan, I think Cthulhu was in my hot tub last night, and I better do something about getting his movie made if I don't want him to eat my soul." With that I got up and left. I didn't have time for games, and besides I could at least tell Olivia I had gone to see her shrink.

THE BLOND LOOKED UP AT ME, HER SMILE SO DAZZLING THAT I almost believed she actually wanted to help me. She sat behind a desk in a small office not far from Paramount Studios and across from the Hollywood Forever Funeral Home. A wannabe actress, no doubt.

"I'm sorry," she began, her voice a nasal drone. Poor girl, with that face and body she could be an actress, but not with that voice. "He's not available today."

I looked around. The office wasn't very big. It had movie posters on the wall, and three closed doors. This office is one of many in the area, but I knew the person I needed to talk to was behind one of those doors. I had made some calls and knew he was in. I'm not going to name any names, but this little place was the production office of a quirky not-quite-A-list director. I knew he was working on an H.P. Lovecraft movie. I had heard it had been shelved. I needed to find out for sure.

You see, it takes forever to make a movie, and most that are conceived of never make it. There are budgets and scripts, actors and directors, studios, and a long gauntlet of challenges before tens of millions of dollars get spent.

My eyes went back to the receptionist's desk. There were a dozen roses on it and a name plate. Doris. I inhaled the sweet scent of the roses, letting it calm my nerves. "Look, Doris. I don't really need to talk to him. I just need to know about his Lovecraft project. I've got a client, a real fan with too much money, who might be interested in investing. I need to know if the project is really on the shelf." I gave her my best, most sincere smile. "That's all I need, can you help me out? I'll owe you one."

She looked to the left and the right before her blue eyes met mine. I actually felt my knees weaken, that's just how beautiful this girl is. "Just between us," she said in her grating voice, totally ruining the effect. "It's not happening, he's moved on."

I sighed and nodded my head. "Here," I told her, handing her my card, "I owe you one, give me a call if I can do anything."

She smiled and nodded. I turned to go and she said, "A part. I would love a part in anything, anything at all."

"Of course," I told her. "I'll keep my eyes open." I tried to smile, but couldn't quite manage it. No one was going to give her a part with a voice like that, and this director had been my best hope for a real Cthulhu movie. Depression descended on me like the early morning L.A. pollution. I slunk back to my car and drove home.

I WALKED OUT OF MY HOUSE PAST THE POOL TO THE HOT TUB. It was empty with Juan, my pool guy, scrubbing it as instructed. The smell of bleach was strong, which I was glad for. After having a tentacle-faced monster and my own waste products in there, I wanted it clean. He looked up, his brow furrowed and glistening with sweat. "You need something, Señor Kelly?"

I sighed and sat down cross-legged at the edge of the tub. I had tried a shrink, why not see what the pool guy thought. "I was visited by a monster last night, and he wants me to get a movie made about him. Made right now."

Juan stopped working, his brown eyes wide. He put down the rag and crossed himself. "And if you don't?"

I shrugged. "He'll eat what's left of my soul."

The reaction Juan gave me was really satisfying. He started a rapid patter of Spanish, which I couldn't quite follow. He pulled out his phone and started texting someone. And then he looked up at me and said, "No worry, Señor Kelly. I make movies. I help."

Most days I would have laughed. Juan the pool guy was a film-maker. Of course he was. Everyone here wanted to be in the business. But I was too touched to laugh. Olivia and her shrink had thought I was crazy, had been worried for my mental health. Not that I could blame them. But here I had found someone who took me seriously, who wanted to help.

I CHOMPED ON A PIECE OF OLD PIZZA: THE CHEESE COLD AND

thick, the crust dry and chewy. My formal dining room was a mess with pizza boxes, Red Bull cans, laptops, and paper everywhere. I hadn't slept in twenty-four hours. I was strung out and punchy. We were making a movie. I was having the time of my life.

I leaned against the wall and took another bite of the pizza while I watched Juan and his wife Susan talk rapidly in Spanglish. After our conversation at the hot tub, Juan had called a friend of his to finish cleaning the hot tub and then called his wife.

Susan was a twenty-something, brown-haired California surfer girl with a laser-like focus. The three of us had been up all night working on the concept for the movie and writing the script. Today we would find actors and deal with props. Tonight we shot. Tomorrow we would have a movie.

I felt my heart thudding in my chest. From fear of Cthulhu not finding our offering worthy, sure that was one reason. From having been up all night and being overly caffeinated, undoubtedly. But, and here is what I was most aware of, we were making a movie. An ultra-low budget indie film, but a movie nonetheless.

"Okay," I said getting Juan and Susan's attention. "I just want to review. We are going old school horror combined with a 'found footage' technique like *Cloverfield* or the *Blair Witch Project*. A series of young people break into a fancy Hollywood Hills home—my humble abode here—and one by one Cthulhu picks them off."

Susan nodded her head. "Right. The actors will film themselves with their phones."

"We do more," Juan began. "A documentary crew films the actors filming. El Cthulhu kills them too. It's..." He turned to Susan. "What is word?"

"Meta," Susan offered.

"Muy meta," Juan finished smiling.

I nodded. "So actors filming a fake found footage movie have a documentary crew filming them, which in the end, after Cthulhu kills everyone, turns out to be 'real' found footage movie.

"Okay, good work everyone," I said. "I am off to find us a lead actress and figure out how we do Cthulhu. You guys are going to work on props and the other actors."

They nodded and I headed outside to get a breath of fresh air and make some calls.

I DID MY PART FOR CASTING. WHEN I THOUGHT OF THE LEAD actress, the ingénue, the last person to die, I could only think of one person. I could see her blue eyes, her smooth porcelain skin, and her big smile whenever I closed my eyes. So, I called her.

"Hi, Doris. This is Frank Kelly."

"Hello, Mr. Kelly," she answered, her voice both nasally and business-like. "How can I help you?"

My rationalization for this choice went like this: She wanted to act, but had a handicap (her voice). We needed a beautiful young woman for the film. Sounded like a win-win.

"I'm making a movie and thought you might be perfect for our lead."

I had to hold the phone away from my ear so loud was her excited reply. It made me smile and feel warm inside. When I put the phone back to my ear, she was saying, "...and who wrote the script? When does production start? What can I—"

"Take it easy, Doris," I said. "It's ultra-low budget and we're shooting tonight. It's a found footage horror movie."

There were a few moments of silence on the line, not what I was expecting. "Are you still there?" I asked.

"You're... you're not talking about an adult film, are you?"

"No. Horror. Straight up. Young people breaking into a Hollywood Hills home and die a gruesome death one by one."

"No nudity?" she asked, her voice serious.

"None. A little blouse unbuttoning, some underwear, but that's it."

Silence again. She was cautious, which meant she had been offered unsavory roles before, had seen some things in this town.

"Look, Doris. I see this as a win-win. You get a part. I get a lead. I know we just met, but people know me in this town. Call around and ask." I dropped a few recognizable names. "Bring a can of mace if you like. If you're in, I'll fax you a contract over—have your lawyer review it."

Silence again, but before I started blathering on some more, she said, "Why? Why me? I don't get offered real roles. With my... my..."

I knew there were a lot of people who never got a shot, I felt like giving her one. "Can I be blunt, Doris?" I asked.

"Um-huh," she answered.

"I need someone who is beautiful, and I need her tonight. You did me a favor yesterday, so I thought I would return it. If you're not interested..." I trailed off. Yes, I was starting to work her a bit, nothing like what I could do, but I needed to get this done.

"No. I'm interested. Really I am. It's just that..."

"This town is full of jerks and freaks," I said. "Well I'll give you a clue, I lean towards the jerk side, but I do right by my people. I'll take care of you, Doris. I promise."

Silence again. She was a hard one to read, this would have been much better in person.

"Tell you what," I continued. "Say 'maybe' and I'll fax the contract over. You'll see then that this is for real and you'll have to come."

There was another moment of silence and then a soft, nasally "maybe."

THE PHONE RANG REPEATEDLY AS I WATCHED THE SUN RISE. A view I almost never saw. I stood next to my hot tub looking down at L.A. as it woke up.

"Frank?" Olivia's answered sleepily. "What's wrong?"

"I've got an acting gig for you tonight."

There was silence on the other end.

"I need you, Olivia." I said.

"What's going on... wait a minute, is this about Cthulhu and your damn hot tub?"

"Just be at my place at sundown. Your show is on hiatus, as I recall, so you should be available." Olivia is a real actress. She is one of the main cast of a major show. She was just a struggling actress when we met, now she's the real thing. "And scrounge up a police-woman's uniform."

"Frank..." she began, but I hung up. Sure, I was pushing it. I was abusing our relationship a bit. But she owed me. I opened a few doors for her, made sure they didn't screw her with the contract when she landed her show. I suffered through the humiliation of her deciding to like girls. She owed me. I needed her. I knew she would come.

In Hollywood you will find some of the happiest people and some of the saddest. The happiest are those that are doing what they love and just can't believe how lucky they are. The saddest—well, that's easy, they are the ones that know what they want to do, but can't do it.

Joan West is the former. She's middle-aged with bright red hair and is a special effects guru. She's old-school, shunning CGI and doing strictly practical effects.

She was poking on an iPad looking at images of Cthulhu, her brows deeply furrowed. I stood looking around her "mad scientist" workshop. There's nothing else to call it with the variety of materials, tools, masks, severed heads, monsters, and other bizarre paraphernalia. No wonder the woman was happy—she plays all day every day.

"And what do you need?" She asked, licking her lips and looking up at me.

"I need Cthulhu. I need him... tonight."

"Sweetheart," she began, "There's not enough time. I couldn't do that for Steven Freaking Spielberg that fast. I sure as hell can't do it for you. I've got other deadlines. I've got my reputation to consider."

I knew Joan pretty well. I've been her lawyer for a while and helped her out of some pretty tough spots. I knew what motivated her. "Okay," I said, "no worries, Joan. I just thought I'd give you first crack at this. I've got Ben Layton waiting in the wings." Ben is a former apprentice of hers, and they did not part on friendly terms. I turned to leave.

"Wait," she said. "This is low budget, right?" She took the bait.

I turned and nodded. "Yup. We're doing found footage. It doesn't have to be perfect, just scary."

"And what time is delivery?" The hook was set.

"Sundown at my place."

"And I suppose I need to provide an operator for the thing?"

I gave her my best, brightest smile. "You are the best Joanie. I will—" I was about to speak more, but I was assaulted by the scent of rotting fish and tar. Joan's workshop faded and I was in a dark room. I could hear something moving, a scraping, a stinking breeze on my face, something slimy running across my skin.

And then I saw him, Cthulhu standing in a pool of harsh white light. The tentacles on his face mesmerizing me again. He spread his wings and marched towards me. He took my head in one clawed hand, and I felt him communicating with me again.

I knew what he wanted and it scared the hell out of me. He wanted to be in the movie. Cthulhu wanted to be a goddamn actor too.

I woke to Joan West slapping my face and the stink of my own urine. I mean, I don't mind so much working for Cthulhu, but I just wish he could find a way to communicate that did not involve my bladder venting itself.

"Wake up, Frank. You Okay? Did you overdo the blow last night? Have you eaten?"

I blinked and roused myself. Joan's hard cement floor was underneath me and the back of my head hurt. "No blow," I said slowly. "I don't do that anymore. Just Red Bull."

Joan snorted. "Jesus, boy. Red Bull does this to you? Wow. What happened to the Frank Kelly I used to know?"

"Not the Red Bull. It's..." I didn't finish. I couldn't tell Joan what was happening, she wouldn't believe me. I needed her to get the Cthulhu costume done and couldn't risk spooking her. My heart was pounding in my chest just thinking of what was coming. A fake, costumed Cthulhu, and the real Cthulhu. People besides me were going to wet their pants when they saw this.

I got myself to my feet and clutched one of her workbenches. "So, Joan, can you do it?"

She grinned, showing crooked teeth. "Look at you, Franky-boy. You're like a goddam weeble. You wobble, but you don't fall down."

The bruise on my hip begged to differ about the falling down part, but this was Joan's way of telling me she was in. "See you at sundown," I said. "Tonight will be unforgettable. I promise"

Kesi is from Jamaica. She's in her fifties with a round face, brown skin, and beaded corn-rows. She don't take shit from no one.

"You want me to buy what?" she asked, her hands on her ample hips. I sat in the kitchen shoveling eggs down my throat. They were loaded with salt, pepper, and garlic, just the way I like. After passing out at Joan's I was starving. I rushed home, changed my soiled clothing, and had Kesi scramble me some eggs.

"Adult diapers, Kesi. I need you to buy adult diapers. A lot of them."

Her mouth turned down and she stared at me as she tried to figure out if I was joking. Her eyes narrowed as her head cocked, and then her expression relaxed. "You got a problem... down there?" Her eyes traveled to the level of my crouch and back.

I felt my cheeks flush hot. "No. No, of course not. It's... I..." I looked down, I couldn't meet her eyes. I needed her help, but I couldn't tell her the truth either.

"It okay, Mr. Kelly. I will take care of you. I always take care of you." She laid her hand on my shoulder and gently squeezed. Kesi has been with me for about five years. My life, honestly, wouldn't run without her.

"And I need you to work tonight," I said. "I am going to have a house full." Her face hardened and she frowned so I offered, "We are making a movie."

"Un huh..." she said, looking away.

"And we need more people to act in it."

"Me?" she asked, her face lighting up like a little girl's. "In a movie?"

I nodded, chewing on more eggs. It never ceased to amaze. It seemed no one in this town didn't want to be in a movie. I briefed her on the supplies we would need—besides the adult diapers—and she moved out of there to the store quicker than I had seen her move in years.

MY CREDIT CARD WAS GETTING QUITE THE WORKOUT. I surveyed the pile of rental equipment that had just been delivered. Lights, digital SLR cameras, tripods, microphones, recorders. It sat there, a jumble of black cases in my living room.

I mean it wasn't like the old days of Hollywood were you needed hundreds to make a movie. The world has changed. Now all you needed was a couple of digital SLR cameras and some knowhow.

Juan and Susan dove into the pile and started assembling equipment like soldiers assembling rifles. They did it with this quick, practiced ease: inserting batteries, plugging in chargers, setting up tripods, trying out the lights. I was mesmerized. They then started showing me how to work the equipment. Most of it is not hard—push this button to start recording, push again to stop recording. But now, focusing, that is another issue. These digital SLRs are not video cameras so you have to focus manually, and that means if your subject moves you have to keep fiddling with the focus.

My sleep-deprived brain was having trouble grasping it. I kept focusing the lens in the wrong direction, hitting the wrong button. I couldn't screw this up. Cthulhu was counting on me and I didn't want to face him if he didn't like the movie we created.

Juan looked at me when I screwed it up for the fifth time in a row. His eyes looked tired, but there was a fire behind them that I didn't feel myself. Cthulhu's last transmission had really taken it out of me.

"Siesta, my friend. Time for you to have a little siesta." I mutely nodded as he guided me to the couch. I think I was asleep before I laid down.

THE HOT BUBBLES TICKLED MY SKIN AS THE WATER BURBLED around me. I smelled the chlorine and my mouth tasted funny, like I just eaten a lemon rind or something. I looked around and found a tall glass of what looked like Tito's and club. I took the cold beverage and sipped out of the blue straw. I then noticed I wasn't alone in the hot tub.

Cthulhu sat sipping his own drink, his undulating tentacles seeming to form some kind of a smile.

"Well..." I began, but my voice caught in my throat. Cthulhu in my hot tub. I knew he wanted something, but I couldn't remember what it was. I knew it was urgent. I knew there would be dire consequences if I failed.

My dream shifted and suddenly I was standing in a court room. Behind the big wooden bench sat Cthulhu wearing one of these silly white wigs judges used to wear. He had a gavel in his clawed hand and he was pointing it at me. In the witness box sat Olivia, her cheeks stained with tears. She gave me the look, the one she had given me the day she had told me she had fallen in love with a woman. It was a look that was full of sorrow and pity.

I stumbled back and ran into something. I turned around and looked at the big desk covered with papers. Briefs, statements, hand written notes—except they seemed to be in another language. I couldn't understand any of them.

I heard the gavel banging down and whirled around. Except the courtroom was gone. Olivia was gone. Cthulhu was not, though.

I stood naked in the desert, sand dunes as far as the eye can see. The sun was high in the sky, and I was sweating. Cthulhu's wings swept out behind him as he leapt on me. I felt his tentacles wrap around my head, pulling me in towards his mouth. The scent of rotting fish and tar choked me. I tried to scream, but I couldn't. All that came out was this pitiful gurgling sound.

I knew I had failed him. I knew that my soul was the price I had to pay.

———————

THE SUN WAS GOING DOWN WHEN I WOKE UP. MY MOUTH tasted like dirty laundry, and my spit had nearly turned to cement.

I silently cursed as I sat up. I had pissed myself again. I looked around, my brain sloshing wetly in my head. My house was a hive of activity. The kitchen was setup with food. The dining room was full of equipment and props. The living room had lights setup and looked ready for filming, except for my sorry, barely conscious ass.

I stumbled into the kitchen and found Kesi. She was frying chicken, and I saw a pot of what looked like her curried goat. She turned and met me with a large smile, her teeth looking very white against her brown skin.

"There you are, Mr. Kelly. You feeling better now?"

"I'm fine Kesi. Can you tell me where the..." I looked around; there were three people I didn't know standing around eating chips and salsa. Actors, I presumed. "You know, that item I asked you to buy."

She nodded, her eyes looking me up and down and her nose wrinkling. She took me by the hand and dragged me into my bedroom. It too had lights setup. "You take a shower now. I will put clean clothes out for you and that... you know..."

I nodded a mute thanks and went into the bathroom and locked the door. I looked into the mirror. I was as white as a ghost. What the hell was I going to do if Cthulhu did not accept our offering?

I took a deep breath and shook it off. After a quick shower, I put on the adult diapers and the clothes Kesi had laid out for me. There was nothing else to do. It was dark. It was time to start shooting. It was time for Cthulhu's close-up.

Doris arrived like the Santa Ana winds in the fall. Her presence was unmistakable and undeniable. And just as the Santa Ana's can make things ripe for a fire in SoCal, her presence made things in the room seem like they were going to explode.

She had on a short skirt and tights with a white blouse. All male eyes in the room went to her and stayed there. She looked around the room and saw me. I was standing next to Juan and Susan going over our shooting schedule.

"There you are," she said, her voice both nasally and commanding. She took off her big, dark, movie star sunglasses. "I have a bone to pick with you."

I smiled because I was glad to "see" her, but I also felt fear. Her tone meant business. "Glad you could make it, Doris. I trust the contract was up to snuff."

"That's just it," she said, pulling a manila envelope out of her big purse. "The pay is substandard, the craft services pitiful, and the back-end... don't get me started on residuals. Are you trying to insult me?"

This was a different Doris. If I didn't know better, I'd think we had hired some kind of big-headed, Hollywood diva. "I'm... I..." I stammered. Juan and Susan were just silent watching the whole affair.

Doris cracked a big smile and relaxed her shoulders, suddenly seeming more like the Doris I had met. "Just kidding," she said in a sing-song voice. "I thought I should, you know, audition, so you all know I can act."

There were sighs of relief from Juan and Susan and a few chuckles from the other actors.

Her brows furrowed briefly before she said, "I asked around about you, Mr. Kelly. Your clients love you, your opponents hate you." She nodded slowly. "So, I've been thinking. If I land a real role, will you be my lawyer?"

"Sure, Doris, just as long as you call me Frank."

She rushed up to me, quickly closing the distance between us, and was suddenly hugging me. Her round feminine flesh pressed against mine. My breath caught, and I found myself hugging her back.

"I brought that mace," she whispered in my ear, "so don't get any funny ideas."

And then just like the Santa Ana's she was gone and I was left there changed by her passage.

IT WAS TIME. THE ACTORS WHERE PRESENT, THE EQUIPMENT was ready, and Juan and Susan had delicately told me I would not be handling a camera. I was the director of the whole thing and, as such, would be "directing" not filming. They had decided to use some stationary cameras and didn't need me anymore. It was embarrassing, but then again I was wearing a diaper, so what the hell?

"Everyone is out by the pool," Juan said, his hand on my shoulder. "Tell them what we are doing."

I slowly walked out to the group of people standing around looking at scripts. There were five cast members, including Doris, playing the reckless youths that break in. Kesi was playing the housekeeper that surprised them. Juan, Susan and myself were playing the documentary crew. I looked around and didn't see Olivia, and Joan West wasn't there with the Cthulhu costume. That was OK. They were pros, they would be here when we needed them.

I cleared my throat and longed for the lime tang of Tito's and club. My gaze went to the hot tub and a bead of cold sweat tricked down my back. I tore my eyes away and looked at the actors.

"Thank you all for coming," I began. I was surprised to hear Juan translating my words into Spanish. Looks like we had some non-English speakers in the cast. "I see you all have a script, so you know what we are doing tonight. This is a 'found footage' movie. You will be breaking into a ritzy Hollywood Hills home filming yourselves with your phones. One by one a monster called Cthulhu will kill each of you. The three of us," I gestured to Juan, Susan, and myself, "are a documentary crew filming the making of the movie. We will have a costumed Cthulhu here soon, and in the final cut, a real looking Cthulhu. The real Cthulhu will end up killing all of us, making the documentary crew's film 'found footage' too."

"Later, a policewoman will show up and we will switch out of 'found footage' as she surveys the damage. Cthulhu will get her too."

Things were quiet after my little speech, which made me nervous. I needed all of these people. I needed this to work. The hot tub kept drawing my attention—I kept expecting to see him there.

"Any questions?" I asked.

The spell broke, and I spent the next thirty minutes fielding actorly concerns. They wanted to change their lines, make their roles bigger, have a more gruesome death, complain about the food, wanted more money. I relaxed. The actors were being actors, and I knew what I was doing here. I placated, cajoled, and sidestepped them until it was time to shoot.

DORIS, A SLIM YOUNG MAN NAMED DENNIS, JUAN, SUSAN, AND I were in my bedroom getting ready to film the first scene when I saw the flash of the police lights outside the window.

Juan spoke rapidly in Spanish to Susan—I couldn't follow much but *deportación*, he thought they were here for him. He ran out of the room towards the back of the house.

"Everyone stay put," I said as I left to go investigate. I opened the front door and walked out into the warm southern California night.

As I approached the car, I couldn't see anything through the tinted windows. I glanced back and saw faces at the door and the windows. Sometimes I feel sorry for the cops; they are never welcome. But, right then, I just wanted to get back to filming. Compared to Cthulhu, the police aren't very intimidating.

I stood there a few feet from the car, it's red and blue lights flashing, and waited. The two front doors finally opened and two female police officers got out. Then the back door opened and my heart skipped a beat. A tentacle-faced monster emerged.

I stared at it, adrenaline running through my veins, but something wasn't right. The tentacles hung limply, and the skin wasn't nearly scaly enough.

"Joan?" I asked. "Is that you under there?"

There was shake of the monster's head and a muffled "un-huh."

"She had you going for a minute," the first officer said. Her voice was very familiar, and I looked past her dark sunglasses and pulled back hair.

"Olivia," I began, excited to see my ex. Then my gaze traveled to the second officer. "Tish," I added with much less enthusiasm. I didn't recall inviting Olivia's significant other to this party. "Thanks for coming. We are just about to start shooting."

As the three of them headed for the house, I grabbed Olivia. "I really do appreciate this."

She smiled, her dark brown eyes boring into me. "You, OK? What's going on Frank?"

I looked away, I couldn't lie to her, but I didn't think I could tell her the whole truth. "Things... well they've gotten complicated. I'm just glad you're here."

———

HOLLYWOOD IS ALL ABOUT HURRY UP AND WAIT. YOU ARE always busting your ass for a contract or a part or a deal and then you have to wait and wait and wait. And the instant the project is a go, it's time to hurry up and do your piece and then wait and wait and wait.

Filming is like that too. If you're an actor it's hurry up and do your part and then wait while the next setup is done or another actor gets their close up. If you're the director you're always waiting for the crew to setup the shot, or the actor to get out of the bath-room, or for Cthulhu to appear.

That last part, I really didn't mind waiting for.

My bedroom was starting to smell like too many bodies. It's not a tiny bedroom but there were a lot of us in there.

Doris and Dennis doing their scene. Two stationary cameras. Juan and Susan with cameras. A little sprite of a girl named Gail with a boom mike. Joan West in her Cthulhu costume off to the side. And me.

I felt like hell and I had a sour taste in my mouth I couldn't get rid of. My constant trips into unconsciousness combined with caffeine and sugar had turned my system a bit toxic.

I was waiting on Juan and Susan as they babysat the gear. I was glad that wasn't part of my responsibility. Being the director was enough.

"Stationary cameras rolling," Juan said, his English particularly good with movie terms. "Camera A rolling."

"Camera B rolling," Susan said.

"Audio rolling," Gail said.

"iPhone video rolling," Doris said.

I checked the clapper I had, walked into the scene, and said, "Bedroom scene, take one." I felt silly as I snapped the jaws shut on the thing, but Susan had explained to me that it was used to sync all the shots up. I stepped back and said loudly. "Quiet on the set. And... action!"

Dennis was lying on the bed, giving Doris a leering grin. We were doing the overly clichéd theme of horny young people getting killed off one at a time. It's a tried and true horror trope and we were using it without shame.

Doris pointed her camera at him and said, "What are we going to do in this big fancy bedroom all alone?" I cringed. Not just from her nasal grate but from how truly awful the line was.

"I think we'll think of something," Dennis said, his grin widening. "How about a game. One button for me, one button for you." He unbuttoned his jeans.

Doris rotated her iPhone around and pointed it at her bosom as she started to unbutton her blouse. "But I've got more buttons than you do," she said with a pout. "That's not fair." She continued unbuttoning, and her blouse fell open revealing a white lace bra.

Yeah, the dialog was bad, the scene was crap, and Doris's voice sounded like a spoon caught in a garbage disposal, but once she started unbuttoning her blouse most male eyes (and some female) would be on her. She really is a beautiful girl, a throwback to the days when women like Marilyn Monroe dominated the big screen.

I felt a twinge of jealousy. I'm the director, why didn't I cast myself in the role of her boyfriend? Sure he was about to die, but he had the better view.

When she turned the iPhone back onto Dennis he had his shirt off revealing a broad chest and six-pack abs. Oh yeah, that's why I wasn't in that part with my doughy lawyer chest.

I gave Joan her signal, and she shambled into the screen. Dennis didn't notice her, his eyes locked on Doris. But Doris did, her eyes widened and she gave a reasonably convincing scream. Turns out that her nasally-ness makes her a pretty big screamer.

Joan, her fake tentacles swinging around, jumped onto Dennis. I groaned inwardly. Not that Joan hadn't done a great job with very little time, but because if this is all we had people would be laughing at the movie.

And then I felt him. Cthulhu. A wave of dizziness passed through me, and I could faintly smell his tar and fish odor.

Of course, we wanted it to look silly—at first. I put my hand against the wall to brace myself for what was to come. And still I was surprised.

The oily rotten smell became overwhelming and then Cthulhu came crashing through my bedroom window, glass shattering, flying all over the place. He stood there in his glory, his chest heaving, his head scraping the ceiling, his wings flexing behind his body, the tentacles on his face undulating. They parted and the roar that escaped him made me glad I had Kesi buy adult diapers.

Doris screamed again—this time it was blood curdling—and ran out of the room. Juan swore in Spanish and backed up a few steps, but being crazy filmmakers as they are (and aren't all filmmakers crazy) Juan and Susan kept the cameras rolling.

Right before shooting I had told them that the real Cthulhu would be appearing. Much to my surprise, they didn't bolt. Juan just crossed himself and Susan shook her head. But that was it, they went back to work. Unbelievable.

Joan couldn't see Cthulhu because of her costume and kept up her awkward undulations. Cthulhu grabbed the costumed version of himself with a distain that was palpable and threw her across the room. She hit the wall and landed in a pile, unmoving.

Dennis then did see the real Cthulhu and let out a scream that nearly matched Doris's. He tried to get away, but the monster pinned him to the bed with one clawed hand. He slowly lowered his mouth to Dennis's neck and bit. Blood spurted forth, hot and red. Juan, Susan, and I all screamed.

Cthulhu paused and looked at us. Hands shaking, Juan and Susan still had their cameras trained on him. He let out another roar and everything went dark.

My last thought as the darkness clamed me was: we are all going to die. This is going to be a real found footage movie. He's going to kill Olivia and Doris.

IN HORROR MOVIES, ARROGANCE IS ALWAYS MET WITH A gruesome death. That, and lust, of course. How arrogant had I been? To involve other people in this mess. To try to make a movie thinking a fearsome Elder God would be content to just be in the movie and not be a real monster.

I heard voices all talking at once. Male and female. Talking fast and urgent.

I felt a cool hand to my neck—someone was checking my pulse. "Wake up, Frank." I heard Olivia say.

My arrogance had gotten everyone here. He was going to kill us all. It would be just what Cthulhu wanted. People would be scared of him again, not make silly jokes on Facebook about him.

"Come on, wake up. What the hell is wrong with you?"

I sucked in air grateful to be alive, for a little while longer, at least. I opened my eyes and all I could see was Olivia. Full, red lips. Deep brown eyes. Hair the blackest black. God, how I missed her.

"Olivia," I said, my voice raw. "I'm sorry."

Her brow furrowed. "For what?"

She helped me get up and I looked around the room. Dennis was sitting up on the bed grinning from ear to ear. The window was back in its unbroken form.

"Oh my God," Dennis said, his words tumbling out. "That was unbelievable. Where the hell did that monster come from? Didn't he crash through the window? I mean, it felt like he did rip my throat out. What a rush, can we do another take?"

My legs buckled and Olivia caught me. This time it was from relief. I had no idea how Cthulhu had done it, but he made it look like he had killed Dennis, but there he was alive with a stupid grin on his face.

"Did we get it?" I asked Juan.

Juan spoke in quick Spanish. I caught *Dios* (God) and *Diablo* (Devil) but most of the rest was lost to me. While he did this he was still filming Olivia helping me up. He ended by lowering the camera and then crossing himself. "I check," he mumbled.

I looked around the room. Susan looked terrified. Joan, in her what now seemed silly Cthulhu costume had taken off the tenta-cled head and looked dazed. Those that weren't in the room looked fine. Tish and a few of the other actors peaked in the door. They hadn't experienced anything but just had gotten worried when they heard all the screaming.

Juan pointed the LCD of the camera at me, and I watched as the real Cthulhu leapt through my bedroom window and ripped Dennis's throat out.

I then remembered Doris. She wasn't there. She had screamed and ran from the room.

"Okay everyone, we are going to do another take. This time after Cthulhu comes in we are going right into filming the police, Olivia and Tish, finding Dennis's body. So reset everything. I'll be back with Doris in a minute."

I could still smell rotting fish so I knew Cthulhu was near. I knew he was listening. I trusted he could take direction and do whatever it was he was doing so that we could capture it on camera.

"HEY," I SAID FEELING THE SLIGHTLY COOLER NIGHT AIR. Doris sat with her arms around her legs, her back against the red brick wall that separated my yard from my neighbor's. The tang of chlorine assaulted my nose; she was right next to the hot tub.

"What the hell is going on?" she asked. Her voice sounded dangerous.

"We're making a movie." I paused and smiled. Not a planned smile but a real one. We were making a freaking movie. The footage Juan showed me was as good as anything Hollywood could do. I knew what we were making was going to be huge. "You're going to be a star."

Her jaw bunched and her teeth ground. "What the hell is going on?" she repeated.

I sighed and sat down in front of her and took her hand. Even in her terror she was gorgeous. Her hand was cold, but she didn't pull away. "I... I didn't tell you because I didn't think you would believe me. But... now..."

"What was that thing?"

"He is called Cthulhu. In the twenties a writer named H.P. Lovecraft wrote a series of horror stories about him."

"That shit is going to scare people," she said with a snort.

"We need to do another cut."

"But... Dennis..."

"Is fine. He got off on it. It was his idea to do it again."

"But... why... isn't he going to really kill us in the end?" Her unwavering blue eyes pierced me, and I felt guilt, like a heavy elephant sitting on my chest, about getting other people involved in this.

"He has assured me he won't."

"He... he talks to you?"

"Well, I wouldn't call it talking. More like sticking a psychic hand into my brains and scrambling them a bit. He just wants a movie. Besides, we've taken precautions."

Her eyebrows furrowed, the lines marring her smooth skin. "Precautions?"

I nodded. "We're filming out of order. The last scene we shoot will require everyone. If he wants this movie made he has to keep us all alive."

She just kept staring at me, so I said, "But, really, is he any worse than most Hollywood producers?"

Doris nodded and took a deep shuddering breath. "I need to fix my face first." I walked her back into the house. She didn't let my hand go until we got to the bathroom. I knew that she was scared and knew that it was my fault, but I liked the feel of her hand in mine.

WE WENT BACK AND FILMED DENNIS'S DEATH SCENE, THIS time with Susan turning her camera on me, the documentary director, as I freaked out after the tentacled one's arrival. We had forgotten our second layer movie on the first take. After that, we shot Oliva and Tish finding the body. When it was all over and the scene was wrapped—poof—everything and everybody was just fine.

Except the actors weren't fine. They had all gotten wind of what was happening in my bedroom and were about to bolt. I could feel Cthulhu's displeasure at it.

If there's one thing I've learned from this little incident, it's this: if an Elder God comes calling and asks you to do something, say no if you can. Simple advice, really. A being like that is going to have motivations and logic you just aren't going to understand. Cthulhu's message, though, was quite clear: Make the movie or die.

I stood barricading the front door with my body, my cast wide-eyed staring at me. Juan and Susan had their cameras and were filming. God bless them, they had the insanity of true professionals, and this scene, which was not in the script and was 100% real, helped make the movie.

"You can't go," I said. "Please."

"We go," a big guy named Raul said as he approached. He was twenty years younger than me and looked like he worked out constantly (or, more than likely worked as a laborer and earned those muscles the old-fashioned way).

"Just give me a chance to explain," I said.

"No," Raul said, picking me up and moving me away from the door with a casual ease.

I smelled Cthulhu then, and knew what would happen if that door was opened, knew what would happen if the movie didn't get made. "Look, you're scared, I understand that."

That stopped Raul in his tracks. It was clear that he was scared, but he was the type that couldn't admit it. He let go of the door knob and stepped back. "Not scared of nothing," he said.

"Well I am," I said as I moved in front of the door again. "Juan can you translate all this for me?" Juan nodded and starting speaking in Spanish while he kept filming.

"Look, I owe you all an apology," I began, wiping the sweat

from my forehead. "But if we don't make this movie Cthulhu will kill us all."

There were shouts in English and Spanish and fear as palpable as a San Francisco fog descended on the place.

Kesi marched forward, her eyes ablaze, and said, "What kind of bad mojo you got going on here, Mr. Kelly? What kind of mess did you get us all into?"

I felt bad about it, I did. But what was done was done. "I'm sorry, Kesi. I truly am, but he's here, right now. He's ready, right now. It's a win-win for him. Either he gets his movie made or he gets us."

Out of context I sounded like a lunatic, but everyone had seen what had happened to Dennis, and that he was all right now. In fact he was in the kitchen eating chips as happy as can be.

The energy of the group was changing, I could feel it. It was going from scared to angry to a mob. And as the mood got worse, my sense of Cthulhu grew stronger. It was like a promise. If I let this get out of control, that would be it.

I was about to open my mouth and say something when a young woman named Helena called to Dennis, "What was it like?"

He sauntered in chomping on his food. "I died, guys. I died twice. I did. I felt it when he ripped my throat out. I felt my blood gush forth. I felt the terror of it all. I knew I was dead. And then..." He trailed off, his eyes taking on a faraway look. "And then I was floating above my body watching it all. Cthulhu lapping up my blood. Joan in her costume slumped on the floor. Frank wetting his pants." That got a good chuckle. My cheeks flushed red, but I let it be. Dennis was arguing my point, and the laughter helped ease some of the tension.

"And then," he continued, "it was all over and I was alive and fine. It was real, I swear to God what that thing did to me was real, and then it wasn't." A big smile crept on his face. "I died, guys, I died. And..."

The room was as silent as a temple as everyone waited for

Dennis to continue. He had this silly, blissful smile on his face, his eyes pointed upward.

"I'll tell you two things you have to know. One: I'll never be the same. I mean life is here for living, and I am going to go grab it by the balls and live it as long as I can!" There was some awkward chuckles at that. "And two: Listen to Frank. If Cthulhu wanted us dead, we would be dead. End of story. That dude killed me and brought me back to life. So let's make his movie so we all get to see the sun rise."

That did it. The energy fled from the room like a popped balloon. Everyone headed into the kitchen and started snacking. They all peppered Dennis with questions. He seemed like the happiest guy in the world and answered with a zeal fitting of a recent convert.

I could still feel Cthulhu, though. His presence hadn't faded... He still wanted something. I looked at Olivia and Doris and Kesi. "You can have me," I whispered. "Please, let them all live and take me."

The scent of Cthulhu receded. He had accepted my deal. I slid to the floor my back against the door.

As the night wore on, more and more of us started wearing the adult diapers, and despite my speech at the door, I had to have more and more talks like I had had with Doris after they had seen the monster. *Yes, Cthulhu is real. No, he's not going to kill us in the end.* We started filming these conversations and reality TV style confessionals too. What we were doing was becoming so meta I could hardly keep it straight—there was a camera shooting everything just in case we needed it.

But, a sliver of me still doubted they would get out of this alive, still felt that elephant of guilt sitting on my chest, but what was I going to do about it? Stop making the movie? I knew that was a sure way to get us all killed.

You know, Elder Gods, you shouldn't make them angry.

One by one we shot everyone dying. And each and every time Cthulhu made a spectacular entrance and got us footage we would have spent months and huge amounts of money creating.

When the deaths were over, we moved on to the group shots. We filmed Kesi coming to the house with groceries and surprising the vandals. We filmed the party the "crazy kids" had out by the pool. We also filmed some interpersonal, shred-of-a-plot interactions between the characters. We had to play lip service to plot, just like almost every other horror movie—yes sir, here's a plot so you can fool yourself into thinking you didn't come to see this just to get the shit scared out of you.

With one shot left, everyone stood around the kitchen, zombie-like. It had been a long and busy night and everyone's caffeine buzz seemed to be waning at the same time. For once, no one was filming. I checked my watch—we had about forty minutes before the sun came up. We were going to use the pre-dawn light as a stand-in for post-sunset light and film the break in to the house.

"Ok, everyone," I began, gathering the shreds of my energy. "You all know why we are here. We have one more scene to film. And once we have that scene wrapped, I want you all to leave. Don't come back into the house, just go."

I took a deep breath and let is slowly hiss out between clenched teeth. "You've all done a marvelous job. We are going to have a hell of a movie. But..." I looked around and all eyes were on me, that elephant was now using my chest as a trampoline. "Just get the hell out of here when we are done. We'll gather again when we have it edited together."

There were some nods. I think they got what I was telling them, but I wasn't about to come out and say, "Run like crazy when we are done. If Cthulhu needs someone, he can have me." My eyes lingered on Olivia,

Doris, and Kesi. I couldn't stand the thought of them paying for this with their lives. I locked eyes with Juan and saw him glance at his wife and then back at me, giving me a small nod. I breathed a sigh of relief. I knew he understood. I knew he would take care of everyone if he could.

"Ok, folks. Caffeine up and let's do this!"

"CUT," I SAID, GLANCING AT JUAN AND SUSAN. SUSAN FIDDLED with her camera and gave me a nod. "OK, folks, that's a wrap!"

We had just filmed our last scene, showing our soon-to-be victims approaching the house they would break into. We were about halfway up my driveway, and I could sense Cthulhu. He wanted me. It was time.

There were cheers and high-fives and hugs. I put a smile on my face but that fatigued joy that happens at the end of a shoot was lost on me. I was worried about what was next. I knew that Cthulhu would require a victim and that victim would be me.

"God bless you, Mr. Kelly," Kesi said, giving me a serious look and then a big hug. "I come back tomorrow. See if..." There was guilt in her eyes along with the concern. She knew I was the sacrifice.

"You've been so good to me, Kesi. Thank you for everything." She was crying as she headed down the driveway to her car parked in the street.

There was a flurry of hugs, slaps on the back, and goodbyes from most of the cast, and then I stood there with Susan and Juan.

"You got all the memory cards?" I asked.

Susan patted her purse.

"I'll call you guys tomorrow, if..." I began.

Juan crossed himself and hugged me. Susan gave me a kiss on the cheek, and then I found myself standing there alone.

After I watched them all leave, I breathed a huge sigh of relief. Everyone was gone, and hopefully safe, but I knew this wasn't over.

I sighed and was about to turn and go back in when I caught some movement at the bottom of my driveway. It's big and slopes down before meeting up with the road. I saw the top of a blond head.

I walked down and saw Doris sitting on the low wall that bordered the sidewalk. Suddenly I was awake again.

"Hey," I said as I sat down next to her.

"Oh. Hi," she said with a weak smile. Her voice was still nasally, but less grating, somehow, than when I first met her.

"What are you still doing here?" I asked.

She shrugged. "I wasn't going to get into the back of Juan's pickup, so I called a cab. And..." she glanced back up towards the house.

So, I'm a male lawyer working in Holly-weird and honest emotion doesn't come easily to me. I bet that comes as no surprise. But sitting next to Doris, smelling her perfume and sweat, seeing her dangerous curves out of my peripheral vision, I was aware that I was feeling *something*.

And yes, as a male lawyer working in Holly-weird sitting next to a beautiful girl fifteen years my junior, lust was part of it. I was fully aware of that part, but there was something else. I was growing fond of the girl—she was trying to make her way in the toughest of businesses and being different (that voice, you know).

"You know..." I began, her blue eyes meeting mine, sending a chill (the good kind) up and down my spine. "You know, Doris. I apologize. This thing got really out of control. I didn't know Cthulhu would be showing up in the flesh when I called about this. I..."

I felt like she was a proxy for me, and I was apologizing to all of them through her.

"Are you sure you're a lawyer?" she asked with a shy smile. "Cause you're kinda nice for a lawyer."

I returned her smile and looked down.

"It's not like I could have told everyone that the executive producer on the movie was kind of the devil himself," I said.

She laughed, a snorting donkey-like braying which made me laugh in return. It felt good to let some of the tension out.

"As if that would have made a difference," she said. "You could have told everyone, and they still would have signed on. This is Hollywood." She rested her hand on mine briefly and there I was, feeling something again.

The cab pulled up and Doris got up to go. "Thanks for everything, Frank."

My mouth seemed glued shut but I managed to open it right before she shut the cab door. "Doris!" I said, rising and walking to her. "Can I buy you dinner sometime?"

She smiled and nodded her head. "I'd like that."

I DON'T KNOW HOW TO DESCRIBE HOW I WAS FEELING AS I walked back into the house. I was exhausted, yes, beyond my ability to put into words. My body was numb—it really didn't feel like my own. Excited, of course, we had just shot the kind of footage no one had ever shot in a single night, and Doris had agreed to go out with me. Beyond question, I was scared, oh yeah. I mean, I had been all noble making the deal with Cthulhu, doing my best to make sure everyone got away from the house, but doubt still plagued me. Maybe there was nothing special about my hot tub and my house. Maybe Cthulhu could go to each of their houses as he pleased and take them there. And, I had a feeling, like a scratch that you can't itch, that I had forgotten something important.

I sighed, and looked around my house. It was completely trashed. Kesi was probably going to have to hire a huge crew just to clean it up. Overturned couches, broken mirrors, dishes, bottles, stains on the carpet. Sure, Cthulhu had undone his spectacular messes when we got done with a shot but not the actor's messes. We were filming them breaking into a rich guy's place and having irresponsible fun. My house showed it.

I shrugged; there was nothing I could do. I went into my bedroom and took of all my clothes, including that damn diaper, and put on the robe that was hanging on the bathroom door. I then slowly walked out back.

This area was a mess too, but I ignored it and went to the bar and stood there with my back to the hot tub as I made two drinks—Tito's and club. As soon as I started pouring the vodka I could smell him, all oily ocean.

I handed him his drink which he accepted with a nod of his head, set my drink down, dropped my robe and got in.

Cthulhu in my hot tub. Who would ever believe this? Well, actually, everyone. Before we filmed the last scene I had Juan set up a camera. If the monster was really going to kill me, at least we would have footage from it. In the back of my mind I was hoping it was some kind of insurance. Every time he had done something with the cameras rolling it hadn't been real (or permanent, at least) —except for the bone-grinding terror, of course.

"Well..." I began taking a sip of my drink. I had made it strong; I needed something to calm me down. "I think we've done well here today. After we all sleep it off we're going to get a rough edit going and then shop it around town."

Cthulhu didn't invade my mind this time, he just bobbed his head in a nod, gave me a scaly thumbs-up, took a sip of his drink, and smiled. Well, it wasn't a human smile, but I swear those undulating tentacles on his face formed a smile for just a moment.

We finished our drinks, and I babbled along in relief thinking that his smile had meant he really wasn't going to kill me. He then rose up, spreading his wings out.

"Time to go?" I asked. He subtly nodded his head. "Well, rest assured, I am all over this. I will make sure this movie is everything you want. People will be scared of you again, guaranteed. I will not rest until—"

One of his clawed hands darted out, and I felt a stabbing sensation in my chest and felt warmth trickling down my body. I looked down and saw he had pierced my heart and watched as my lifeblood ran down my chest and began to mix with the hot tub water.

I looked up at him in time to see him turn towards the stationary camera. He let out a roar that set car alarms off half a block away and knocked the camera over.

I looked back down and remembered what had been bugging me. We hadn't filmed my death scene. In all the rush, I had forgotten. Cthulhu hadn't.

Soon I wasn't looking at my chest anymore but looking down on my body as it bled into the hot tub. I watched as my limp flesh slid into the tub, my face swallowed by the reddening bubbles.

Huh, I thought, *I guess he did need a victim after all.* I looked around but Cthulhu was gone. My spirit, I guess you would say, slowly rose above my house, thoughts running through my mind. *Well, at least I got to make a move. Cthulhu's roar knocked the camera over. I hope the footage is still there. Wow, this is not so bad, this being dead thing—I see what Dennis was babbling about. Damn! I guess I won't get to keep that date with Doris.*

THE SOUND OF A SIREN, PIERCING AND SHARP, SLOWLY penetrated my consciousness. I felt strange, my limbs heavy, my breath coming in shallow gasps. Something was wrong. I slowly opened my eyes and found myself slumped in my hot tub, my mouth barely above the water. I fought to bring my limbs under control and lumbered over to the stairs and used the shiny metal handrail to drag myself out of the tub.

I was so hot, my mind sluggish. I dragged myself onto the cement, wanting to cool my body off. How long had I been in there?

As I crawled, my eye caught the stationary camera, the one Cthulhu had roared at, the one he had knocked over, except there it stood, its red "recording" light on. It all came rushing back to me.

I collapsed on the cement and giggled like a little girl. I was alive. He hadn't really killed me. I then promptly passed out and didn't wake up until the next morning.

As we worked on the movie, I kept worrying that Cthulhu would come back, that he had only spared me long enough to finish the movie. But he never did return. I consider it my bonus for a job well done.

"MY AGENT IS OUT OF HIS MIND ABOUT THIS," OLIVIA SAID IN my hot tub. She sat right where Cthulhu had sat a few weeks earlier.

I glanced up from my drink preparation and smiled. It was good to have some Olivia time without Tish around. She was, though, wearing a bathing suit. Back in the day she never wore a bathing suit in my hot tub. For once that thought didn't cause me pain.

"Really?" I asked as I handed her a drink and got into the hot tub. I was wearing a bathing suit too.

"He's seen the clip Juan put up on the website. He is freaking that he didn't know anything about this. That I somehow snuck off and shot this effects-heavy movie without going through him."

I smiled and let the bubbles massage my sore lower back. I had continued my lawyer duties as well as producing and directing the Cthulhu movie. I was tired.

"He's worried it's going to go big and I'm not going to make anything—or rather, he's not going to make anything."

I nodded. "I'll forward him the contract you signed. If any money is to be made, you'll get your share." I had taken care of Olivia. Just reflex, I couldn't help it.

I closed my eyes and let the water do its job. It is moments like this that I think hot water must be the very foundation of civilization. We were savages until we learned to deliver the wonders of steaming water on demand.

When I opened my eyes again Olivia was staring at me, a smiling playing on her lips. "So, who do you think will end up in your hot tub next?"

I smiled. "I'm hoping for Marilyn Monroe—many wrongs that need righting there."

Olivia shook her head. "Well, from what I hear, you've already got a Marilyn Monroe visiting your tub."

Hollywood, it's a small town in so many ways. Everyone knows your business. She was referring to Doris. We had become something of an item after the film. "She's a good kid and I think she has a fair shot as an actress."

"That voice..." Olivia said.

I smiled. Doris's voice had grown on me. "I've got her in with a plastics guy. He thinks he can fix it. But, I don't know, the voice makes her different. I think she should keep it."

Olivia gave me one of those looks, a mixture of penetrating gaze and bemused smile. "I'm happy for you, Frank." She swam over and kissed me on the cheek. "I gotta go. Tish and I are meeting up for dinner."

When she got out, I didn't even turn to watch her go. I sat there wondering who was going to show up in my hot tub next and what they would want.

BACKSTORY—LIGHTS, CAMERA, CTHULHU!

BACK IN THE TWENTIES, H.P. LOVECRAFT WROTE A LOT OF very creepy horror stories. Cthulhu was a staple of them. I am not a horror aficionado or a Lovecraft fan (although I've read a bit of his work), but when I started seeing Cthulhu become a silly meme on Facebook, it tickled something in me.

If Cthulhu were real, what would this ancient Elder God feel about his treatment? Enabling this memeification of Cthulhu was the fact that Lovecraft's works were no longer under copyright.

So, mix those two pieces with the low-tech approach of a movie like *The Blair Witch Project*, add a dash of romance, and out pops this strange tale.

This is not straight-up horror, but even playing there is an anomaly for me, and this is, frankly, a weird story.

So weird it just makes me smile.

PART TEN
CAFFEINE AND DIMPLES

CAFFEINE AND DIMPLES

It all started with that cute little redheaded barista who made me macchiato every morning. That small, shy smile, those adorable dimples—the indent of her left cheek deeper than the one on the right—that lilting southern accent. And, as I was leaving, she would always say, "Have a beautiful day John." And for some reason I believed her; silly me.

I know, I know, it's ironic, I get that. In the lobby of the corporate offices of the country's largest android manufacturer, humans are serving coffee. Quaint, right? And I was furious at first; I mean how would it look? We were barely holding on to the number one spot. How long until the news feeds did a piece on this, how long until I was a laughing stock CEO. So the moment I found out, I stormed down there, ripped open the door to the little place and made ready to unleash my wrath when—

"Good morning sir, welcome to Coffee Heaven. My name is Annabel. How can I make your day brighter?" I was stunned to silence, and had to swallow all the words and vitriol I had ready to launch. That wavy red hair, the slim delicate fingers, the melodious voice, and most of all—yes—the dimples turned me back into a stupid stammering teenager. "Ahh... Umm... A venti macchiato please."

She wasn't a normal woman, this wasn't my normal reaction. Normally I went for what I wanted, compensating for my short stature and bald head with confidence and wealth. But her, but this, was something I had never experienced. I was out of my depth, and it had been a long time since that had happened.

And to add to the irony, once it got around that I bought coffee there, the place was crowded with patrons. You see, all other tasks in the building that can be performed by androids are: janitorial, security; secretarial; etc. It turns out people are willing to pay more for a coffee and pastry from a cute southern belle than from a metallic android. Yeah, I know, I know, not surprising. I was just expecting some, you know, loyalty.

Now, I could wax poetic about love and the human soul and how neither can be truly known, but that is a *load of crap fresh from the farm*, as my Pa would say. It's not like I didn't go in dutifully every morning like a stammering idiot for some caffeine and dimples. I did, and I did it like a pimpled adolescent. It's just that I lacked the normal romantic idealization; I look at my reaction as a problem, and tried to solve it like I solved every other problem in my life.

"So nice to see you this morning John," she said my second day there. I thought, *John? How the hell does she know my name is John?* Then, of course, I remembered I was the guy on the top floor with the corner office and the killer view. Of course she knew my name. "How about a bear claw with your macchiato today? First one's free. I just know you'll love it." I just nodded my head yes like a mute idiot, staring at the left dimple and the sweep of her wavy auburn hair.

I HAD HER INVESTIGATED. THOROUGHLY. WHEN I ARRIVED IN

my office, my hands sticky from the bear claw and my eyes starry from the dimples, I was greeted by Greta, my assistant.

"Good morning sir, how are you today?" she said, a slight smile on her robotic face.

"I want to know everything about the redhead slinging coffee down stairs. Everything! Top priority, top secret."

"Very good sir," she said with a sharp nod. "Will there be anything else?"

Greta was our latest model executive assistant; I always used our latest model. Partially for show—it was good PR—and partially so I could find out what needed improvement and drive those lazy-ass engineers to fix it. She was smart, capable, and except for that damn bald metal head, quite beautiful. As she stood there, something quite uncomfortable occurred to me.

"Greta, who choose your accent?" I asked. She had an English accent, Birmingham specifically.

"Why, you did sir," she said, "during our intake session."

"Right. Thank you Greta, that will be all for now."

I sat there stunned. Do I have an unconscious thing for woman with accents?

IN THE MORNING WHEN I ARRIVED AT THE OFFICE—COFFEE and bear claw in hand—Greta said, "That dossier you requested is on your workstation, ready to be viewed.

Annabel Harper was 26 years old, born in Luverne, Alabama, graduated from Harvard Business School in the 90th percentile of her class. She lived alone with a boxer named Rex in a small brownstone she bought with money she inherited from her grandmother.

I nibbled on the bear claw as the presentation rolled; tearing small chunks of it off and eating it like I was eating popcorn at the movies, licking the sticky cinnamon glaze off my fingers.

The presentation had video of her college graduation, pictures of parties, boyfriends, and family; status on her social network; a credit report; college and high school transcripts; parking tickets; the contents of her sealed juvi conviction for possession of marijuana; and on and on. In a word, it was thorough. She had gotten the same treatment that a competitor of mine would have gotten.

And as thorough as it was, it wasn't enough. If this was a potential competitor, or an ally, my next move would be to spend some time with them, to learn what dry facts like these cannot tell.

"Greta!" I yelled.

"Yes sir?" she said as she ambled in.

"Is there any pending business we have with Ms. Harper? Like, signing a lease or waivers or something?"

She paused for a moment, her head cocked to the side; she was searching. "No sir, all paperwork is in order."

"Well then, make something up! I want to have her up here in my office this week."

I HAD PREPARED FOR THIS ENCOUNTER. I HAD FIRST ROLE played with Greta, and then had her wipe the memory of it. I then had a VR simulation put together—which was top secret with the damaging bits outsourced; my people just couldn't know about this. But it wasn't enough.

When she walked into the office, her dimples on full display, and said, "John? I wasn't expecting you. Well, what a pleasant surprise," I just sat there with my mouth agape.

I think what did me in was what she was wearing; or rather what she wasn't wearing. For once she didn't have her apron on, revealing more of the curves I had only imagined.

"Umm... Ahh... Please, please sit down." I said, indicating the chair across from me as I hastily stood up, knocking my own chair over.

I had planned, and practiced, to come around and stand next to her and show her the points of the document she was to sign. But I ended up fumbling with my own chair, giving her a fine view of my ass while I did it, and sitting back down with my face, I am sure, red.

"You want my permission to upgrade security in the shop?" She said, once I got myself back in a dignified position. She had already read through the document—fast reader, her dossier didn't mention that. But Harvard Business, what the hell was I thinking? That she would need it explained to her?

I nodded yes; it was the best that I could manage.

With a quick and graceful scribble the document was signed, and she was gone, leaving the strong scent of coffee and roses behind.

NEXT CAME THE PARADE OF THE ESCORTS. MY THEORY WAS that if I could find a woman that made me feel even half as weak as Annabel did, I could user her to conquer the flaw in my psyche, and maybe be able to talk to Annabel, or at least get over this silly infatuation.

Greta sent out a sketch of a woman who looked similar, but not the same, as Annabel (this was a top secret after all), and one by one the escort agencies sent them over to meet me.

And they were beautiful, and sexy, and many of them intelligent and witty, and even a few had lilting southern accents, but not a one of them made me weak in the knees. I needed something that looked, sounded, and acted just like her.

"THE UNCANNY VALLEY," I SAID TO THE ASSEMBLED engineers, scientists, and artists, "can one of you kindly explain it to me."

A middle aged dweeb with glasses and a greying ponytail raised his hand. That made me smile; it had taken a lot to get these creative types trained. "Go ahead," I said, glancing at Greta, who transmitted his name to my earbud. "Go ahead Mr. Humold."

"Sir. The uncanny valley is a hypothesis that states that the more human in appearance a non-human is, the greater the revulsion humans feel towards it."

"Right," I said. "When androids appear nearly human, but not fully human, it scares the shit out of us." There was a smattering of laughter. "And Humold, can you tell me why my otherwise lovely Greta is sporting this stylish, metal face?"

"Well Sir, to use your phrasing: so she doesn't scare the shit out of you." The laughter was louder this time, and I let it be. As long as they got the point.

"Right. Greta's appearance does not put her in the uncanny valley, which is important to our sales. We can't have our androids creeping people out. But it is time for that to change." That got their attention. Silence descended in the room. "From this day forward crossing that valley is our top priority, and I will be down here each day until we cross it."

WANT TO KNOW WHAT THE BEST WAY TO SCARE AN ENGINEER is? Tell them that management will be looking over their shoulder every day, that the big boss will be rolling up his sleeves and working besides them.

"With all due respect sir," Humold began. He was sitting in my office across my desk from me. The poor sap had been drafted to try to reason with me. He was clearly nervous and looked uncomfortable in the suit he had put on for the occasion. "We feel that deadline you have given us is unreasonable, and that daily inspections won't help, but in fact, will hinder our process."

When he was done, I let him squirm for a while. He kept

pulling on his collar, like the tie was strangling him. Poor dweeb probably didn't know his own neck size and had on a shirt that was too small. "Is that it?" I asked.

"Yes sir."

"And what do you think will be a reasonable deadline to cross the 'uncanny valley'?"

"Sir, I don't know. It has never been done; the problem has been worked on for decades without success."

"Exactly. Without sufficient motivation this project will drag on and on. You have six months." I waved him towards the door and turned my attention to some paperwork.

I heard him sigh and slowly get up. When he was at the door he asked, "And the daily inspections?" I was impressed, I knew he had wanted to ask, I just didn't know if he had the guts.

I looked up and saw that he was scared. Good, that is just the way I wanted him. It would motivate the whole lot of them to perform. "Tell you what Humold. If you are up here every morning at 7 am presenting the previous day's progress I may feel less inclined to go down to engineering."

"Yes sir. Thank you sir."

I chuckled after he left and yelled for Greta.

HERE LIES JOHN "THE TERMINATOR" FOSSEN, LAID LOW BY A *pair of dimples*, read the tombstone in my dream. I woke up terrified and sweating, and yelled, "Greta!"

"Yes sir," she said from my door as the lights slowly came up. This wasn't my office Greta, this was my home Greta. They shared files and memories and were, in all intents and purposes, the same. Having two saved me the annoyance of transporting her everywhere.

"Show me the goddamn footage again."

The screen rolled down from the ceiling and the footage

played. The scene was a small lab and a few dweebs in white coats and a redheaded woman sitting on a stool. Humold was not visible, but it was his voice narrating the scene. "As you can see Mr. Fossen, we have nearly crossed the valley when she is at rest." And I had to admit, they had. The dimples were intact, the red hair silky smooth, the green eyes shining. "But," Humold continued, "We still have a long way to go to deal with the face while in motion. Jane, how are you today?" He said coming into frame talking to the woman.

"Well, I am just fine. How are you?" She said. The voice was right, dead on, but when her face moved, the materials did not move right, and she went from cute to scary.

"Greta, I want to go to the lab tomorrow, set it up. Humold only, have everyone else clear out."

"Yes sir."

That was it for sleep; I spent the rest of the night pacing. My first attempt to cross the valley had been an abject failure. I had called a halt to it after 3 months. I then created a smaller, top secret, highly incentivized team led by Humold. They had made solid progress, but it wasn't enough.

Annabel had a boyfriend now, and it was looking like it was getting serious. I had to get over this, and soon, if I was to have even the smallest chance. After close to 5 months, the best I had done was—

I stopped pacing and said, "Play video named 'Stupid, Stupid John'."

The scene that came up on the screen was of the coffee shop. A sharp dressed, bald man of diminutive stature (me) walked in and cut to the front of the line. The redhead, Annabel, looked up and said, "Why good morning John. Your usual?"

"Yes..." the man began, swallowing hard. "Yes Annabel, that would be *appropriate*." Damn! Why had I said appropriate? I had practiced my one line over and over before I can come in. "That would be lovely," was what I was supposed to say.

The woman's eyes brightened and her dimples deepened into a smile, "Why John, I didn't think you knew my name."

That man on the screen is clearly sweating, his brow deeply furrowed, "I... Why... Of course I..."

"Here you go John, have a beautiful day," she said.

Once the man left the shop there were some whispers and snickers. None of those people worked for me anymore.

"SHE IS THE SAME MODEL AS GRETA," HUMOLD EXPLAINED, wearing a tie again and pulling at his collar. "It is only the head that is different, and some software modifications to manage the face."

"Excellent," I answered. This was the first time I had been in her presence. "Leave, now. Take the rest of the day off."

He looked puzzled, he was probably wondering if I was about to fire him. "Leave!" I yelled. He scurried out.

"Greta, shut down the video and audio security and guard the door. I am not to be disturbed under any circumstances."

"Yes sir."

I pulled up a stool and just sat in front of her. She was in standby mode and completely still. The face was really remarkable; they had gotten the skin right, which was far from easy. Skin is translucent, and it is the light reflecting off its surface, as well as deeper layers, that makes it look like skin.

"Greta, take a note." I whispered. Even though she was on the other side of the room I knew she could hear me. "Review the files on this skin. Do we have any patents in process? Where are our competitors on this?"

I touched the face, gently probing it with my fingers, feeling tremors deep in my belly. The face didn't quite feel normal. It was cool to the touch, and while the hard surface underneath it felt right, the skin and the tissue below it were too stiff and a little too thick. I began to sweat.

"Wake up Jane," I said after I had pulled my hands away.

"Why hello Mr. Fossen," she said, her dimples more creasing than deepening as she smiled. I turned away.

"You look lovely today Ana— Jane."

"Thank you Mr. Fossen, that is so kind."

"John, please call me John." My palms were sweating. I closed my eyes and concentrated on my memory of her face, what it felt like to touch even a simulacrum of it.

"OK. John."

"Tell me about yourself."

"Oh, I'd love to. I am a Fossen Industries android prototype—"

"Power down," I growled as I stomped my way out. "Greta, wipe her memories of our encounter. And setup another lab with a copy of that thing that only I have access to."

———

You see the dweebs that work for me forget that I used to be one of them, that I started this damn company in my parent's barn 25 years ago. I get it; it's easy for them to forget with me running around making unreasonable demands of them. It's not like I ask any more from them, than I ask of myself.

Greta, bless her silicon heart, set up a private lab for me that adjoined my office. She had to kick out some VP of Marketing to do it, but she did it. I am sure it was the talk of town: did the short guy still have it?

And if truth be told, I doubted it myself. Briefly.

I stopped wasting time watching Annabel work and went to work myself. I would plow through the corporate work as soon as I could and got to the lab usually by 4 pm. Around midnight Greta would drag me out and send me home. And I fought her, most every night, but she was strong enough to force me if she needed to.

I didn't worry about the face, at first. It was the personality I was concerned with. So I put those hundreds of hours of surveillance footage to good work and started in depth analysis of how she spoke, how she moved, her mannerisms and the like.

It was slow going, but I loved it. It forced me out of love-struck pimple-headed-teenager mode and made me really analyze what made up, what was to me, such an attractive package.

I would isolate something, like the way she would always look down briefly before making eye contact, run that through a simulated virtual reality Annabel, and once it was working there, move it over to the android Annabel.

And on it went: wiping her hands on her apron before she took your credit card; the abbreviated curtsy and "thank you so much" when a sizeable tip was left; the twirling dance she would do when she was cleaning and alone in the shop.

A month of this passed and when I went for my morning caffeine and dimples I could actually get a few words out.

"Good morning John, it's a beautiful day, isn't it? I am so glad spring is finally coming," she said.

"Lovely Annabel, lovely."

"OK John, there you go. You have a beautiful day."

"You too."

It wasn't much, but it was something, and it gave me hope that whatever sickness had plagued me, could be cured. I also took to paying in cash so I could stuff the tip jar and get the extra "thank you".

As the android's personality developed, I used her as practice. The face wasn't quite right, but I really didn't care. I would turn the lights down and just practice on her. It was just silly little stuff, like the weather and the news, but it made a difference. Soon I could actually hold a real conversation with the real Annabel.

In fact, I think we were starting to develop a little bit of a friendship. It's kind of hard to tell when your interactions occur in 30 second snippets, but it felt like progress to me. Through all that I learned from having her investigated, and watching the security footage, and imprinting her personality on the android, I thought that I was getting to know her. But, really, I was wrong. So wrong.

I WAS HAVING A VERY HAPPY MORNING. I HAD JUST DELIVERED Annabel a personal invitation to the company picnic and told her that I hoped to see her there, to which she replied with a thrilling, "I wouldn't dare miss it." I was on top of the world. I knew she had recently gotten engaged, but that didn't matter to me. I had conquered my irrational fear of her and that is what counted.

I was in an early afternoon meeting with my VPs when she came storming into the office.

"I... I... I can't believe you. What you did!"

"Sorry sir," Greta said from behind her, "she slipped passed me."

My heart was pounding in my ears, and I experienced a level of fear that it had been years since I had felt. It was thrilling.

"If you'll excuse me gentleman, it looks like I am double booked and I'm afraid I need to talk to Ms. Harper." The VPs rushed out, with looks of surprise and delight on their faces. I am sure the gossip was epic.

Annabel held her tongue, her face red, until they had all left and Greta had closed the door. "This... this is an outrage!"

Her standing there alone in my office so outraged, her green eyes flashing dangerously, her hands clutching an envelope to her chest, well... it turned me on.

My inhibitions nearly gone, in my mind I grabbed her and kissed her hard. She struggled at first, briefly, and then kissed back with an unexpected strength, her teething biting into my lip. I swept my desk clear and threw her on it, ripping her blouse open, buttons flying all over the place. I then began kissing her neck, moving lower and lower—

"John! John!" she said interrupting me from my fantasy. "John, did you hear a word I said? I know what you have been up to. And why do you have that damn silly grin on your face?"

"Photos," I said, regaining my composure, "you said something about photos."

"Here they are!" She opened the envelope and spilled them onto my desk. Large 8x10 glossies of me and android Annabel. "What the hell do you have to say for yourself?"

I looked at her, my face stony. This was serious now. "Hold that thought Annabel, you deserve answers and I promise, I will give them to you, but first I have something very urgent to attend to."

"I... I..." she stammered and stuttered.

"Greta! Lock the building down. Now. Code red! No one gets in or out until all security bots have been replaced. All current bots need to be scanned for viruses." I turned to Annabel, "Please, Annabel, tell me where you got those photos."

She still looked furious, but answered my question. "A man just came into the shop and handed me the envelope. He said, 'I thought you might want to know what your friend John is up to.'"

"Excellent!" I said, her anger turning puzzled. "Greta, I need security footage from Annabel's shop from about 15 minutes ago. I need it now! Also, call the SFPD and let them know what we are up to. Tell them if they send a few cars around, sirens blazing, I will owe them one."

Greta strolled in as the screen descended from the ceiling. "Lockdown complete, SFPD has been notified, here is the footage you requested."

With Annabel's help we located the man that had delivered the envelope and using the "enhanced security" we had installed in her shop we were able to get a good facial image of the man. This was transmitted to my investigative team.

When there was a moment of quiet Annabel asked, "What is this about John?"

I was about to answer, but we were interrupted by a team of sweepers that scanned my office and then moved into the lab. After they had passed, and found several monitoring devices, I said, "Industrial espionage. That man who gave you the pictures is trying—"

"I'm not stupid John," she answered, her cheeks starting to flush red again "I know what he was doing. That is not what I meant, and I think you know it."

I sighed and got up and led her into the recently vacated lab. Sitting there demurely on a stool was android Annabel. I heard a gasp when Annabel saw her. I wasn't surprised; a picture was one thing, seeing it was something entirely different.

"Annabel," I said to the android, "I want you to meet Ms. Harper."

The android got up, smiled, looked down briefly before meeting Annabel's eyes, and said, "I am so glad to meet you Ms. Harper."

Annabel ran.

I HAD GRETA TELL SECURITY TO LET HER OUT OF THE building and had her followed, discretely, to make sure she was OK. She ran out of the building, walked around the block several times and then took a cab home. After I had finished up supervising the fallout from the security breach, I went to see her.

When she opened the door of her brownstone for me, she was pale.

"Tea?" she asked once we were in her living room.

"That would be lovely Annabel," I replied. I was still thrilled that I could talk to her, and that I could put "lovely" and "Annabel" together in a sentence and not sound like a crazed stalker—I hoped.

When she came back with the tea, her face had hardened. She put down the tray, with its tiny china cups and teapot, poured for us and said, "Explain yourself. Now. No bullshit."

I took a deep breath, a sip of tea, cursed when I burned my

tongue, stared at my shoes, ran my fingers through what remained of my hair—

"Now!" she yelled.

No one got away with a tone like that with me. No one. It created an energy in me that overrode my traces of shame, and lingering shyness.

So I told her. All of it. I told her in a gush of words about how her presence affected me and everything I had done to master it, including all the surveillance and the millions of dollars I had spent developing android Annabel.

She was silent the entire time taking it in, staring at me, unmoving. It helped that she was so still, it was almost like I was in my lab practicing my speech with the android and not with the real Annabel.

When my speech was over, she got up, squatted in front of me, and kissed me.

It wasn't the hard aggressive kiss I had imagined; it was softer and more delicate. Her lips were silky, like rose petals, and as her lips met mine a band of butterflies started rioting in my stomach. Quite out of character, I let her take the lead. She placed her hand on the back of my head and held me there for what felt like an eternity and also like a fleeting instant.

When it was done she looked at me with her brows furrowed, her face frozen in a question. I wondered, was it: wow, that was amazing; or wow, I didn't feel a damn thing; or strange, he tastes like bacon. I didn't recover fast enough to ask. Before I knew it she stood up, smoothing her skirt, and said, "John, I think you should go."

My mouth opened as if to say something, but nothing came out. So I just sat there like a gaped mouth idiot.

"And from now on," she continued, "just phone your order down and I'll have someone bring it up."

She turned then and walked into the kitchen, leaving me alone to let myself out.

I SENT HER A DOZEN ROSES FOR A DOZEN DAYS; EACH DELIVERY was refused. I had gifts of jewelry left in the shop; each of those was moved out to the lobby for some random stranger to acquire. After that, I got the message, and left her alone. She didn't want to be wooed.

I don't understand women. I know, I know, this is a problem as old as mankind. But I wish I did. I wish I understood what made her kiss me and what made her turn me away. Well, after all I did, I fully understand why she didn't want to have anything to do with me—invasion of privacy and the like—but the kiss? I just don't get it.

And wouldn't that be a fabulous business to be in: divining the motivations of women for men. Now there's a business with a high profit margin in it. Love sick pigs like myself would pay a fortune to understand.

What came next, I was more capable of understanding.

First came the couriered contract, followed by a call to Greta to setup an appointment between me and her lawyer. Finally, she wanted something, I was hopeful. Irrationally so, but hopeful.

The contract had two major features: Annabel would work with my engineers (but not me) to perfect the android Annabel in exchange for a sizeable lump sum payment and royalties on the "uncanny valley" technology; and that I would cease all surveillance and agree not to knowingly come within 100 yards of her. A civil restraining order, if you will.

Her demands were not unreasonable. If we could cross the uncanny valley, it would mean a large amount of money, and secure Fossen Industries in the number one spot. Her cooperation would help; her unknowing cooperation (with all the surveillance) had already helped. But with her help, we could do body scans, motion capture, and MRIs of her face to get the structure down better. The business aspect of it really excited me. How many people out there would pay big for a near duplicate of somebody?

"Greta!" I yelled. "Get our lawyers involved in this and have them negotiate the amounts down and come up with some stupid changes and send the contract back. Also add a stipulation that Annabel and I must sign the contract in person, and that she must give me 30 minutes of her time alone."

ANNABEL PACED BACK IN FORTH IN MY OFFICE WHILE I SAT behind my desk. The negotiations had taken a few weeks, and the contracts were laid out ready to sign.

"Why did you want to see me John?" she asked.

"You know why," I answered.

"Pretend I don't. Explain it to me."

"I want you."

That stopped her pacing. She stood with her hands on her hips and stared at me. I don't think she expected so direct a response. "There is only one way—one way—that is going to happen..."

She had my attention, but left it hanging there. "What?" I asked when I couldn't stand it anymore.

"Make a fully-skinned, sexually-enabled android version of me, then you can do anything you want with it."

I was stunned into silence. It wasn't what I wanted, I wanted the real thing. But, my god, what an idea. Why hadn't I thought of that before? It would take years and years, but it would change everything.

She must have read something on my face. She said, "What? You hadn't thought that? The mighty John Fossen being out thought by a barista?"

I just nodded my head in ascent. "You have outdone me in every way Annabel."

"Flattery is not going to help you here."

"I know. And, for what it is worth, I am sorry."

Her face softened then, she must have believed me. "Thank you John, I appreciate that."

"And I wish we could at least be friends."

Annabel laughed, sat down across from me, and began signing the contracts. "John, you know you're not that kind of person. You don't have female friends, except maybe for your mother and your sister... and *maybe* Greta."

I nodded. "But I would try," I said meekly, but she just laughed again.

Soon the contracts were all signed and Annabel got up and moved towards the door. "Stop," I said. "I still have a few minutes left."

"Really?" she asked.

I felt terrible, pitiful, for asking for them, but they were mine and I wanted them. "I just have one more question."

She sighed and said, "OK."

"Why did you kiss me?"

She shrugged her shoulders, laughed, and said, "Why not?"

"GOOD MORNING JOHN," ANDROID ANNABEL SAID FROM behind the counter. "You want the usual: macchiato and bear claw?"

"That'd be great Annabel." She wasn't perfect, not quite. Five years running and that damned uncanny valley was still not completely crossed. We compensated for it though: the lighting; the way her hair fell on her face; and much smaller dimples.

But on the plus side there was one of these manning each of the 150 Annabel's Coffee Heavens throughout the country. Consistent, flawless service delivered by an adorable redhead with a lilting southern accent. She produced more income than a metallic android, so all in all it was working out well.

And me and the real Annabel? Nothing more to say, that day we signed contracts was the last day I ever saw her. And I can't really say I am unhappy with how it turned out. Fossen Industries is solidly on top of the android biz, and the developments on the "fully-skinned, sexually-enabled" android that she suggested are well under way. There is no stopping us now.

So what did you expect? I'm not some sappy, incurable romantic. That caffeine and those dimples didn't take me where I expected, but honestly, for a guy like me, what could be better?

BACKSTORY—CAFFEINE AND DIMPLES

THE UNCANNY VALLEY IS A REAL TERM AND A REAL PROBLEM. If you've viewed any early attempts at realistic CGI humans you know what I mean. We have so much of our brains dedicated to recognizing faces that when they are slightly off it's creepy.

This story was inspired by a fairly good novella I read (whose title has escape my frail memory) that featured an unlikeable protagonist. Most of the time my protagonists are very likeable, but this book made we want to try one that wasn't very likeable. His shyness is, hopefully, relatable, but he's not my typical protagonist.

It was fun to imagine that shyness and lust just might be the reason we finally find ourselves at the other end of the uncanny valley.

This story received an honorable mention in the Writers of the Future Contest.

PART ELEVEN

CONNOR BRIGHT AND THE CASE OF THE PURPLE UNICORN

CONNOR BRIGHT AND THE CASE OF THE PURPLE UNICORN

THE RINGING OF THE PHONE IS LIKE A DENTIST'S DRILL TO MY sodden consciousness. I groan, realizing I hadn't managed to get undressed when I tumbled into bed. Again. I feel for my cell phone on the nightstand, my hand connecting with a half-eaten microwave burrito before finding it.

"G'day, you got Bright," I say, remembering even in my hungover state to use my B-movie quality Australian accent.

"Got a job for you, but you've got to get here quick." The voice is feminine and a tad husky. Detective Trisha Sanchez. Why the hell is she calling me? After that jacked-up stakeout, I'm her least favorite private investigator in the Phoenix metro area.

"What kind of a job?" I say, my voice rough from too long in a noisy bar working as a bouncer and too many cheap beers afterward. I look around my shit hole of a bedroom. Dirty laundry, trash, the spring heat of the desert morning flowing in the open window. "And can they pay?"

An Australian accent is easy. Just elongate your vowels—"paay" instead of "pay"—and throw in the occasional "mate" and "g'day."

In the desert southwest, that and changing my name to Conner Bright, keeps my past at bay.

"They can. It's a murder, Bright, so get your ass out here now. No booze or I'll throw you in the drunk tank."

"Aces. Happy to help."

"Texting you the address now." She hangs up.

After some mouthwash for breakfast, I stop by the old cookie tin that sits on the top of my little entertainment center. It's got a shameful layer of dust on top and holds the ashes of my father inside. "Hey, Dad," I say, without a trace of an Australian accent. "I've got a case. An important one."

Sitting next to the tin is a DVD of *Crocodile Dundee*. My dad took me to that movie in 1986 when it came out. I was thirteen and loved it, but not as much as he did. When we exited, he'd said, "Now that's a man, son. That's a man."

I GET OUT OF MY 1976 EL CAMINO, MY COWBOY BOOTS crunching on the dry ground as I approach the murder scene. It's a hot day, and since the El Camino doesn't have air conditioning, I'm already sweating. I'm at a little ranch in the desert between Phoenix and Wickenburg, Arizona. This is a big deal. There's lots of cowboys and lots of guns around here, but not that many murders in the sticks.

I get the usual assortment of looks as I duck under the yellow tape. Looks of surprise from folks that don't know me, looks of recognition or disdain from those that do. The disdain belongs to Trisha Sanchez, the detective who called me in.

And the looks from the others, it's what I expect. I'm tall and slim; at 6'5" and 170 pounds, some people call me scarecrow. I've got a bowie knife with an eleven-inch blade on my belt, a crocodile claw hanging around my neck, and a wide-brimmed bush hat on my head, all to go with my Australian accent.

"G'day, Detective," I say, tipping my hat to Sanchez as she strides away from the murder scene. She's in her late-thirties, short and wiry, wearing reflective sunglasses.

"Your client's in the house," she says, grabbing my arm and pulling me away. I resist a moment, watching Helen Montana, one of the medical examiners, leaning over the prone form of a gray-haired Mexican man that has a ragged hole in his chest.

"Where we goin'?" I ask.

"To see your client, Irene. She asked for someone to help her solve this murder."

"And you called me?" Something isn't right.

She pauses, her hand still locked around my bicep, her head jabbing back to the scene. "At this point we're ruling it an accident. The victim, Edwardo Campos, has got a big hole in his chest, and we found a bull running loose with blood on his horn."

She starts to pull me forward again toward the one-story ranch house. It's small with blue vinyl siding that was popular in the seventies. The blue has started to fade, and the house looks like it has seen better days.

"Then what the hell am I doin' here?"

Sanchez smiles, showing her perfectly white teeth, looking something like a shark. "The kid says she saw it happen."

I shrug.

"She says it was a man riding a purple unicorn that killed her great-uncle."

I ALMOST DON'T GO IN. I ALMOST MARCH BACK TO MY EL Camino until Sanchez says the magic words. "She's got cash." I think of the delinquent notices stacked on my little kitchen table. I think how I'd love not to buy the cheapest damn beer in the store.

It's surprisingly neat inside the house. Not fancy, but everything's put away, the wood floors swept, the old throw rugs shook out. The living room isn't much—an old couch with a brown blanket thrown over it, a wooden rocking chair, and a shelf full of books. No TV, no stereo. It looks very much like what this house probably looked like a hundred years ago.

Sitting awkwardly in the rocking chair is a tall deputy with blond hair. He gives Sanchez a brief look of relief before scurrying out.

And then I see the girl. She's got long black hair, big brown eyes, and is maybe eight years old. I almost leave again.

"Irene," Sanchez says, "this is Conner Bright. He's the private detective I was telling you about. He's got a reputation for dealing with unusual cases."

With that Sanchez leaves. I stand there awkwardly, my hands shoved into my jeans, wishing I hadn't answered the phone this morning.

The girl's wearing a purple shirt and has a stuffed unicorn on the couch next to her. On the table in front of her is a battered hardcover of *The Last Unicorn*.

Great. Of course she saw a purple unicorn. She's obsessed with them.

"Where are you parents?" I ask.

She just shakes her head. Ah hell, she's an orphan too.

I lower myself into the rocking chair, wishing the hard seat was padded. The room smells of must and wood polish. "You got any family?"

She shakes her head again, her hands sitting placidly in her lap.

"I'm sorry about what happened to your great-uncle out there."

Her brow furrows and she stares at me a moment before saying, "Where you from?" Judging from her uncle and her appearance, I expect her to have a Mexican accent, but she doesn't. Not a trace.

"Australia," I lie. But it's a lie I tell everyone. "A little place called Scatterwood deep in the outback."

"You don't believe I saw a unicorn." She says it straight up, her voice steady, her eyes clear.

I shake my head.

"I did," she says, her voice too hard for someone so young. "And you have to prove it." She pulls out a wad of hundred-dollar bills from her pocket and slaps them on the coffee table in front of her. I notice light red stains on her hands and I imagine them pressed against her dead great-uncle's chest.

I know I should say no, but three thousand is a lot for me. A whole lot. I rub my suddenly sweating palms on my jeans. I'm dying for a drink. That would clear my head. Help me think this through.

"Well?" she asks.

I get up and start pacing. "Why don't you tell me what you saw."

THE GIRL TALKS, I PACE, MY FEET FINDING SQUEAKY BOARDS IN the old floor. The money is in a jumbled pile on the coffee table in front of her. I want it even more than I want a drink.

"Been here for a few months," she says. "Came after the accident . . ." Her face darkens, and she blinks several times. "We moved around a lot, Mama, Papa, and me. We picked grapes in California, pecans in Oregon."

"Your parents were illegals?" I ask.

She nods. "But I was born here. After the accident, Uncle Ed came and got me. He was afraid they'd send me back to Mexico."

"Tell me about your great-uncle," I say.

She shrugs. "He raises cows, rides horses."

I look at the wad of hundred-dollar bills and then back to her, doubting that was all he did.

"And last night?"

Irene pauses, her hands finally leaving her lap as she wraps them around her chest and shivers. "Uncle Ed was so happy. Said things would be changing today, like a birthday party but better.

Said it would be good. We were reading when the animals started making noise. He took his gun and told me to stay.

"I wasn't scared until I heard a shout. I went to the window and peeked through the curtain. That's when I saw it."

"The unicorn?" I ask, keeping my tone as even as possible.

She nods. "The moon was full so I could see good. At first I thought it was a horse with a man riding it. But then I saw the horn and the dark purple fur. Uncle Ed was real surprised. That man spurred the unicorn hard, and it ran down my uncle, its horn hitting him . . . right in the . . . He . . . I . . ." She trails off into soft sobs. I feel for the kid. She's suffered way too many losses in the past few months.

The tears don't last long. She takes a deep breath, holds it for a few beats, and slowly lets it out. She wipes the tears from her cheeks, her eyes hardening. "The man got off the unicorn and came in here."

"What did you do?"

"I hid behind the door. He walked in like he had been here before. Went right to the kitchen. I hid behind the couch and watched. I couldn't see much. There was banging, crashing, and a bunch of beeps. He marched out holding some papers."

"Did he see you? Did you get a good look at him?"

She shakes her head. "He had a bandana over his mouth. I don't think he saw me. He walked right out, got on his unicorn, and rode away."

I nod and walk into the small kitchen. One of the plain hand-made wooden cabinets is open, cans spilling out onto the counter and the floor. In the cabinet is a small metal safe embedded into the wall. The door is ajar, and the safe is empty.

"Is that where you got the money?" I ask after I walk back into the living room.

Irene nods, her hands back onto her lap, her eyes way too calm.

I'T'S A HOT DAY AND THE CORPSE OF EDWARDO CAMPOS IS going to stink to high heaven soon. The smell of blood and urine and horse manure is already overpowering.

"It looks like a horn did this," Helen Montana says, pulling away the bloodied cowboy shirt that used to be a powder blue. There's been a lot of foot traffic, but I did find a few fresh hoof-prints leading to the corpse. She gets up, brushing absently at her ponytailed blonde hair. Helen is a tall, big-boned woman with blue eyes and a great smile. She's my age at around forty. There's been sparks, and we've briefly dated a few times, but never a sustained flame. Working with her is always a bit awkward.

She walks several paces back to a yellow CSI marker where I located the hoofprints right next to a shotgun. "It looks like he was hit here and thrown back."

"The bull did it?" I ask.

"I'll know more when I do the autopsy."

I nod, glancing back to the faded blue ranch house.

"Sorry, Conner," she says, and I hear that sweetness in her voice that makes work hard.

"Did they get a blood sample from the bull's horn?" I ask.

She chuckles and looks over to a corral where two deputies are trying to get a rope around the bull. He's a big Hereford and doesn't appear to be cooperating. "Maybe you should go show them how it's done."

I shake my head, feeling uncomfortable. Helen was born in upstate New York and has a thing for cowboys. Could explain her interest in a mess like me.

Sanchez walks up, her arms folded. "You taking the case?"

"Any other witnesses?" I ask, pointing at a smaller building back behind the blue house.

Sanchez shakes her head. "Campos used to have a ranch hand living there. The neighbors told us he left a few months ago before the girl got here. Said they were close, that the old man treated him like a son, but something happened."

"Did you call CPS, Child Protective Services?"

She nods. "Doesn't look like they can get out here today."

"Why the hell not?"

"Budget cuts. Short staffed. You know the drill."

"And what about Irene?"

Sanchez chuckles and smiles at me again. "You take the case, you take the girl." She walks away looking like she's having the time of her life, paying me back for that stakeout with this mess.

I GO HELP THE DEPUTIES WITH THE BULL. NOT THAT I WANT to get into the corral with a ton of pissed off beef. I need to think. And to think, I need to move. Everyone, including Detective Sanchez, knows I need the cash. But taking a little girl's money on a wild-goose chase doesn't seem proper.

I climb over the fence and hop down onto the churned brown dirt of the corral. It stinks of horse and cow, but at least it doesn't smell of death. The jolt of the hop doesn't do my sacrum any good, and I feel each and every one of my old rodeo injuries. I rode bulls for a while, but mostly worked as a rodeo clown—keeping other riders safe was the right kind of crazy for me.

"You're just makin' the old boy mad," I shout to the two deputies. One is the lanky blond from the house. "Back away." They comply promptly.

I scrape some oats out of the bottom of the feed trough and get the specimen collection swab from the tall deputy and amble over toward the bull.

Those deputies may have been born and raised in Arizona, but they ain't no cowboys. They were afraid and trying to overpower an animal that's five times their weight. Stupid.

"Hi ya, boy," I say gently as I approach, the hand with the oats outstretched. I keep my eye on the bull and walk slowly. This is no rodeo bull used to bucking guys like me off. This fellow's older, probably kept around for stud duties. He didn't want to fight, but he didn't want to be bullied either.

People think cows are dumb, but they ain't. They seek safety and comfort just like the rest of us. The bull's big brown eyes finally leave mine and flick to the handful of oats. I'm two paces away and I stop walking, the final choice has to be his.

My left hand has the swab in it, and I hold it just back from the oats. I'd be a fool to spring it on him while he was eating. His nostrils flair and his eyes flick to the swab and back to the oats. He doesn't like the sharp alcohol scent of the swab, but he wants the oats.

I stand there like I don't care and just keep talking to him. He eventually takes two steps forward, his soft mouth in my hand as his rough tongue licks up the oats. I wipe the swab against the red stain on his horn, and when he's done eating, I back slowly away.

A crowd has gathered, and there's a smattering of applause. When I'm clear of the bull, I look back and see Helen holding Irene on the other side of the corral. Detective Sanchez is there, a question on her face.

"THE GIRL IS TRAUMATIZED," I SAY TO SANCHEZ. WE'RE OUT of earshot of Helen and Irene, who are both staring at us as we walk the dirt driveway. "She needs a professional."

"The system sucks," she says, "but the girl needs something to do, and running around with you trying to find a purple unicorn might be better than her hanging out in the sheriff's office."

I'm about to say something stupid when it occurs to me that this must be Sanchez's way of looking out for the girl. But why me? "What about the robbery? There's somethin' that ain't right."

She shrugs and points towards the bull. "I've got the killer right there. As to the money, the old man just realized he bought a bunch of Home Depot stock on a whim back in the eighties. He's suddenly rich, that explains the money, and besides, the safe wasn't forced open. Until I have evidence to the contrary, I'm done."

I nod and look back at the girl. Helen has her by the hand and is walking her away from the crime scene and towards the pasture. The girl needs someone, that much is certain. But me? A mostly drunk, past-his-prime cowboy pretending to be Australian?

"Look, Bright," Sanchez says. "Just take the girl for the day. Take any clue you can find and run it down with her. I'll call you when the social workers are ready for her."

Sanchez walks away and starts barking orders. I don't fight it. I owe her.

I keep Irene in the house while Helen finishes with the corpse and hauls him away.

It's odd that the murderer wanted those papers, but didn't care about the money. And that damn unicorn keeps tripping me up. Maybe there was no robbery. Maybe Irene knew the combination and got into the safe herself.

I'm standing in the mess of a kitchen staring off into space when I notice Irene looking at me. Her eyes have that too-wide look of shock. That's why she's been so restrained. The poor kid is in shock. Sanchez was right, she needs something to do.

"All righty then," I say, stooping down and picking up a can. "Get over here and help me clean this up."

"Clean?" Irene says.

I nod. "There could be a clue here, so we're gonna clean up this mess and see what we can find."

While Irene is in the kitchen, I go searching Edwardo's

bedroom. It's small and neat, with a twin bed, an old wooden chest at the end, a small closet, and a cross on the wall.

I start in the closet, going through the pale blue cowboy shirts—the man liked to dress the same every day—and patting down the two dark blue blazers. Each of them has a matchbook from the same place. The Sugar and Spice, a "gentlemen's club" in downtown Phoenix.

So the old man liked to look at young women.

"Did your Uncle Ed go out much?" I ask Irene back in the kitchen.

Irene nods. "Every Saturday night. He didn't think I knew, but he snuck out after I went to bed. Stayed out real late. He always came back smelling like smoke." She wrinkles her nose.

It's Monday morning, Edwardo was killed Sunday night. Maybe something happened at Sugar and Spice. I show Irene the matchbooks.

"What is it?" she asks.

"A clue, Irene. It's a clue."

THE SUGAR AND SPICE IS A PINKISH BUILDING WITH BRIGHT neon that sits between a bank and a fast-food joint off a busy street in central Phoenix. I shift uncomfortably in the seat of the El Camino as I drive by for the fourth time. It's Irene sitting next to me that makes me feel uncomfortable.

The fifth time I drive by, Irene sighs and says, "Just pull in."

I park behind the building.

"Are we going in?" Irene asks.

"You're kiddin', right?"

"I know what goes on in there. Men look at girls." She ends by rolling her eyes.

My reputation's bad enough without dragging an eight-year-old into a strip club right before turning her over to CPS. "Not gonna happen, love," I say as I get out the car. I walk over and open the door for her. She looks puzzled, but gets out and follows me to the McDonald's next door. As I do this, I'm convinced that I'm not the only man that's dropped off a little girl at this McDonald's before ducking into Sugar and Spice.

She doesn't complain, but she grabs my hand and holds it as we cross the hot asphalt. Her hand feels so small in mine, and I look down at her and she's looking at me with a tiny smile on her face. That look of trust scares the hell out of me.

THE INSIDE OF SUGAR AND SPICE SMELLS OF DESPERATION, with a bored blond dancing and a few rumpled men watching. I give the bartender a twenty and show him the picture of Edwardo Campos that Irene gave me. He tells me Edwardo was there the night before last, buying drinks and celebrating like he'd just won the lottery or something.

On the way out of Sugar and Spice, I'm confused. I have no motive for murder, and no idea why a robber would leave behind a wad of cash—or ride a purple unicorn, for that matter.

I'm not looking and collide with a man on his way in while I'm on the way out, the Phoenix heat swirling around us.

"Sorry, mate," I say, looking at the stranger. He's got on alligator-skin cowboy boots, a Stetson hat, sharp green eyes, and a sneer. He's almost as tall as me, but a lot beefier.

"Watch it, buddy," he grumbles, moving past quickly. I'm distracted by his boots, which would make a fine addition to my Australian cowboy look.

I get halfway to the El Camino when Irene runs up and wraps her arms around me. "That's him," she whispers between gulping breaths. "The man that came into my house. That killed Uncle Ed."

"How do you know?"

"The boots. The eyes. I'll never forget them."

AN EL CAMINO IS A CRAPPY CAR TO TAIL SOMEONE IN. Especially mine. With its shiny blue paint job and tricked-out rims, it stands out. This car is the one thing in my life that I truly take care of. I love it. It's a car, but it's got a bed like a truck. It's rare. It used to be my dad's.

Irene is sitting right next to me, eyes wide. She smells of cheap beef, french fries, and fear. Her closeness feels strangely good.

We follow Alligator Boots in his red Ford F-150 from Sugar and Spice to a Circle K where he stops for gas. I pull into the carpet place next door. When he ducks into the Circle K, I make to get out of the car, but Irene grabs me.

"Don't go," she says. "Please."

I get lost in those big brown eyes of hers. I'm not used to someone needing me.

"I'll be right back. No worries." Those eyes don't look like they believe me.

I walk casually over to the truck and place my cell phone in the back. What I see there makes me gasp. It's a long horn with spiral ridges running its length. It's an honest-to-god unicorn horn. I'm dizzy for a moment. Did Irene really see what she thought she saw?

As I look closer, I see that the tip of the horn is rough, as if it broke off, and the other end has an odd leather harness on it.

I rush back to the car, my heart pounding hard.

IT FEELS STRANGE, LIKE I'M MISSING SOMETHING. I'VE LEFT Irene with the morgue's receptionist. I had called in on a burner phone I bought at the Circle K to have Sanchez trace my cell so I could keep tabs on Alligator Boots. She told me Helen needed to see me and it was urgent.

Helen is pacing when I walk in. Her blue eyes are a bit wide and remind me of Irene's. Does Helen need me too?

The corpse of Edwardo Campos is laid out on a metal table, the wound to his chest all that much more shocking being exposed—no shirt to hide it, no blood to mask it. It's a big, red hole near his heart.

The morgue is pretty small. A couple of shining tables for the dead with bright lights mounted above. A wall of drawers for bodies to be stored in. Except for the ragged wound in Edwardo's chest, the place is spotless and smells strongly of antiseptic.

Helen's biting her lip and stands me next to the body, showing me a stainless steel tray. In it is what looks like a piece of bone about the size of an almond. Like a piece of rib or something.

"So?" I ask, shrugging my shoulders.

"The blood you got from the bull's horn is his. But . . . I pulled *this* out of him," she says, like she's telling me the Pope is secretly a woman or something.

I give her a blank stare. I'm clueless.

She drags me over to big round magnifying glass and holds the tray underneath it, giving me a pointed look. I lean close and look at the little piece of bone. It's pointed and has a distinct spiral ridge. When I look back at Helen, I'm smiling. She looks worried.

"That ain't no cow horn," I say.

She shakes her head.

"Good on ya, Helen," I say, kissing her on the cheek. "You just made my case."

"What? Conner, unicorns don't exist. How can this be?"

I shrug. "Don't know. What I do know is I just saw the mate to that piece in the back of an F-150."

WE'RE BACK IN THE EL CAMINO HEADING OUT OF PHOENIX

towards my place. I'm tired and hungry and don't know what else to do. Sanchez won't go after Alligator Boots. Won't tell officers to look for an F-150 with a unicorn horn in the back, says she'd be risking her reputation and won't do that for me. She wants more evidence.

Irene's smile is a mile wide. She looks so much more like a kid now. She's happy because I told her what Helen found and what I saw in the back of that F-150. Told her that I believe her. Her smile warms my wilted old heart.

It's near rush hour and the Phoenix traffic is thick as ants on honey. We're moving slowly forward in the stifling heat.

Phoenix is a flat and boring expanse except for the occasional outcrop of craggy stone. The city streets are a monotony of urban sprawl with strip malls, cookie-cutter houses, and the ubiquitous Circle Ks.

"So do you think it was a real unicorn?" Irene asks, her voice all bubbly and light.

I shrug my shoulders. Given the harness that was on the horn, I doubt that. I didn't get to telling her that part, and with her lit up like this, I just can't.

In the rearview, I catch a flash of a bright red truck weaving its way through traffic. My face falls.

"What's wrong, Conner?" Irene asks.

"Nothin', love," I lie. I point at the glove compartment. "There's a bottle of water in there. You best drink in this heat."

She nods and dutifully pulls out the water bottle and takes a drink. My eyes keep flicking to the rearview mirror looking for that red truck. Maybe it's Mr. Alligator Boots. Maybe he got wise to me following him.

At a stoplight, I pull out the burner phone and text Sanchez, *Check location of both phones.*

A minute later, as the traffic is finally starting to ease up, she texts back. *Same location.*

WE DIDN'T HAVE THE TAIL LONG. I SAW HIM BRIEFLY RIGHT behind me and then he was gone, talking a left and speeding off.

When we're past the city and closer to my house, we pull into yet another Circle K, my stomach grumbling and my head pounding. I needed food and a drink. A stiff drink. I take Irene in. She holds my hand the whole time while I pick up a few microwave burritos and some cookies for us, and she picks out some potato chips.

I stop in front of the refrigerated section. I have to let go of Irene's hand to open the door. My hand's shaking a bit, my body screaming for alcohol. And there it is. Row after row of beer, an obscene number of choices. Dark beer, light beer, fancy beer, cheap beer, foreign beer.

Beer reminds me of Tommy Wilkins. Of the sickening sound of his scream when I ran him over. You'd think it would make me drink less, but it's done just the opposite.

I was sixteen and at a high school party near Globe, Arizona, where I grew up. Tommy and I fought over a girl whose name I can't even remember. We were both drunk, and I was trying to leave and he wouldn't get out of the way, banging on the hood of my old Toyota pickup and screaming at me while I revved the engine. My foot slipped off the clutch and . . .

It was big news in Arizona. I did my time in the juvenile system, had my records sealed, but people around here remember my name. That's why I changed it, even though it broke my dad's heart. That's the reason behind the whole fake Australian thing. That's why my life is such a—

"What?" I ask. Irene had just said something.

She smiles and points at the vitamin water. "Can I have one of those? The purple one, please."

I blink at her a few times and nod, grabbing two of the plastic bottles and handing them to her. I turn my back on the obscene array of alcohol. Maybe tonight I can sleep without the beer.

I'm not thinking well. I drive right to my ten acres, a few miles from the Circle K, and pull in. Irene is babbling on like happy kids do, her words bright shards bouncing around my car. My fatigue and her happiness seem to lull me into a peaceful state. She goes on and on that when she grows up she's going to make a "My Little Unicorn" toy for girls, like the one already made for horses. That since unicorns are real, and once she finds one and gets her picture taken with it, everyone girl in the world will want one.

I still haven't told her about the harness.

"Maybe instead of 'My Little Unicorn,'" she says as I unlock the door to my dingy single-wide trailer, "I will name it after you." She's beaming at me now, like I'm someone important. "I'll call it 'Unicorn Bright.' That's a wonderful name."

I step into the house and am nodding when the clenched fist of Alligator Boots connects with my jaw, fiery pain radiating through the left side of my face. He was waiting behind the door.

As I go down, I curse my fatigue. He had tailed me long enough to get a look at my license plate. From there it wasn't hard to get my address or break in.

Irene screams and our food goes tumbling to the floor. On my way down I get a look at the chaotic mess of my living room. Dust covering the flat screen, piles of clothes, trash, dirty carpet.

I have a horrible realization: If I can't take care of my own living room, how am I going to take care of Irene? The thought doesn't last long. My head bounces off the carpet with a sharp crack and darkness descends.

I wake up with a start, the light of the full moon shining above me, hard ground below me, and cool air on my skin. My head is pounding and my jaw aches. My mouth is dry and my stomach clenches. I roll over and try to vomit, but there's nothing in me.

I hear the snort of a horse and bolt upright, the motion making my stomach try to empty itself again.

"Stand up," Alligator Boots says. He's mounted on what looks like a purple unicorn, a white horn jutting from its forehead, its coat a dark purple. In the moonlight it's hard to see the harness on the horse's head, but I know it's there.

"Why might I be doing that?" I ask, trying to hide the pain and desperation in my voice.

"Because if you don't, it will go badly for the girl."

We're back behind my trailer. It used to be a horse corral, back when I could afford to keep a horse. Now it's a falling down fence and a weedy expanse of dirt. Back behind the horse and Alligator Boots, I see the trailer, my El Camino, and his F-150 with a horse trailer attached.

"What?" I ask, trying desperately to get my mind to turn over.

Alligator Boots staged Edwardo Campos's death as an attack by a unicorn. Why? So Irene, a little girl obsessed with unicorns, would see it. Would talk about it. Would be dismissed. He put Edwardo's blood on that bull's horn. He also took something from the safe, just papers and not money.

This was all about Irene. The way her great-uncle had died had been a show for her.

Alligator Boots points to his right and I see Irene. She's tied to one of my cheap plastic chairs. She's gagged and her eyes are wide, her cheeks stained with tears.

I nod, make a show of getting up, and then slump back to the ground with a grunt. "What is it you needed from that safe?" I'm leaning on my right side, where my bowie knife should be, but he's taken it.

"Stand up!" he yells.

"You're the ranch hand Mr. Campos had a recent falling out with, ain't ya? The one that was once like a son to him."

He pulls a gun from his side and points it at Irene. "Stand. Now." He's not yelling anymore and that's a bad sign.

I slowly get into a squatting position. I feel in my right boot. That knife is still there.

I remember what Sanchez had told me about Edwardo Campos's recently remembered stock. What the bartender at Sugar and Spice had said when I showed him Edwardo's picture. How Edwardo had hinted to Irene that things were about to change for her.

"He wrote you out of his will," I say as I pull the knife from my boot and hold it behind my back, shakily standing up. "That's what ya took, the will that left everything to Irene. I'm guessing he hadn't signed it yet, but was about to. He had told all his buddies at Sugar and Spice about his windfall, about how he was leaving it all to his delightful niece that loves unicorns and the color purple. Someone there told ya."

Alligator Boots doesn't speak. He spurs the horse hard, and it leaps forward. As I stand there, I have empathy for Edwardo Campos. He came out in the middle of the night under the bright moonlight expecting a coyote and saw a galloping unicorn bearing down on him. He had the shotgun in his hand, but he didn't use it. His grandniece had been babbling about unicorns, and now seeing one made him dumb for an instant, just one small instant.

Adrenaline dumps into my bloodstream, my heart pounding in my ears in time with the thundering of the hooves. But I don't move. I stand there swaying, still trying to get my bearings, hoping my body still remembers my time at the rodeo.

I wonder what Detective Sanchez will do if she finds my body just like Edwardo's, if she has a hysterical girl that talks about yet another man being run through by a purple unicorn. Once, she might brush off, twice, never. It's all over for Alligator Boots, even if I don't survive. This thought gives me comfort. Briefly.

But what of Irene? I remember how she clung to me outside Sugar and Spice, how she sat so close to me in the El Camino, how she held my hand in the Circle K. It felt strange, but good, to be depended on. My eyes flick to her. I can't hear her over the pounding hooves or through her gag, but it's clear she's screaming.

The unicorn is upon me. I smell dust, paint, and its sweat. I quickly rotate my body around, moving just to the side. I pull the knife from behind my back. I do what I need to do.

I WAKE UP SLOWLY AND GROAN, REALIZING I'M FULLY DRESSED again. I'm slumped in a half-seated position, my lower back and my neck aching, my mouth dry as the desert.

"Take it easy." I'm not sure who it is at first, a woman with a sweet voice. Helen.

And then the events of the last day tumble onto me like a monsoon cloudburst. I bolt upright and open my eyes. "Irene," I croak.

"She's fine," Helen says, putting a hand on my back, a gentle smile on her lips.

"Where is she?" Part of me feels silly. I hardly know the girl. Another part of me is desperate for her to be okay.

"CPS came while you were sleeping. She's just fine, Conner."

I nod and rub at my face, trying to wake myself up, feeling several days of stubble. I remember the charging unicorn. I remember rotating out of the way and jamming my knife through one of those alligator skin boots. I remember him screaming and falling off that spray-painted horse, struggling to get up. Me punching him in the face. Him lying still. Untying Irene. Her sobbing and clinging to me while I call Detective Sanchez.

"They took her," I mumble, mostly to myself.

Helen is looking at me, her soft blue eyes searching my face like I'm not the man she knows.

I remember what it had felt like as Irene clung to me while we waited for the sheriff's deputies to arrive. How the ambulance had come and I had refused it and Irene had refused to leave me. How they had hauled Alligator Boots away. How Helen had finally come and we had gone into the trailer. I had given Irene my bed and held her hand for hours until she fell asleep and then stumbled out to the couch. Helen had insisted on staying.

"That horn," Helen says, pulling out her phone and showing me a picture that looks like a whale with a unicorn horn sticking out of its head. "It was real. This is a narwhal, that tusk is some crazy tooth."

It all makes sense . . . except for how I feel.

I look up to the tin of ashes on top of my entertainment center. I lever myself up, stumble over, and say, "Hey, Dad. The girl's safe." I reach down, my head screaming at me, and pick up a stray piece of paper, a microwave burrito wrapper.

"What are you doing?" Helen asks.

"I'm cleaning up." She's staring at me, like she doesn't know me. Like we've never danced or touched or had meals together. "Will you help me?"

THE DOOR IS A FADED YELLOW AND THE NEIGHBORHOOD'S somewhat faded, too. It might have been cheery three decades ago, but now it's looking a little sad.

It's been ten days since I met Irene, and two days since I've had a drink. I would have come sooner, but I swore to myself I wouldn't do it unless I had been dry for at least two days. My hand is shaking as I knock.

A plump woman with a pinched face answers the door.

"I'm here to see Irene," I say. "I called earlier."

She nods, lets me in, and leaves me in the living room. There's a TV playing loudly with strange blue creatures on it dancing around. There's a couple of kids, much younger than Irene, watching it, their eyes wide.

And then she's there. This time I'm expecting it and kneel down before she gets to me. "You okay?" I whisper.

She hugs me hard. She nods and sniffs. I can feel her tears on my shoulder. I can feel my own tears on my cheek. "What took you so long?" She says it gently but it feels like a horse kicked me in the chest.

"I was . . . I . . ." I stammer. "I was trying to . . ." I can't finish. I can't tell this girl that I was trying to be worthy of her. That I have been ever since we met. That I will be as long as she'll have me.

I don't know if she understands, but she hugs me even harder and that's enough.

BACKSTORY—CONNOR BRIGHT AND THE CASE OF THE PURPLE UNICORN

THERE IS SOMETHING QUITE COMFORTING ABOUT THE procedural detective trope. Just look at TV, how many of these shows have there been? How many murder mystery books have been written?

The addicted detective hiding from his past is also common, and fairly cliched.

This is my take on those two things, with an Arizona flair. The part I had fun playing with was making this feel like there was a paranormal component, when in the end, it ended up being an entirely contemporary tale. The TV show *Castle* did this from time to time, often to good effect, and was part of the inspiration.

It's that "contemporary tale" part that puts this in the anomaly column for me. I do write them, but not that often and usually quite on accident.

I wrote this for an anthology about purple unicorns, and one thing that is a good idea when writing for something like that, is to try to produce something different, in other words, create an anomaly. A story with an alcoholic detective and not one bit of fantasy in a purple unicorn anthology was just that.

I hope you enjoyed getting to know Conner Bright. I hope to get back to him soon and see what mystery next greets him.

This story originally appeared in *One Horn to Rule Them All: A Purple Unicorn Anthology*.

PART TWELVE
FOR A HORSE NAMED CORWIN

FOR A HORSE NAMED CORWIN

EVAN WILCOX REIGNED IN HIS HORSE AND STOOD UP IN THE stirrups. The desert of planet Valdrin stretched before him in all directions, seeming to be an endless expanse of sage brush, sand, and prickly pear cactus. He felt a tingle go up and down his spine. Something wasn't right.

"Bad," his mount, Corwin, said, shaking his head and rattling his tack.

Wilcox nodded and then remembering the horse couldn't see the gesture, added, "You got that right, brother." Wilcox sniffed the air and smelled nothing but sweat, horse, and dust. He scanned the horizon but saw nothing but the distant mountains and heat rising off the land. He closed his eyes and listened carefully and heard-- nothing. Not the slithering of a snake as it moved from one rock to another; not the scamper of a jackrabbit, scared into motion by the snake's approach; not the sigh of a coyote as it slept through the hottest part of the day. Nothing.

Wilcox adjusted his wide brimmed hat, eased back into the saddle, and brushed his thumb against the back of his left ear. There a nerve bundle triggered the release of a hormone that made his cochlea more sensitive, enhancing his sense of hearing. Wilcox, while purely biological, was no longer purely human.

Still he heard nothing but the rattle of the brush in the slight breeze and the breathing of his mount.

Wilcox swallowed hard; he had a sour taste in his mouth, like a rotten lemon. The taste of fear. "Git, Corwin," he said with a grimace, urging the horse from a standstill to a gallop. Wilcox didn't know what was wrong, but he knew something was. The animals knew it, none of them moving a muscle. And Corwin knew it too; he cooperated with unusual vigor. Wilcox rose up in the saddle as the animal galloped beneath him.

When he was a hundred meters out, Wilcox turned and looked back; the spot he and Corwin had just been occupying was shimmering. Not with the heat of the desert but with the hum of the Ancestors.

It had been more than a generation since the Ancestors had visited, long enough so that the young began to doubt their existence, and the old had stopped telling the stories about how they survived. Long enough for vigilance to end.

But Wilcox knew better. He had long dreaded their return. Valdrin is a preserve, formed in the mold of a long dead society from humanity's past, and intent on keeping humanity pure. A place where a strict level of technology is enforced and altered biologicals, like Corwin and Wilcox, are not welcome.

The shimmering resolved into a tight spherical shape with a fuzzy splotch of color in the center starting to come into focus... starting to look like men on their horses. Above the sound of Corwin's hooves striking the ground Wilcox could hear a high-pitched hum that hurt his ears. He thumbed the back of his left ear again, returning his hearing to normal.

"Real. Bad," Corwin gasped as his pace quickened.

Wilcox turned away from the scene of the arriving Ancestors and leaned close to Corwin's neck. "You said it," he said. "Run, my friend, run!"

WILCOX COULD FEEL CORWIN'S FATIGUE, THE HORSE'S BREATH ragged, sweat coating his body. The horse had run long and hard as the flat desert had turned into rolling hills, but Salkin City was still a good ways off. "Ease up, boy," Wilcox told him and the horse slowed to a walk.

He looked behind and didn't see anything. He hoped that they hadn't seen him. He didn't want the Ancestors to ever see them. They wouldn't look kindly on him or Corwin.

Wilcox's plan was simple. Make it to Salkin City before the Ancestors, pick up supplies, head for the mountains, and don't look back.

But, even Corwin couldn't run forever. Wilcox saw a thin tendril of smoke in the distance and let out a sigh of relief. Maybe, just maybe, he could get what he needed there and not have to go to Salkin City. He reigned in Corwin, dismounted, and wrapped the reigns around the saddle horn. He wobbled briefly, his legs weak from the long gallop, before walking towards the smoke.

"Thirsty," Corwin said as he followed.

"I'm working on it, buddy."

"MA'AM," WILCOX SAID HOLDING UP HIS HANDS, FEELING A trickle of sweat slide down his back, "there is no need for that."

The woman brought the shotgun to her shoulder and said, "Well I think there is. Now get off my property."

Wilcox studied her. She wore pants and a shirt made of coarse cloth and had her long black hair braided in the back. Her hands were rough and her face was dirty. Even so, Wilcox caught a whiff of soap among the sweat. All in all, he reckoned she knew how to use that shotgun. He backed up a step, his right hand going to

Corwin's neck. "It's my horse, Ma'am. He's ridden long and hard and needs a drink, if you would be so kind."

She lowered the shotgun and studied the horse, her eyes quickly appraising Corwin's condition.

"What kind of a man rides his horse that hard?" she asked.

"A desperate man," Wilcox said lowering his eyes. "I have news that might make your hospitality worthwhile."

"What news?" she asked raising her shotgun again.

"I'm sorry, Ma'am, but can you tell me your name? I haven't been in these parts for a while, and I'm afraid I don't recognize you. And, it just seems impolite to have a conversation with someone I haven't been introduced to. My name is Wilcox, and this is Corwin."

"I'm Sadie Larkin," the woman said with a sharp nod. "Now say your piece."

Wilcox nodded. "The information I have is valuable. And after I tell it to you, I hope you will consider not only watering Corwin, but giving me whatever food you might that is travel worthy. I--"

"Spit it out, Mr. Wilcox," Sadie said, cocking the shotgun.

"Yes, Ma'am," Wilcox said with a tip of his hat. "The Ancestors have returned."

Wilcox watched as her jaw opened and she blinked rapidly. He followed her eyes to a relatively fresh grave and met her gaze when it returned to him.

"You lie," she said.

"I do not, Ma'am." Wilcox said.

"Ancestors," Corwin said the pronunciation a bit garbled. While Corwin's tongue and vocal cords were more suited to speech than a standard horse, it wasn't as flexible as a person's. "Thirsty. Please."

Sadie lowered the shotgun and held it limp in her grasp. She nodded from Corwin towards the watering trough, her gaze returning again to the grave. "The Ancestors are here?" she mumbled.

"Yes Ma'am," Wilcox said, "and they'll be about the Purge. If you have anything to hide, like Corwin and I do, I suggest you pack up and go."

"SORRY, BOY," WILCOX SAID AS HE RUBBED THE HORSE DOWN, apologizing for the long gallop. He had removed the saddle and blanket and was rubbing the horse's white flank with fresh straw Sadie Larkin had provided. He loved the scent of horses, all clean sweat and power. People often smelled bad when they sweat but horses didn't. It was a purer, cleaner thing, free of the tangle of the darker human emotions.

"Ancestors," Corwin replied.

Wilcox sighed. He feared there was no escaping them. That the decisions of his youth to go off planet and alter himself were finally going to catch up to him. That they had too far to go, and even Corwin did not have the stamina to take them there.

"He's so big, so beautiful," Sadie said as she led another, smaller horse towards Corwin and Wilcox.

"That he is, Mrs. Larkin," Wilcox agreed. "What's the mare for?"

"She's for you."

"I don't understand, Ma'am."

"You are going to ride her to town. You are going to warn those in Salkin City of the coming of the Ancestors."

Wilcox just stared at her, his mouth open.

"You need supplies," she continued. "I have them. Corwin needs rest. You warn the city, and I'll have the cart packed by the time you return. We can leave then."

He studied her face. It was earnest and serious, not a trace or hint of humor. She had washed it while she was inside, and he saw that she was more than a little pretty, with a sprinkling of freckles perched on her high cheek bones. She had eyes that seemed to reflect the blue of the sky and full lips. He had been calling her Ma'am, as was respectful, but he finally saw her as a woman.

"Sorry," he said, turning back to his horse. He pulled a curry comb out of his saddlebag and began brushing Corwin. He noticed that the horse was watching the exchange carefully.

As the seconds slowly passed, he expected her to argue with him. To tell him it was the right thing to do, that everyone should have a chance to avoid the Purge and the judgment of the Ancestors. He stood there pretending to be totally absorbed in what he was doing, pretending he didn't know warning Salkin City was the right thing to do.

The minutes ticked by. He brushed; she stood there with the mare. He wasn't used to this. In his experience women made a big fuss when men didn't do what they ought. The silence weighed on him until he couldn't stand it anymore.

"Corwin..." he began.

"Go," the horse said. "Help."

Wilcox nodded and took the reins of the mare from Sadie. He expected to see a smile on her face, but instead he saw a look of grim resignation, a look that seemed at home on her face.

"You best be ready when I come back," he grunted as he mounted the mare. "We'll be out of time and need to head towards the mountains." He pointed southwest towards a tall snow covered peak.

"I'll be ready," she said and he believed it.

WILCOX KNEW HOW TO RIDE A HORSE. HE HAD BEEN RIDING before he was walking. But this mare was not Corwin. She would not turn at the slightest pressure of his knee, or heed his verbal commands. It took him a few miles to get the feel of riding a normal horse. A natural horse.

And that was it. Natural. The Ancestors would judge this

horse as natural and Corwin as unnatural. They would judge Wilcox with his enhanced senses and his improved nervous system as unnatural. And he and Corwin, they would...

What would they do to them? It had been more than a generation since they came and the tales the grandfathers told grew each year in the telling. If the oldest were to be believed, those that have lived through several visits from the Ancestors, then Wilcox and Corwin would be tortured and killed.

On this planet only that which is natural is allowed. Only limited technology is tolerated. All else is punishable.

Wilcox spurred the mare into a gallop as he headed for Salkin City.

The Hitch Up Saloon was crowed for mid-day. It wasn't just the desperate and lonely, the saloon was so full that Wilcox had to push his way through the crowd as he made his way towards bar.

"What's going on?" he asked Martin Aster, who had a mug of beer in his hand. Aster was the undertaker and didn't frequent the saloon during the day.

"It's Taylor, he struck a rich vein of iridium. He's been buying drinks for hours." The plump man's speech was slurred as he raised his mug into the air, sloshing beer on the stained wooden floor.

Wilcox nodded and continued plowing towards the bar, his nose wrinkled against the smell of sour beer, urine, and too many bodies. Maybe this was his lucky day, so many citizens of Salkin City in one place. As he approached the bar he spotted the muscular form of Herbert Taylor. Taylor caught his eye as he approached and said, "Wilcox, my friend. Have a drink." He nodded to Hunter, the old wisp of a man that was tending bar, who poured Wilcox a whisky.

"Now you are not the only Salkin native," Taylor continued, "to hit it big. To me!" he cried.

A chorus of "To Taylor!" echoed around the big man as everyone drank. Wilcox shot back his own whiskey, letting it burn its way down his throat, and then without saying a word climbed up onto the bar.

"Excuse me, might I have your attention," he shouted. But the men kept drinking, the saloon girls kept flirting, and the piano man kept playing. Wilcox knew he didn't have much time, that none of them had much time. He pulled his gun out and shot into the floor. He knew what the upstairs of the saloon was used for, so he shot down for fear of his bullet hitting someone up there.

The piano came to a jangling stop as the noise in the saloon decreased, and all eyes found their way to Wilcox. He saw a few hands go to their guns, and Wilcox quickly holstered his. He wasn't here for a fight. "Sorry, folks, I have an announcement, and I'll keep it quick."

The saloon grew quiet, a chorus of annoyed faces looking at Wilcox.

"The Ancestors are coming," he said.

The saloon erupted in noise but a different kind of noise. There were shouts of fear, cries of doubt, and the scuffling of boots as some of the patrons left. Wilcox stood there and let the sound wash around him until one shout rose above the rest.

"Liar, you're a liar, Evan Wilcox," Taylor yelled.

"I am not lying, Taylor," Wilcox replied. "I was far to the east on the flat desert. I had been scouting around Diablo Canyon, heard told there might be some iridium deposits there. On my way back, the desert got dead quiet and I saw the sphere. I saw the bodies materializing in it. It was the Ancestors, no doubt."

"Liar," Taylor repeated. "The Ancestors are just a story our folks used to scare us. They ain't real."

"Then why don't we have electricity?" Wilcox asked. "Why don't we have flying ships or land machines or engines that run on anything but steam? Why are we so backwards when the rest of the worlds are so advanced? I've been there Taylor. I've seen these wonders. It's the Ancestors that enforce our low level of technology, keep us scratching in the dirt."

Taylor snorted and took a drink of his beer. "Truth told, we are a low technology world. It is the basis on which we were founded, the charter on which this planet was settled. That's it and nothing more. We don't need no boogey man to enforce this. We do it by choice."

"You always were dumb, Taylor, weren't you?" Wilcox said. He raised his voice and spoke to the crowd. "Listen to Taylor if you all want. But I am telling the truth. The Ancestors are coming and if you've got tech to hide, you best go hide it and hide yourself. For my part, I'll be headed out of here now."

"Truth is, Wilcox, some of us like it the way it is," Taylor growled. "Some of us will keep our riches here on this planet, will use it to make this a better place, and not run off to see what kind of sick depravities humankind has come to. Some of us won't change what we are no matter how much money we have." The big man paused, taking out a handkerchief and wiping his sweating brow. "Ah hell, forget Wilcox. I'm buying!"

The chorus of agreement was deafening. With a shrug Wilcox got off the bar. Let them think what they think. Wilcox sighed, Taylor had told the truth about him--he had left Valdrin, he had immersed himself in the other world's high tech societies, he had changed himself. He elbowed his way through the crowd until he was outside the saloon standing in the bright sunshine.

"Is it true?" a voice said lightly.

Wilcox turned and saw Jimmy Oster. He was the apprentice barber but had a side business in black market goods. Small things like flashlights and GPS units. Things that ran on electricity. Things made off-world. Things that were forbidden. "Yeah, Jimmy, it's true." Wilcox moved to the mare and unwound her reins from the hitching post.

"But... but..." Jimmy stuttered. "Aren't they just legends? Stories our parents tell to scare us, keep us away from tech? I mean, why would a man choose to sleep the centuries way just to... to..."

Wilcox looked him up and down. Jimmy was just twenty. He hadn't been born when the Ancestors were here last. "They're real, Jimmy, and they're coming. When I was six I saw them take our neighbor away." Wilcox's eyes unfocused and his face went blank. "They looked like gods in their glittering armor, sitting tall on their horses." His eyes snapped back into focus as he looked back at Jimmy. "And I just saw them rise up out of the desert." Wilcox pointed east. "They're coming, I swear it. Spread the word."

Jimmy nodded and took a stride down the dirt street before Wilcox stopped him when he said, "And tell the mayor and the sheriff if you come across them."

"Didn't you seem him?" Jimmy asked, "Mayor Bailey is in there. He's drinking Taylor's whisky and laughing at you."

Wilcox kicked the hitching post and swore. "Damn this town, damn them all to hell. Let the Ancestors take them." Wilcox saw Jimmy's pinched look and added. "You get, Jimmy. You take care of you and yours. There's not much time."

He watched as the young man ran down the long street.

It took him longer to get back to the Larkin ranch than he wanted. He was impatient to get moving on towards the mountains, to get back to Corwin. But the mare was not Corwin and couldn't keep up the pace he wanted.

He slowed the mare to a walk to let her rest some. He stood up in the stirrups and scanned the landscape. Small evergreens, a smattering of cacti, and big clumps of cheat grass covered the rolling landscape. He spotted hints of dust in the air between him and his destination.

"Damn," he mumbled, moving the mare towards the south. He

didn't know who or what was headed this way from the vicinity of the Larkin ranch, but he didn't want to run into them. "Damn," he said again as he spurred the mare into a trot.

———

He smelled it first... oil. Well maybe not oil, but something petroleum based, something that you almost never smelled on Valdrin away from the railroad. The rest of the worlds of the Alliance are filled with that smell--but not this one. It was just a tentative whiff, just a hint, but his olfactory senses, just like his hearing and eyesight, were the best that his money could buy when he was off world. He urged the mare into a gallop as the Larkin house came into view.

He breathed a sigh of relief when he spotted the cart and the horse. But his relief didn't last. The horse harnessed to the cart wasn't Corwin.

Sadie Larkin came striding out of the house carrying a large sack as Wilcox approached. "Where is he?" he asked.

"They came," she said with a set-jaw, determined look on her face as she swung the sack into the cart. "They seemed to know to come here. They took him." Her grim face met his as she added, "I'm sorry."

Wilcox slowly got off the tired mare and led her to the watering trough. He left her there to drink, walked several meters away, picked up a branch from the ground and started beating the fence with it. He didn't speak, he didn't make a sound, he just pounded the wrist-thick branch against the split rail fence until the branch broke. He then stood there panting, his face pinched in bitterness, holding the remaining piece of wood, looking around the Larkin ranch.

There was a small house with a tin roof. A lean-to and corral for the horses, now empty, an extensive garden, and the grave.

Except the grave looked different. Gone were the crude

wooden cross and the signs of freshly turned dirt. On top of it were some recently cut branches and straw.

Wilcox walked over, his eyes dangerous as he started clearing the grave with the branch he still held. Underneath the debris was fresh lye. The smell of it stung his nostrils as his efforts kicked it up into the air. He spit out the sour taste and turned and saw Sadie Larkin staring at him, her arms folded in front of her breasts.

"What is that you have to hide, Sadie Larkin?" he asked. "What the hell happened to my horse?"

"They came," she said, her eyes looking at the uncovered earth and not the man she was talking to. "They knew to come here. They knew to look here." Her eyes were wide, and Wilcox could smell the fear on her.

It helped diffuse his anger. "What is it you have to hide?" he repeated.

She nodded at the grave, her eyes filling with tears. "My husband, Jilop. He wasn't human. It's why we settled so far out of town."

"Not human?" Wilcox asked.

She tore her eyes away from the grave and looked at him. "Well, he looked human enough; he could pass if you didn't look too close or spend too much time with him. He was an anthropologist. He was here illegally, studying our 'technology constrained society.'"

Wilcox nodded. "And you were afraid they would find the body?"

She nodded looking back at the grave. "And his possessions."

Wilcox's eyes widened, but he didn't comment, he had other things on his mind. "And Corwin?"

"He saved me. There were only two of them. One had this device, a scanner I think, the other a gun. They would have found him... they would have found out..." She trailed off, her eyes going blank before she took a deep breath. Her face hardened and she squared her shoulders, walking back towards the house. Wilcox followed.

"Corwin spoke," she said looking back at him. "He saw what they were doing and he spoke. They would have found Jilop's body... they would have searched the house... they would have taken me away." She turned and looked at Wilcox. "Why did he do that?"

Wilcox shrugged and said, "He's a better man than I am."

Sadie wiped at her eyes and said, "Well, we must go. If they think about it too much, they'll be back to search." She marched towards the house and stopped when she got to the door and looked back. Wilcox hadn't followed. He stood still, his eyes vacant. "Are you going to help?" she asked.

He shook his head slowly. "I need your other horse, the stallion, the mare is spent."

"What?" she asked, walking back towards him.

"I can't leave Corwin to them, I can't. I'll either get him back or I'll put him down, but I will not let them have him."

"But..."

"Listen, I've got a place up in the mountains, up towards Helgold pass. An old mine I found while prospecting. You can go there. You'll be safe. It's hidden, hard to find, but I can draw you a map."

"Corwin... I'm sorry..." Sadie said, her hand coming to her mouth. "You'll never... they are too powerful."

"Can I take your other horse?" Wilcox asked, the muscles in his jaw bunching and releasing.

Sadie Larkin just stood there staring at him.

With a sigh, Wilcox asked, "How did you husband die?"

Her eyes went to the grave, and her mouth turned down. "He got sick, some damn virus foreign to him."

"Why didn't you take him to the doc in Salkin City? Our medical technology is less restricted--he might have been able to help."

Tears sprung to Sadie's eyes. "They would have exiled us, and I couldn't imagine leaving Valdrin. He said he would rather die than live without me."

Wilcox nodded sharply. "Then you understand why I have to go. Can I have the stallion?"

She shook her head as if waking from a dream, her eyes meeting Wilcox's again, "Yes, of course. But, please, just come with me. No good can come of this. You can't win."

"Yes, Ma'am, I know that. But for Corwin, I have to try."

WILCOX RODE THE STALLION HARD, NOT SAVING IT FOR A return trip. He was planning to ride Corwin out of Salkin City or not ride out at all.

The Ancestors weren't hard to find. They were in the center of town where the two main streets of Salkin City crossed, right out front of the Hitch Up Saloon.

He rode slowly down the road and studied them. They looked the same as he did--they were human--but he felt in awe of them. Men centuries old that had settled this planet, men his mother and father had taught him to revere. They had on what looked like glittering grey armor and held strange devices. Some looked like guns, others were small pieces of technology that fit in the palm of their hands that might do most anything.

There was a pile of contraband: flashlights, GPS units, cameras, batteries, solar chargers, mineral sniffers, and a few rock cutters. Wilcox wondered how they had done this so quickly. How they had found it all.

There were four of them gathered. Wilcox knew there were many more, but these four were making a display right in the center of town. A display, he knew, that was designed to chastise them all.

He let the stallion walk slowly towards them, and when he was fifty meters away, he slid off the horse and started walking towards the Ancestors.

"You don't steal a man's horse," he said loudly, his heart ponding in his ears.

"Do you speak, descendant?" One of them asked sharply. He was tall and thin with short black hair and a pinched look to his face. He rose up from the pile he was inspecting and turned towards Wilcox. The Ancestor pointed a device, some kind of sensor, at him and studied its readout. Wilcox could hear the faint whir of motors in the Ancestor's armor and smelled the stench of oil. He hated the hypocrisy of the Ancestors, using technology to enforce their ban on technology.

"You don't steal a man's horse," Wilcox said again. "We have laws against that around here." He swept back his duster so that his revolver was exposed. He didn't think a bullet could penetrate the Ancestor's armor, but his head was exposed, as well as gaps at the neck, waist, and joints. An Ancestor could die just like any man. It felt sacrilegious to even think it, but he had to for Corwin.

"And we have laws about the abuse of technology, laws that you seem to have no respect for."

Wilcox nodded. "I have no forbidden devices. Just me and my horse, the way God intended. Where is he? Where is Corwin?"

The man laughed and looked back down at the device in his palm, holding its display towards Wilcox. "No, you don't have any devices, just yourself. That is enough of an abomination."

Wilcox felt his anger overwhelming his awe and fear. He blinked once, then twice, his lips twitching into the briefest of smiles. During that span of blinks, he drew his gun, fired, and holstered it. When he was done, the device the Ancestor had held up was destroyed, and the Ancestor was holding his hand grimacing in pain.

"Where is Corwin?" he asked again. "I am just about done being polite."

The tall Ancestor shrugged and said, "There are many horses. How am I to know which one is yours?"

"He talks," Wilcox said. "He was taken from the Larkin Ranch east of here."

"Ah," the Ancestor said, "that thing. It's not too far."

Wilcox stiffened at hearing Corwin called a "thing," but he didn't comment, gesturing that the Ancestor should lead the way.

The armored man said to his fellows, "I'll take this descendant to his horse, you stay here." He then started walking down the street, his hands held awkwardly, well away from his body. Wilcox followed.

"Do you know why we forbid advanced technology on this planet?" The Ancestor asked. "Why we settled it this way? Why we enforce it so vigorously?"

"Valdrin is a preserve, created for a purer way of life, where man is not separate from nature or his creator, where man can live as God intended." Wilcox said, reciting the phrase all children learn.

The Ancestor looked over his shoulder and smiled at Wilcox. "Then you understand why we can't let a horse like Corwin, created as he was with advanced technology, be on this planet."

"I do not," Wilcox said. "His DNA is altered, sure, but he's pure biological. No 'advanced' technology in him. And he's sterile, so his DNA can't spread, can't ruin your precious balance. So, with all due respect, I think you got this one wrong."

The Ancestor stopped and turned. They were standing in front of the barbershop, and Wilcox could see multiple faces pressed to the windows. "Man is weak," the Ancestor said. "It makes me sad that I have to live the life I do." He flexed his armored arm. "That I have to live surrounded by technology, that I live only for a few months every generation to do this work. That I can't live the life we have afforded you. A life you don't seem to want." He sighed, his brown eyes looking through Wilcox as if at something far, far away. "I was born on the generational ship that brought us here. My ancestors taught me how this dry desert of a planet was all our movement was given, and we were lucky to have it. How we had to seed it with plants, animals, and a way of life from our past that was purer, simpler. That my generation had to guard it, had to keep coming back to make sure the intent was kept pure and not diluted by the passing generations."

His eyes snapped back into focus. "I know who you are, Wilcox," he said. "I know you struck it rich mining. I know you could have stayed, but you didn't. You turned your back on this life. If you wanted a life of technology, why didn't you stay away?"

Surprise registered on Wilcox's face as he struggled to understand how the Ancestors knew his story. "I was young and stupid when I left, a kid with way too much money. I learned a lot when I was gone. I missed my home, and what was done was done."

"And the horse?"

"One does not discard one's friends," Wilcox said, his voice low. He heard footsteps behind him and whirled around, his gun ready, but it was too late. One of the other Ancestors pointed a two-barreled contraption at him. It had a single grip, with two barrels about five inches apart. Wilcox felt an assault of sound slam into him, and his hands went involuntarily to his ears as he fell to his knees.

He knew what it was: a sonic gun. Non-lethal, the two barrels focused complementary sound waves on a single spot, silent to everyone but him. He thumbed the back of his left ear, turning his hearing down, but it wasn't enough. They knew him; they must have turned the thing all the way up. The sound crashed into him relentlessly. He couldn't think. He couldn't move. He screamed.

THE SMELL OF URINE ASSAULTED WILCOX AS HE SLOWLY WOKE up. His tongue felt swollen, his saliva thick, his mouth cottony. He felt a cot beneath him and could hear someone breathing nearby. He sat up slowly and held his head. It hurt like a railroad spike had been driven into it. As his eyes focused, he saw that he was locked in a cell, and Taylor was sitting outside it on a chair watching him. Wilcox's frown became a grimace.

"Good morning," Taylor said with a big smile.

"What do you want, Taylor?"

The big man shrugged. "To gloat. I'll admit it. I'm here to gloat. Your fancy mods, your horse, your wasted money, and you end up right where you belong." Taylor's chuckle was as irritating as fingernails on a chalkboard.

Wilcox took a slow deep breath and sighed. "Well, get it over with, Taylor." Wilcox raised his head and sniffed the air. "Is that you I smell?"

Taylor chuckled. "No, my friend, I believe you pissed yourself when they shot you with that gizmo. It's you that stinks."

Wilcox looked down and saw that Taylor was right. "At least I know right from wrong," Wilcox said.

Taylor chuckled again. "Sure. Going off planet and smuggling back your highly modded self and that abomination of a horse is the right thing to do. In the only place where humanity is still pure. Why don't you explain how that was the right thing to do?"

Wilcox stared at him and noticed the big man's new clothes, hat, boots, and pair of revolvers. He remembered Taylor buying drinks, getting half the town drunk right before the Ancestors came. Something sparked in his mind. "You didn't find any iridium. You're helping the Ancestors, and they're paying you, aren't they? You were buying drinks so no one would notice them coming."

Taylor stood and clapped, coming close to the bars of Wilcox's cell. "I guess it turns out you're not quite as stupid as you look."

"And that's how they knew where to go, how to take me down, about Corwin."

Taylor spat on the floor when Wilcox said "Corwin." "Thank God that abomination won't be alive much longer."

"What?" Wilcox asked, coming fully awake.

"You, they're going to exile. Him, they're going to make an example of."

Wilcox surged to his feet. Taylor saw the movement and shoved himself back, but he wasn't quick enough. Wilcox thrust his arm through the bars and got his hand around Taylor's throat.

"Hands where I can see them," Wilcox said. "Now you know so damn much about me, you know I can snap your neck long before you can draw."

Taylor nodded his head imperceptibly, his eyes wide.

"Where is Corwin?" Wilcox could feel Taylor's pulse against his hand thumping like a locomotive.

"He... he's behind the general store. They built an iron cage big enough for him."

"And what are they planning?"

"They are going to execute him at noon in front of the whole town." Wilcox's grip tightened and Taylor began to choke. "You kill... me... they hang you," he spit out.

Wilcox relaxed his grip but didn't let go. He looked around. His cell was in the little jail at the back of the Sheriff's office on the main strip. Sheriff Yost might have let Taylor back here to have his fun, but he wasn't dumb enough to give him a key. Wilcox jerked Taylor forward, his head bouncing off the iron bars of the cell, and he fell to the ground unconscious. Wilcox took the shiny new revolvers out of Taylor's holster and sat back on the cot and thought.

He needed to escape and quickly. But how? He could call for one of the deputies and force them to unlock him. And then what? Shoot his way out of the jail? He had no quarrel with Yost and his men.

As he sat there thinking he started to smell something. It was subtle at first, barely even noticeable, and then the alkaline stench of burning rock became apparent. He looked around and saw nothing but felt heat emanating from a corner of his cell.

Soon the rock cutter, the kind often used by miners to lay in dynamite charges, the kind the Ancestors were now confiscating, was visible as a red glow running along the rock forming a rough circle. Someone was breaking him out.

He searched Taylor, reaching through the bars of his cell, while the rock was cut. Wilcox took his money and put on his gun belt, holstering the revolvers.

When the red glow stopped, Wilcox moved the bed so it was up against the bars and sat on the floor of the cell, his back to the bed and pushed the rock with his feet. The wall was thick and the rock was heavy--it took everything he had, but he managed to slowly push it through.

"Hurry," a voice whispered through the open hole.

Wilcox squeezed through the opening and stood up in the alley behind the jail. There he saw Sadie Larkin, her black hair disheveled, the rock cutter at her feet. "We've got to go. Now. I've got the cart hid just outside town." She pointed south.

"Corwin?" Wilcox asked as he patted at his smoldering clothing, burned by the still hot rock

She shrugged her shoulders.

"I thank you for the escape, Ma'am, but I've got to go get Corwin. They're going to execute him. Head for the mountains. I'll catch up with you if I can."

She looked at him and frowned. "I won't be breaking you out of jail again. I felt bad about getting you mixed up in this and losing Corwin, but we're even now."

"I understand. But I can't leave Corwin to them." He headed further down the alley towards the general store.

Two guards, Wilcox knew them both, stood right in front of the cage holding Corwin. He had seen three ancestors around the corner within shouting distance. Wilcox studied Corwin from his prone position at the edge of the alley. The horse looked fine and calm. Wilcox was neither, his heart pounding loudly in his ears.

Five minutes passed and a plan, one that had any chance of succeeding, eluded him. He didn't want to just throw his life, or Corwin's away. He didn't want to kill people he knew and liked. He didn't want to land back in jail, only to be banished from his home.

Ten more minutes passed, and he heard the clock tower strike once. It was 11:30, and with Corwin's execution happening at noon, time was running out.

With a shrug, Wilcox pulled himself up, dusted himself off, pulled out Taylor's shiny new revolvers and stepped out of the alley.

The first guard, Adams, made to draw his gun. "I wouldn't do that, both you boys know how fast I am."

Adams bit his lip and put his hands out to the side.

The other guard, an apprentice mortician named Haut, did the same. He said, "You can't get away with the horse, Wilcox. Just turn back around, and we won't tell no one that you were here. Go hide, wait out the Ancestors. I hate to have to fit you for a coffin."

Wilcox nodded and stepped forward, a gun trained on each man. "That is some good advice, Haut. Sorry to say I can't take it. The Ancestors stole my horse and I can't let that stand."

Haut nodded his head, and Adams kept looking over his shoulder.

"You okay, Corwin?" Wilcox asked.

"Okay," Corwin replied. "Go now."

"That's the idea, my friend."

Just as Wilcox was wondering what Adams was waiting for, an Ancestor came around the corner. It was the same one he had talked to in front of the saloon. "Is it ready yet?" he asked. "We need to get it to..." He trailed off when he saw Wilcox, his face becoming more pinched than normal.

"Hands where I can see them," Wilcox said.

The Ancestor smiled and slowly raised his hands. "You don't want to do this," he said.

"Now you know my mind?" Wilcox asked. "Go over there and unlock the cage."

The Ancestor slowly walked to the cage. As he approached he said, "Getting the key, don't shoot." He reached into the pocked on the right leg of his armor and came out with an iron key. He unlocked the cage and stepped back, moving away from Adams and Haut.

"That's far enough," Wilcox said. "Now all three of you kindly stand together, over there." He indicated the other side of the alley with his gun. The three of them complied. "Now Corwin, just push the gate and you can walk out."

The big horse shook his head and stamped his front hooves. "Locked," he said.

"It's okay, boy. He unlocked it; you can just push your way out."

"Locked," the horse repeated with a snort.

Wilcox cursed under his breath. Smart, though Corwin was, he was also real dumb in some ways. All closed gates and doors were locked to him. "Don't follow me," Wilcox said as he backed over to the cage, his guns trained on the three men. "I will be much less kind if we meet again."

"You can't hide," the Ancestor said. "We will find you."

Wilcox hooked the cage with his boot cracking it open while watching the men. He stepped back, and now that the gate was cracked, Corwin pushed his way through. "Free," the horse said.

Wilcox holstered one revolver while keeping the other one trained on the three men as he mounted Corwin.

"Coming," Corwin said as Wilcox heard voices from around the corner. He pulled the second gun and began shooting. He shot over the heads of the three men and at the corner of the building he heard the voices coming from. The three threw themselves to the ground, covering their heads. He heard shouts from around the corner.

"Run, Corwin!"

WILCOX STAYED LOW ON THE BACK OF CORWIN AS BULLETS whizzed past them. He didn't urge his horse or even use the reins. Corwin knew what the stakes were so Wilcox stayed out of his way.

They had four mounted pursuers, three Ancestors and Taylor. When returning fire he always aimed at Taylor. Despite his recent history with them, he couldn't bring himself to shoot at the Ancestors. They were the Ancestors, beings of legend, centuries old, one did not shoot them. But Taylor was another story; Wilcox thought of him as a traitor. Eventually Taylor dropped back and it was just the three Ancestors chasing him.

They wound through the dusty streets of Salkin City at a gallop. Past the slaughterhouse, the cloying scent of blood clogging the air. Past the lumber mill, the scream of the saws assaulting their ears. Past the brothel where painted ladies waved and shouted as they went by.

Corwin was fast and soon his speed gained them distance from their pursuers, and they broke out of town with the Ancestors far behind.

Wilcox knew that Sadie Larkin and her wagon were headed south, so he headed north and west into the rough foothills of the mountain. He let Corwin slow his pace, keeping the Ancestors out of rifle range. This was now a marathon, not a sprint. There was a long way to go to reach safety.

THE ANCESTORS WERE ARMORED AND HEAVIER ON THEIR mounts than Wilcox. Soon the gap between them grew enough so that Wilcox was comfortable giving Corwin a break.

He let the horse drink his fill at a small creek and then walked with him up a mountain trail for a while.

"Ancestors gone?" Corwin asked as he followed Wilcox.

"No, Corwin. Not really. They are still chasing us."

"Where go?" the horse asked.

"I'm not sure. The plan was to hole up in that old mine. But with them on our trail I don't want to lead them to it." Wilcox stopped when he realized that Corwin wasn't following anymore. The horse was still, his nostrils wide. Wilcox thumbed the back of his ear and listened. He heard the creek they had left behind as it made its way to the low lands. He heard the wind whistling through the pinon trees. He heard a grunt and the click of a rifle hammer being pulled back.

"Run!" Wilcox yelled as he leaped for cover. A sting and then a sensation of fire burst forth from his shoulder before he heard the shot. His dive turned into an awkward roll as he heard the sound of Corwin's hooves thundering up the trail.

He looked at his shoulder. It was bleeding but looked to be only a flesh wound. He crawled behind a rock and listened again. More shots and the sound of Corwin's receding hooves. The pattern of his run didn't change, so Wilcox guessed they didn't get him. That was something.

He wondered how they had caught up with him. The three pursuing Ancestors were far behind. Radio, it had to be radio. While the Ancestors didn't allow modern technology on this planet, they were using it in the pursuit of their goal. The irony of it was bitter in Wilcox's mouth.

He listened carefully and heard some whispers and men moving in the forest above him. He counted four different sets of footsteps moving in to flank him on either side.

"Hold on, boys," he shouted. "Let's talk this over before people start dying."

"Surrender and no one has to die," a voice said back. It was deep and gravely like stone against stone. It wasn't a young voice; it was a voice hard with the lessons of age.

"Let me go and no one has to die," Wilcox said.

"I can't do that," the gravel voice replied.

"And you've got me backed into a corner. I won't go down without a fight." Wilcox paused as he checked his revolvers. Six bullets in both of them, twelve more bullets in the belt. Not enough. "I was taught to revere the Ancestors. Please don't test me. I don't want to kill you."

The man with the gravel voice chuckled and said, "Hold it there, boys. Take cover and watch his position." Wilcox could hear that the movement stopped. "Wilcox, I am laying my gun down and coming to your location. I want to talk, are you willing?"

"Willing, I am. One hostile move, though, and I will kill you."

"Understood. Here I come."

Wilcox listened to a single set of footsteps approach him. "Hands up, if you don't mind," Wilcox said, pointing one of his revolvers at the Ancestor. He was tall, over two meters, but wasn't wearing armor like the other Ancestors. He wore buckskins and looked at home in the forest. He had a weathered face and short grey hair. The only thing that betrayed him as an Ancestor was the radio perched on his right ear.

His hands remained in the air as he walked below Wilcox and turned around.

"See, unarmed," he said.

Wilcox pointed at the large knife strapped to his leg. "You call that unarmed?"

The Ancestor smiled again, betraying his origins. His teeth were straight, white and perfect. The perfection of them was disconcerting in his weathered face. "Oh come now, we both know how fast you are."

"Say your piece," Wilcox said.

The Ancestor squatted down, his grey eyes boring into Wilcox.

"You can't escape. If you give yourself up, we won't hurt you, but you will have to leave the planet."

"Sorry, done that. Not doing it again."

"Why waste your life like this?"

Wilcox's shrug turned into a grimace as the pain in his shoulder intensified. "When I went off world, I thought it would be this grand adventure. And it was, but soon it soured on me like fresh milk in the noon-day sun. It wasn't for me. This is my home, I ain't leaving."

A brief smile danced on the older man's face before he reached into his vest. Wilcox cocked his gun and the older man withdrew his hand. "My name's Blane," he said. "And I was just going for a flask, if you don't mind. I figure we ought to have a drink before the dying starts."

Wilcox nodded but kept his gun steady on him as Blane withdrew a metal flask, unscrewed the top and took a sip, a sigh escaping his lips. He handed the flask to Wilcox. He sniffed it and took a sip, the liquid burning his throat as he suppressed a cough. "Strong stuff," he said. This wasn't any fancy whisky Blane had given him, but plain old corn mash gin. The kind of drink a man makes for himself from corn he grew himself.

Blane nodded, "If it ain't gonna kick you in the head, why drink it?"

"Are you really an Ancestor?" Wilcox asked, taking another sip and handing the flask back.

Blane chuckled and nodded. "I reckon I am at this point. I've been through two long sleeps, so that does qualify me as an Ancestor."

His eyes wide, Wilcox looked Blane over again. He wasn't an original Ancestor. Wilcox had never heard of them recruiting. But, it didn't matter now; he had bought Corwin enough time to get away. "Well, we've had our drink. Shall we start this dance?"

"I reckon," Blane said as he put the flask away and rose. "Okay, boys," he said loudly. "Hold your positions until I am back to where

I put down my gun. And then..." he trailed off not finishing the thought.

"Thanks for the drink," Wilcox said as the older man walked away. "I'll be sorry to kill you."

THE ROCK WILCOX HID BEHIND WAS HIS SHIELD AND HIS downfall. It offered protection, but it didn't give him an avenue to strike back without exposing himself. He tried, multiple times, but there were two riflemen keeping him pinned down. Each time he showed his head it nearly got shot off. The other two were moving into flanking positions and it wouldn't be long.

He looked at the rough terrain that sloped down below him to the creek. There were a few pine trees, but it was mostly smaller pinon still. Not much good cover. And if he did get away, what then? Was he going to outrun four horsed men? Ones that could call in reinforcements from a different direction. Ones that could watch him from satellites.

Wilcox grunted and refilled his revolvers with the last of his bullets and prepared to continue the fight. He had gotten a bead on one of the riflemen keeping him pinned down, and it was time to make them pay the price. If he was going to die, he wasn't going to do it alone.

He took his hat off and held it with his left hand while holding one of the revolvers in his right. Still hunkered behind the rock, he raised his hat and was rewarded with gunfire from both riflemen. They were a bit overzealous, and he knew they would both need to reload soon. When the fire abated, he rose up enough and fired at the one of the riflemen. His effort was met with a cry of pain, but he had been too soon. The other rifleman had been bluffing, another shot rang out, and Wilcox went down.

WILCOX FELT THE WARM, VELVET NOSE OF CORWIN IN HIS hands. "Hold on, boy, I'll get more," Wilcox said, reaching into the bag of oats and taking out a huge handful and holding it for him. The horse ate eagerly, gently scooping the grain into his mouth with his soft lips and chewing them with his large teeth.

Wilcox laughed as the horse pushed his head against Wilcox's chest, asking for more. "Still hungry, huh?" he asked, but the horse didn't answer. The man thought it strange but was so happy to be with his friend that he didn't think anything of it.

As he reached into the bag of oats again, he felt his scalp burning, a line of bright pain on the right side of his head where he parted his brown hair. He felt the warm trickle of blood and the pain wax and wane with each heartbeat.

Nausea flooded him, and he felt the hard ground underneath him and smelled gunpowder and blood. Dreaming, he had been dreaming.

"He's down," a voice shouted. "Looks like I got him in the head. Is Lindstrom Okay? The freak just winged him right?"

Wilcox heard the cautious steps of the Ancestor that had shouted. The one that had shot him. The one that would kill him if he realized he wasn't dead. He felt the smooth grip of a revolver in his hand and was glad.

Adrenaline flowed through his veins, and ignoring the pain in his head and in his shoulder he sat up quickly cocking the revolver and pointing it at the Ancestor.

A wave of dizziness assaulted him and he wanted to throw up, but he pushed the sensations down and focused on his target who was turning back towards him. "One move," Wilcox hissed, "and you die."

The Ancestor had blond hair and a beard and wore the segmented armor of the Ancestors. He looked at Wilcox, eyes wide, and started to pull his rifle up.

"Was I not clear?" Wilcox asked, and the Ancestor lowered his rifle. "Slowly set the gun down. Keep your hands where I can see them." The Ancestor complied. "Now back up a pace." Wilcox moved slowly, he didn't want his enemy to see how dizzy he was, and took the rifle.

"Well?" Blane shouted as he walked down towards Wilcox and the other Ancestor, "Is he dead?"

"Not quite," Wilcox said as Blane came into view. He had drawn his second revolver and had one pointed at each of the men.

Blane smiled and held his hands out to the side, one of those hands held a rifle. "Good," he said, his gravel voice loud. "I would rather you not die. You seem a decent sort to me."

"Toss your rifle this way, easy," Wilcox demanded. The older man complied. Wilcox scooted the rifle towards him with his foot. "Now the revolver, I..." Another wave of nausea hit Wilcox as his vision blurred. In that brief second, Blane's hand reached his revolver and had it half pulled. "Oh, no you don't. Two fingers, easy, toss it to me."

Blane complied, a sour look on his grizzled face. "You should just kill us and get it over with," he said loudly.

"I thought I was a 'decent sort,'" Wilcox replied, licking his lips. He knew he was right; there were two more Ancestors out there and both of them armed. "Go stand next to your buddy there."

Wilcox watched as Blane slowly moved to stand next to the blond-haired Ancestor. He moved slightly so the two men were between him and the rifleman he had shot.

"Now," Wilcox shouted, realizing that Blane had signaled to the other two Ancestors that he was alive when he spoke loudly, "If I hear one branch break, one footstep come towards us, I will kill these men. Got that?"

"Understood," someone yelled from the where the rifleman was.

"What now?" Blane asked. "Two more armed men out there, reinforcements on the way. We've got radio and satellites. What do you expect is going to happen here, Wilcox?"

"I expect that I'm going to get away. The choice you need to make is if I will leave with you alive or dead."

"Well, I would prefer alive, if you don't mind."

"Very well then. Both of you turn your backs to me and call your other two boys over. Have them approach with their hands up holding their guns well away from their bodies."

Blane sighed and turned around, as did the other Ancestor. "Did you hear that boys?" he yelled.

"Yes, sir," a voice said from the trees.

"So you all do as he said. That's an order."

Wilcox gritted his teeth against another wave of nausea. He was glad Blane couldn't see him. The bleeding had slowed, and the trickle of it dripping down his face was an aggravating tickle he was desperate to deal with, but he needed both hands.

The third and fourth Ancestors walked over, one supporting the other. The one had his hand pressed to his neck, blood running freely.

"Stand with your comrades and toss your weapons onto the pile," Wilcox said. After they had complied he added, "Now turn around, hands up."

Wilcox considered killing them. They had tried to kill him, they would keep following him. But he couldn't do it. He couldn't shoot a man in the back, much less four Ancestors. He holstered one gun and began pulling the lacing out of one of his buckskin boots. He squatted down and used the lace to roughly bind the rifles and pistols together, so he could carry them with one hand.

"Where are the horses?" he asked.

"They are tied up the hill a bit," Blane answered his upraised hand pointing.

"Now this is how it's going to go, gentlemen." I am going to move away and ride out of here. As I leave I will keep my eye on you. If you all move one muscle I will shoot to kill. Understood?"

"Understood," Blane said.

Wilcox paused, rubbing the blood off his face with his sleeve. It was beginning to drip over his right eye. As he bent to pick up the guns he had bound together, he groaned, another wave of nausea hitting him.

Out of the corner of his eye, Wilcox saw the blur of movement and instinct took over. He dropped all the way to the ground and fired at his prisoners. A knife whistled over his head, a man fell, the other men ran. Wilcox continued to fire from his prone position at the receding Ancestors until his gun emptied.

The smell of gun smoke and blood assaulted him and he vomited, unable to hold down the nausea any longer. He slowly rose, his remaining loaded gun in hand, his shoulder sore and his head throbbing. He saw one body on the ground. Blane. He could hear the other three Ancestors as they ran through the forest away from him, the one with the neck wound moving slowly and still visible.

He ignored them and approached the fallen Ancestor. Blane had thrown the knife. Blane had not been armored. He lay flat on his back, his eyes blinking slowly, blood seeping out of his chest soaking the ground beneath him.

Wilcox squatted down, Blane's wide eyes meeting him. "Why?" Wilcox asked.

The man gasped for breath, but did not speak, his mouth moving like a fish out of water. It didn't last long. Soon the gasping ended and the eyes, now vacant, stared up at the sky.

Wilcox swore loudly before gently closing the dead man's eyes. "I'm sorry," he whispered, nausea rolling over him again. But this time he couldn't tell if it was from the head wound or the aftermath of killing a man. Killing an Ancestor.

He slowly rose, holstered his guns, and gathered the guns he had taken from the Ancestors. He made his slow way up the hill to where the Ancestors had left their horses.

"Hurt," Corwin said as he nuzzled Wilcox with his soft

nose. The horse had found him shortly after he had gotten clear of the ambush site with the Ancestor's four horses.

"Yeah," Wilcox said, his head aching. "We need to move, though. They are going to be after us."

"Why?"

"Because we're different Corwin. You are different than other horses, and I am different than other men."

"Good."

Wilcox chuckled as he tied the rope that he had been leading the four horses with to Wilcox's saddle. He mounted Corwin and said, "Take us up, boy, up over the mountains."

Corwin snorted, turned back to the four horses and whinnied, like he was telling them something, and then surged forth.

———

THE CAMPFIRE BURNED LOW IN THE COOL NIGHT. WILCOX squatted on the ground studying it. A lone figure sat at attention next to it. He smelled rabbit stew and heard the crackle of the fire. He studied the profile of the figure until he was as sure as he could be.

He walked slowly into the fire light, holding his hands away from his body. The woman by the fire leveled a double-barreled shotgun at him and said, "That's far enough. I don't want trouble."

"Seems to me," Wilcox said, "that a woman alone all the way out here with the Ancestors on the loose, purging Valdrin of illegal tech, has already found trouble."

"Wilcox?"

"Yes, Mrs. Larkin, it's me."

"I thought..." she began as she studied him in the dim firelight. "You're hurt." She threw another log on the fire, new flames illuminating Wilcox's face. "Get over here, now, and let me tend to you."

"Yes, Ma'am." Wilcox said as he brushed at the ugly scab on his scalp. He hadn't given it the tending it needed.

"Corwin?" she asked, her voice a whisper.

"He's fine," he said. "I left him back a ways, just in case."

She dabbed at his wound with a cloth and Wilcox winced. "What happened?"

Wilcox told her, or rather he summarized briefly the chase of the Ancestors and how he got away.

"Did they follow?"

He shook his head. "We went over the mountains into the Great Waste. I nearly killed Corwin and myself doing it. It was more than a normal horse could have done. If they followed, they died, and I don't think their satellites could find us once we got back into the forest."

"And now?"

"And now we go into hiding. It occurred to me that I never got around to drawing that map, so I came back to find you. I have that old mine setup and ready. It won't be much of a life, but it will be a life."

Sadie Larkin looked into Wilcox's eyes and slowly nodded.

Evan Wilcox sat back in the mouth of the damp cave, hidden in the shadows. He could see the land rolling away from his high perch, but even the Ancestors wouldn't be able to see him where he was. He was alive and safe, but he missed being in the open, he missed riding Corwin.

It wasn't too bad. He had Corwin and Sadie Larkin for company. He had food and snuck out at night to go hunting. It wasn't much of a life, but...

He inhaled slowly and sighed. While his physical wounds were healing, he still hurt. He kept seeing Blane's fluttering eyes as the man breathed his last breath, as the Ancestor died.

He heard the sound of hooves on the ground behind him, but he didn't turn. He could smell a mixture of dirt and straw and horse flesh. He loved the smell of Corwin, almost more than the look of him. He breathed it in and felt himself calm.

"Think too much," the horse said, as he knocked Wilcox's hat off.

Wilcox laughed as Corwin's lips tugged at his hair as if he were going to eat it.

"Alive good," Corwin added.

"Yes it is, my friend. Yes it is."

BACKSTORY—FOR A HORSE NAMED CORWIN

A FEW YEARS BACK, WHEN I WAS TRYING TO BECOME comfortable with the blank page, I spent morning after morning writing openings. I did this for months. I would start with nothing, no ideas, a blank screen, early in the morning before food or caffeine.

I wrote opening after opening after opening, until the blank page didn't scare me anymore. It does intimidate, I don't expect that to go away, but I don't fear it like I used to.

While I was doing that, some openings wouldn't leave me alone. The opening to this story is one of them. It was so curious. Who are these ancestors? How can a society that can engineer a talking horse be like a western? It wouldn't leave me alone.

I had horse as kid, living on a ranch outside of Globe, Arizona. I rode him nearly daily for years through the cactus filled, high desert foothills of the Pinal Mountains, herding our milk cows back to the ranch. In some ways westerns are a bit of a natural fit for me, but I hadn't written anything in that genre.

I hadn't ridden in many years, but right before I wrote this opening, a good friend of mine let me take a ride on her horse. It felt... well, it felt good, and natural, and I remembered how much I had loved my horse and loved parts of that ranch life.

Horses are a tremendous commitment in time, money, and energy. If you look at our modern culture and see how we tend to get attached to our cars and our pets, now imagine combining those two. How attached would you become to a strong, intelligent animal that you depend on for survival?

That ride turned into this opening that wouldn't leave me alone and out popped this gritty sci-fi/western about the bond between a man and a talking horse.

This story received an honorable mention in the Writers of the Future Contest.

PART THIRTEEN

THE JUDGMENT OF EDWARD TILLINGHAM

THE JUDGMENT OF EDWARD
TILLINGHAM

EDWARD TILLINGHAM WAS THE SIMPLEST MEN WITH THE hardest of jobs—he decided who lived and who died. For the good of all.

"Hi, Eddie," his wife said when we walked into their small, neat dwelling in Habitat Tower #6. "How was your day?"

"Sparkling, dear. Sparkling," he answered, lowering himself into his chair.

They performed this ritual every day. She would ask about his day, he would say it was sparkling. He would ask about her day, and she would say the same. It was a simple semaphore, but contained no meaning, no essential data, just an acknowledgment of each other; a holdover from centuries ago.

His wife, Adeline, didn't know what he did with his days. She thought he was a Processor, just like her, just like most of the people they knew, but he wasn't. He was a Justitia, deciding who lived and who died.

"I think System has chosen us a fine story for tonight," Adeline called from the kitchen.

"Oh?" Edward asked.

"Yes. It is a pre-Devastation era murder mystery crossed with a romance."

"That sounds nice," Edward said. He loved murder mysteries, how, by the end, the murder was caught and all the loose ends were tied up. She loved romances with a "happily ever after" ending. They both loved stories set before the Devastation when humanity wasn't confined to the Dome and could travel.

The chair encased him and moved him into a horizontal position, as it massaged his shoulders, and bathed his lower back in heat. He sighed and closed his eyes chasing out the pictures in his mind of those he had just sent to their deaths.

———

EDWARD AND ADELINE MET FIFTEEN YEARS EARLIER PLAYING the Cell Games. Edward was a master, consistently at the top of the ranks. The games were beautiful and simple; a visual display of the organic beauty of life.

Each person was a single cell in the game, and it was their job to follow a set of simple rules.

The shield over their eyes displayed game information and a feed of their communal creation taken from a camera high above. They could not see their surroundings and had to follow the rules carefully to keep from colliding with other players. Their wands fired a beam of light at the end of each turn, and they had the slow tick of a metronome in their ears timing their movements.

The moves were simple: crouch, stand, step forward, turn to the left, turn to the right, stay still. The moves where dictated by their last move and how many beams of light hit them (displayed on their eye shield).

The day they met it was a larger group, 100 citizens playing the part of cells in a larger organism. The patterns they were making were diverse and beautiful. Coming together, moving apart, opening like a flower, collapsing like a black hole.

Edward found it soothing, reassuring, how such simple rules could create such order, such diversity, such beauty.

Crouch, stand, one step forward, turn to the right, one step forward, turn to the left, crouch, stand, one step forward. He felt his body crash into another and he heard a feminine cry of pain.

In the games, for those less experienced, this was not unusual. For Edward, this didn't happen. He knew the rules, he didn't make mistakes.

He took the shield off his face and saw her. Adeline wasn't beautiful, not by the standards of Entertainers, but she wasn't plain either. She had arching, expressive eyebrows, and bright blue eyes. She was sitting on the grass holding her foot. "Freeze," Edward shouted. There were two other Citizens with their faces covered about to run into her. The calls of "freeze" echoed throughout the park and everyone stopped.

"Sorry about that," Edward said. He was surprised to hear himself taking blame for the accident. He extended his hand, "Here, let me help you."

She leaned on him heavily as he guided her to a bench out of the way.

They bonded quickly over their obsession with the Cell Games and soon found love in their pairing. They were both delighted when System approved their union six months later. They had been a good match and found contentment together. Their only true sorrow as a couple was that they had wanted to procreate, but System had never approved it.

EDWARD STARED AT THE POD WAITING FOR HIM, BUT HE wasn't ready. Once again, it struck him how like a coffin it appeared.

Being a Processor, he thought, was so much simpler. Eight

hours of confused dreaming while System used your brain to augment its processing power.

Both his parents where Processors, simple citizens that had a simple life. Eight hours a day hooked to System, eight hours a day sleeping, the other eight hours a day eating or playing or resting. Simple. Easy. Guilt-free.

He would even prefer being a Laborer, using his body to tend plants, or clean, to build, or to carry. But he wasn't gifted with a Laborer's physic. He was a small man with a bald head and weak lungs.

His sister was an Enforcer. She spent her days being the eyes and ears of System. Listening to System's voice in her ear and maintaining a peaceful atmosphere for the good of all. A worthy contribution, but not one Edward was psychologically suited for.

Edward was not a Processor anymore, he was a Justitia. He had to remain conscious, had to know what he was doing.

He sighed, let his robe drop, and climbed in. He clenched his teeth while the pod mated with his elimination systems, and gasped when the interface hardware wrapped around his head, and the world disappeared.

The blackness faded as the room appeared. Grey stone walls and a grey stone floor. In the center was a wooden desk raised on a dais. Before it were the Defender and the Accused on the right, and the Accuser on the left. They were seated in simple wooden chairs. "All rise for Justitia," a booming voice said as he climbed the dais and took the chair behind his bench.

Everyone rose. Edward gestured lazily at them as he took his seat.

"The people versus Felston Xander," the booming voice said.

"Plea?" Edward asked.

"Not guilty," the Defender said. It was the only thing they ever said. Another ritual of communication that contained no meaning. Guilt meant death. For lesser infractions System ruled, but for life and death judgments a human mind had to make the final decision. It was the Law. For the good of all.

"Present arguments," Edward said, gesturing for the Accuser and the Defender to approach him. He took the data pod from each and allowed the information to flood into his mind.

Xander, Felston. Laborer. Accused of sedition. Evidence presented: video of Xander organizing small gathering of citizen to discuss leaving the dome, leaving the protection of System, starting a new society.

Defense presented a video of one Ilan Opon talking to Xander over a period of time and swaying him onto the side of the Outsiders; turning him into an Outsider. Opon had been convicted of sedition last month and put to death. For the good of all.

"Leave me," Edward said. "I will call you back when I am ready to rule."

EDWARD HAD BEEN HAPPY AS A PROCESSOR. IT WAS A SIMPLE life, one that suited him as such a simple person. He was happy to obey the rules; he knew that they were needed for the good of all; he knew that System had kept humanity alive for many centuries since the Devastation.

But a decade ago, that had changed. He woke up in the middle of a shift and was in a small white room.

"What? Where am I?" he had asked.

"Testing," the voice of System said.

Edward had heard of Testing, whispered rumors from those who failed. No one ever talked of passing the tests.

At first they were simple logic puzzles, Edward loved these.

His father had loved puzzles, and would play with the holographic images that System provided for him for hours at a time. Edward inherited this love from his father.

Then came short dramas played out before Edward that would

stop right before the climax. The voice of System would then ask him what should happen, what was best for each character in the drama. These were harder, but Edward enjoyed them too.

Then came the questions. System would quickly explain a situation to Edward and ask him to "judge" it. Edward liked these less, but the answers were always clear to him.

At the end of what seemed like days System said, "Edward Tillingham, you have passed the test."

Edward swallowed hard. He knew there was danger, he had never heard of anyone claiming to pass the test.

"Edward Tillingham, from this day forward you are Justitia. You may tell no one of this. Do you accept this honor?"

Edward nodded his head. He knew of Justitia, everyone did. He also knew it was a lifelong appointment, one that could only be terminated with the life of the Justitia. "Yes, I accept," Edward said.

"Justitia is a sacred honor and duty. For the good of all you must fulfill this duty, you must keep your role secret, you must never speak of this."

"For the good of all," Edward intoned.

"Two hours has passed," the booming voice of System said. "Are you ready to rule, Justitia?"

Edward stopped pacing and looked up towards the vaulted ceiling of granite. He was stalling. His decision was clear, the law was clear, but he didn't want to make it.

"I want to recuse myself," Edward said, wishing System would enter the environment with an avatar, like the rest of them, but it never did.

"On what grounds?" System asked.

Edward paused, searching his mind for a viable reason. He could feel the pressure of System's questions in his brain. He knew it was monitoring his mind and body on enumerable levels. He knew that this course was dangerous and ill considered, but he couldn't... couldn't do this again.

"I am no longer fit to be Justitia," he said, his voice cracking.

"Please elaborate."

"These decisions are becoming harder and harder. The faces of the dead haunt me in my dreams."

"I see," System began.

Edward took a deep breath, anticipating what System would say.

"You know, of course, that there is only one way to end your role as Justitia," the voice said as it echoed around the granite walled room.

"I... Well... Yes. Yes, of course I do."

"Perhaps a course of Therapy is in order, and Rest. Then you can resume your duties. I can bring in another Justitia to rule on this case."

Justice was blind, and all Justitia had the same avatar—a tall woman in flowing robes with a blindfold on—so no one would know he had been replaced.

"Yes... Yes, thank you."

THERAPY HAD LASTED A FULL CYCLE AND EDWARD Tillingham felt better. His sleep was peaceful again, his shoulders no longer tied up in knots. Each day he had entered the pod for his shift at Therapy, and each day he had exited with only echoes of strange dreams. It was almost like being a Processor.

Edward whistled as he slowly walked around the garden. He was on his prescribed Rest, and had found himself touring the dome they lived in. Here, on the edge of the dome, where the clear substrate that protected them wasn't very high, they grew the plants of the past. Rose bushes, thorns and all; dwarf apple trees with small green fruit; daffodils and pansies. The air seemed fresher, the smells odd and tantalizing. Edward found it very relaxing.

His mother had loved plants. When Edward was a child, she would tend them endlessly on their small balcony high in the habitat tower. She would grow red tomatoes and green peas. Edward had inherited this love from his mother.

His feet took him to the edge of the dome as he traveled the paths of the garden. The place wasn't crowded, with only a few Citizens, Laborers, and the occasional Enforcer in view. He stopped, looking beyond the bed of small wildflowers out through the dome to the outside.

He kept looking down at the small flowers, red, purple, and blue, but his eyes would not stay there. You didn't look outside, not if you were a good Citizen. You just didn't do it. His eyes slowly climbed up and he stared. A vast flat plane of dirt, brown and dry. Lifeless. Why did the Outsiders want to leave? What did they think was out there?

System took care of them. System knew best. He bit his lip, turned his head, and quickly walked away. The tension that had recently disappeared with Therapy and Rest, crept back into his shoulders.

"I FIND THE ACCUSED, FILLIN TALBEN, GUILTY OF SEDITION," Edward as Justitia said from behind his ornate wooden desk.

It wasn't always sedition that caused him to send Citizens to their death. It was sometimes violence, or the extreme listlessness of acedia. In those cases he had leeway with sentencing. If he found that rehabilitation was possible he could send them to Therapy and Training. But not sedition; there was only one sentence for that.

"Before I read your sentence Citizen Talben, I have a question for you," Edward said. He felt System probing his mind, this was a deviation from protocol.

"Yes, Justitia?" the thin man asked, licking his lips.

"Why do you want to go outside? It is just a wasteland." Edward could hear System whispering in his mind, but he ignored it. He was Justitia, this was a capital case, System had to let him rule.

Talben's eyes widened in surprise. "Freedom, Your Honor. A man needs freedom. System takes care of us, but the price is our freedom."

"And you would rather die on the outside than live here under System's care?"

"Yes, Your Honor. I would. And..." Talben trailed off his eyes widening as he looked around.

"Speak, Citizen. I command it."

"There is talk, Your Honor. That the wasteland is no longer. That System hides the truth from us. That—" All three avatars, Talban, the Accuser, and the Defender disappeared.

"What are you doing, Justitia?" The voice of System boomed above him.

"Trying to understand," Edward said looking at his hands.

"What is there to understand? Sedition is a crime. Sentence must be carried out, for the good of all."

"But sedition is spreading. I hear more and more of these cases. Shouldn't we find out what the cause is?"

There was a pause, which surprised Edward. System didn't pause. System always knew what it wanted to say.

"If this trend continues," Edward interjected, "our population will start to decrease. That would not be for the good of all."

"I have run those scenarios," System said. Edward believed that the pause was System running them. "If we allow the Outsiders to leave our population will decrease even faster."

"It will?"

"Yes. The Outsider phenomenon will spread like a cancer once the penalty of death is lifted. It is your work, Justitia, that keeps things in balance."

Edward nodded, thinking. His mind was just one mind, not as vast and powerful as System's. How could he think of something System couldn't? He didn't hope to, but yet he continued to puzzle over it.

"Is the wasteland habitable?" he asked after a time. He felt himself shaking inside as he questioned System. He knew it might mean the end for him, but he asked it anyway. It was a question, a direct question, not sedition.

"No," System answered immediately.

"When will it be habitable?"

"Another century or so."

"Are you hiding what is happening out there from us?"

"Yes," the booming voice said. "There are small changes, very small changes. A form of algae has adapted and is growing in the waters and plants are beginning to grow again. If the Citizens knew, the Outsider movement would grow and threaten our society. I do this for the good of all."

Edward shook his head, his eyes wide. He wanted to see the plants, no matter how small or weak. He wanted to see them, see the signs of life that had so long ago left their planet.

He knew the history, before System was in charge, man roamed the planet, and man destroyed the planet.

Edward was the simplest of men, and he knew that the longing he felt would be multiplied in normal men. He knew that the knowledge he had was not safe, he knew—

"You are going to terminate me now, aren't you?" Edward asked.

"Yes," the booming voice of System said.

"Then why did you tell me?"

"A small gift in return for your service. One day Citizens will leave this dome, one day humanity will spread across this planet. But not today. Humanity must be preserved, for the good of all. This is the only way."

Edward nodded. He understood. He felt fear, but not too

much, he knew the kind of death that System brought was painless. Drugs pumped into your body that brought a dreamless sleep followed by death.

"But, you can't carry out capital punishment without a sentence, without a Justitia. Who will rule?"

"You will, Justitia," System stated.

THE HOURS HAD TICKED PAST IN SILENCE. EDWARD SAT behind his wooden desk, on the dais, in the chamber of granite. The Hall of the Justitia.

System would not let him go until he ruled against himself. Edward was having trouble finding the courage to sentence himself to death.

He was Justitia, he decided who lived and who died. How could he decide to terminate his own life?

There was no way out. Edward knew that he was not guilty of sedition, but that if his life was allowed to continue, he would be. It was clear. It was truth. It was for the good of all.

"SYSTEM," EDWARD SAID.

"Yes, Justitia."

"I am ready."

Before him in the chamber appeared the avatar of Edward Tillingham, flanked by the Accuser and Defender. Edward studied it. It was him with his bald head, and his protruding belly.

He found it disconcerting, both avatars, the Accused and the Justitia, were him, both controlled by his thoughts.

"The people versus Edward Tillingham," the booming voice said.

"Plea?" Justitia asked.

The defender was about to speak when the avatar of Edward said, "I wish to speak to Justitia alone."

"Granted," Justitia said with a bang of his gavel, and the avatars of the Accuser and Defender disappeared.

Edward as Justitia sat staring at himself. "I am sorry," he said to himself. "This is the only way."

His avatar nodded, licking his thin lips. "I know. But..."

Edward smiled. He could feel both sides of himself in the conversation. He knew what his Edward-self was going to say; he knew what his Justitia-self was going to say. But having it played out felt right; it served.

"Yes, what is it Citizen Tillingham."

"I would ask a small boon of System," Edward said.

"What is it?" Justitia asked.

"In exchange for entering a plea of guilty, I want to see."

"See?"

"I want to see what is really out there. I want to see our planet for what it is. I want to know that what I am doing is the right thing. For the good of all."

Edward as Justitia paused. He was giving System a chance to say no. To tell him it wasn't possible. But System was quiet. "Granted," he said as he banged the gavel.

Everything disappeared. All was dark.

BELOW HIM EDWARD COULD SEE THE LARGE ROUND DOME humanity called home. The tall buildings in the center, the shorter ones surrounding it, the parks and gardens along the edges of the dome. He began to move quickly towards the ground past the dome. The dirt was dry, a fine dust lay over everything, the sun was yellow and hot above him.

There was no life here, no life that he could see. The ground was infertile and bleak. He moved quickly and low over the ground, when he was several kilometers away from the dome, his view paused. A small robot was poking at the ground. Edward's view zoomed in close, it was a small green sprout, pale and wan, but green nonetheless. The robot grabbed the sprout with its tiny pinchers and deposited into its cargo area.

"This growth would be to the dome by now if uninterfered with?" Edward asked.

"Yes," the voice of System answered.

"And this would destabilize us, wouldn't it?"

"Yes," System answered again.

Edward rose up and the ground began moving below him again. When the dome was out of sight the plants became higher and healthier. They weren't much more than weeds and grasses sparsely populating the ground, but they were represented life where once that had been none.

Man could not live out here, but seeing it would cause hope, would cause longing, would cause chaos.

AFTER HIS TOUR, BACK IN THE DARKNESS EDWARD FELT questions welling up in him. "Since... well... can I ask some more questions?" he asked.

"Yes," System boomed.

"Did you cause Adeline and I to meet? Did you feed us incorrect input to cause us to crash together like that during that Cell Game?" It had always bothered Edwards; both of them were too good at the games to make that kind of mistake.

"Yes."

"And you never approved us for procreation because you knew it would come to this?"

"Yes."

Edward took a deep breath and sighed. It made sense, System always made sense, at least to a mind like Edwards.

"One more thing," Edward began before trailing off. "I... I don't want Adeline to think me an Outsider. I don't want her to question who I was when I am gone. Can you..."

"Yes, Edward," System said. It surprised him, System rarely used his name. "Your death will be reported as an aortic aneurysm."

Edward nodded, relieved. "And help her find another mate."

"One has already been chosen."

"WHAT IS YOUR PLEA?" EDWARD AS JUSTITIA ASKED. BEFORE him, again, was his other avatar, the Accuser and the Defender.

The Defender said to the Edward avatar, "Are you sure?" His avatar shook his head and smiled. "Guilty," the Defender said, his face twisted into a sour frown.

Edward as Justitia smiled. Finally a message with meaning. Finally something different. "The accused, Edward Tillingham, is found guilty of sedition by his own admission. Sentence is death to be carried out immediately by System."

All three avatars disappeared and it was just Edward in his Justitia avatar that remained.

"Thank you," the booming voice of System said.

"For the good of all," Edward replied as the world went dark.

BACKSTORY—THE JUDGMENT OF EDWARD TILLINGHAM

Humans overcoming an evil AI is a common, cliched trope. Almost any movie that involves truly intelligent AI has the AI going off the rails and the brave humans, somehow, barely, defeating it.

What if the AI was right?

Designation Null asks this question, as well as this story.

For the opening of this story, I envisioned a far-future, AI controlled world. As I was writing it, I came to the point where Edward could take on the AI (the system) and fall into that cliched rut, or he could sacrifice his individual existence for what was best for the whole.

We have egos for a reason, we need them to survive, and we need to survive so the race survives. This survival instinct has worked remarkably well for the human race, but it has also caused a lot of suffering.

Perhaps the choice Edward made in this story is the more heroic one.

AUTHOR'S NOTE

THANK YOU SO MUCH FOR READING. WHAT FOLLOWS IS AN afterword and the acknowledgments (that ever import task of me thanking all the people that helped with these stories).

But first, if you've enjoyed the science fiction stories in this collection, you might want to check out my novel *Seeing Forever*. It explores life, love, and loss in a post-biological existence. Here's what *Kirkus Review* had to say about it:

"In this quiet but far-reaching thriller, author McCarter explores the essence of what it means to be human... Sci-fi as it should be: engaging, moving, and grand in scope."

If you are interested, more information, sample chapters, and an extended sample e-book are available at: *RobertJMcCarter.com/books/SeeingForever*

AFTERWORD

Sometime soon, probably in 2018, I will complete short story number one-hundred. It's such a feeling to complete a story, and an even better feeling to revisit one with months or years in between and experience it more like a reader. But, one-hundred feels like a big number. It will be somewhere near 500,000 words, and comprise many, many hours of work.

Even so, each story still feels like a miracle to me. The mechanics are simple: learn your craft and keep your butt in the chair (or feet at the standup desk). But the results... they still feel magical as I watch my subconscious conjure story after story and continue to surprise me.

Easy? God no. You have to mine your own flaws and fears, reflect deeply on the world around you, confront imposter's syndrome at every corner, and frequently believe you should just quit and be a whole lot more normal (whatever the hell that is).

Rewarding? Absolutely. Partially because it is so hard to learn that craft, to get to the point of finishing, to put your art out there and experience rejection after rejection for those few yeses that come your way. But at a deeper level, it's because the act of creation is so fulfilling. I can't explain it, but if I'm not deep in the middle creating something—even with the doubts, frustrations, and fears— I don't feel whole.

(And if you are an artist trying to find your way like so many of us, I encourage you to keep at it. Grow in your craft and you will grow as a person and it's rather hard to be bored that way. Create what is unique to you, put it out, let it get rejected and, sometimes, it will be loved.)

These thirteen stories are anomalies for me, at least when I look at the body of my work. Or maybe they are something different, a corner turned, a new phase, the restless subconscious looking for the new and different and interesting.

As I change, my stories change. As the times get tough, the stories get darker. I've recently been straying into even different territory with stories that are so much fun to write (yes, even then the doubts don't go away) and are a lot lighter. I think this cycle of fun stories is a reflection of difficult times survived, my inner child wants to play for a while. (These fun stories will start appearing later in 2018.)

Thanks for reading. I hope you found something worth your time in these anomalies, these curiosities. I'd love to hear what you think, there are lots of ways to reach out. You can let me know by writing a review wherever you buy books. Go to my website, *robertjmccarter.com*, and fill out the *contact page*. I'm on Twitter at *@robertjmccarter*, or you can join my *Facebook group*.

If you want to keep track of my writing, the best way is to *join my email newsletter*.

ACKNOWLEDGMENTS

There are always people to thank. These stories span 2010 through 2016, but I've been lucky to have a hearty band of beta readers, so thanks to: Chris Kalinich, Peter Klein, Roni Hornstein, Gary McClellan, and Eliot Schipper.

Also thanks to Meg and her horse Nellie for bringing back such fond memories.

I got to work with some great editors on some of these. Thank you Edwina Harvey and Lisa Mangum for making these stories better.

As always, thanks go to Diana Cox, my amazing proofreader.

I would like to thank my mother, Ellie, who is gone now. She taught me by example to be kind, considerate, to put others first, to try to live a life that makes things better for those around me. I would not be who I am with out her, I wouldn't be a writer without her, and while the end was enormously difficult, I miss her so very much.

And last, but certainly not least, thanks to my first listener and amazing wife, Aleia. I read everything to her first before anyone else reads them. Reading aloud is so helpful in catching silly mistakes and hearing the rhythm of the words. I could not do this without her.

ABOUT THE AUTHOR

Robert J. McCarter is the author of six novels, three novellas, and dozens of short stories. He is a finalist for the *Writers of the Future* contest and his stories have appeared in *The Saturday Evening Post*, *Adomeda Spaceways Inflight Magazine*, *Everyday Fiction*, and numerous anthologies. His short stories have been published along-side such luminaries as Brandon Sanderson, Peter S. Beagle, Jody Lynn Nye, and David Farland.

He has written a series of first person ghost novels (starting with *Shuffled Off: A Ghost's Memoir*) and a superhero / love story series (*Neutrinoman and Lightningirl: A Love Story*). Ten of his short stories were published in *Life After: Stories of Life, Death, and the Places in Between*.

He lives in the mountains of Arizona with his amazing wife and his ridiculously adorable dog.

Find out more at:
robertjmccarter.com

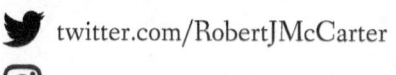 twitter.com/RobertJMcCarter

instagram.com/robert.j.mccarter

BOOKS BY ROBERT J. MCCARTER

Novels in the "Ghost's Memoir" world:

- Shuffled Off: A Ghost's Memoir, Book 1
- Drawing the Dead
- To Be a Fool: A Ghost's Memoir, Book 2
- Of Things Not Seen: A Ghost's Memoir, Book 3

Other Novels:

- Seeing Forever

Books in the Neutrinoman and Lightningirl Series:

- Meteor Attack! Lightningirl and Neutrinoman, A Love Story. Episode 1
- Toxic Asset: Lightningirl and Neutrinoman, A Love Story. Episode 2
- Protocol X: Lightningirl and Neutrinoman, A Love Story. Episode 3
- Season 1 (Omnibus edition of Episodes 1 - 3)
- Off Book: Lightningirl and Neutrinoman, A Love Story. Episode 4 (*Coming soon*)

Short Stores and Collections

- Anomalous Readings: Thirteen Curious and Confounding Tales
- Life After: Stories of Life, Death, and the Places in Between
- Probability: Resolve
- The Turing Test Will Be Televised
- Ghost Hacker, Zombie Maker

For a complete list, go to RobertJMcCarter.com

www.ingramcontent.com/pod-product-compliance
Lightning Source LLC
Chambersburg PA
CBHW050916250626
47155CB00001B/255